TRAFFIC

Robin Gregory

Clan Destine
P R E S S

First published by Clan Destine Press in 2020

PO Box 121, Bittern
Victoria, 3918 Australia

National Library of Australia Cataloguing-In-Publication data:

Gregory, Robin

TRAFFIC

ISBN: 978-0-6485236-0-4 (paperback)
ISBN:978-0-6485236 (eBook)

Cover Design by © Willsin Rowe
Design & Typesetting by Clan Destine Press

Clan Destine
P R E S S

www.clandestinepress.net

In memory of my beloved mother, Leslie Gregory, who
loved a murder mystery.

The author would like to acknowledge that this novel is set on
the land of the Kulin nation.
She pays her respects to Elders past, present and emerging,
and recognises that sovereignty of this land has never been ceded.

REGRET

When sunlight fades, I'll vanish like footprints of an ant
My bed will be the coffin of the next crushed girl.

1

Blood oozed from her neck and formed a mini-lake around her body. The wound was open and you could see what you're not meant to see in a person; some kind of tissue, maybe muscle.

I used to be immune to gruesome scenes, or so I told myself. This image was going to be etched in my brain, like the murdered man I'd discovered last year. His smashed-in face continued to flash into my mind, especially on the cusp of sleep. That wasn't the worst part. His mother's hollow eyes had torn my heart apart.

After that case, I'd sworn I'd never investigate another homicide.

If only I'd remembered.

'How's the rescue pooch?' I asked my favourite barista as I inhaled the rich scent of coffee.

Before he could answer, my mobile sang and Maria's name popped up. Maria Luisetto and I had studied law together at Monash for a year – and had a brief fling. She went on to complete her degree. Maria had been the first person in her family to go to university, which made her folks mighty proud. These days she was earning enough to have a mortgage with her girlfriend on a single-fronted terrace in Carlton North.

'Sandi, *bella*, where are you?'

'Just heading home after an intense session with wild kids.'

Twice a week, too early in the morning, I taught kids to swim. Sometimes it was rewarding, but after doing it for five years, it was mostly like swimming in the ocean against a gale-force wind. On the upside, having some regular, if meagre, income was a lifesaver.

The screech of the coffee machine at the Corner Shop café made me scoot outside, latte in hand, onto the AstroTurf carpeted mall.

'How's life in the fast lane?' I leaned against a rust-coloured pole sprouting geraniums.

'You know,' Maria always sounded like she was getting laryngitis, 'swamped, but getting there. I need a favour. Generous conditions as always.'

I wouldn't have started the Sandi Kent PI business without Maria's promise of some cases. It was handy having a solicitor to toss you bones. Maria's work was usually run-of-the-mill – investigating affairs, insurance fraud, that kind of thing – but once in a while she threw me a curve ball.

'Look, Sandi,' she said, as if anticipating my reaction, and I knew it was about to be a doozy. 'I'm representing a man who's been charged with the murder of a sex worker.'

'You know I love being your sidekick, but murder isn't my forte,' I said firmly.

I imagined Maria, ready to convince me with her charming smile, her extra-white teeth, the crowded lower set exposed, and resolved to withstand her pleas.

'I know it's not really your thing, but just hear me out. Don't be a bull in a yard.'

'A bull in a china shop you mean,' I said. 'Why are you dealing with a murder case? Not your normal clientele.'

'Not my choice. I've been asked to take this on, given my prior experience. I could use your help; I'm up to my ears in cases at the moment and this one has more layers than a tiramisu.'

She must have heard my intake of breath, because she said in a rush, 'The accused – his name is Ricardo – comes from Colombia. Hardly speaks a word of English, in spite of being in the country for five years. Not usual for someone so young. He's our age. Point is, I need to know more in order to defend him.'

Clouds dominated the sky. I focused on the Art Deco cinema opposite, with its crown of a half sun, belying Melbourne's grey skies. The Sun Theatre created an impression of frivolity in the otherwise downtrodden western suburbs. The theatre had survived hard times, picking itself up after being derelict for 20 years.

I jumped over a green stool and dodged prams before turning the corner towards my parked car. The glare speared my eyes; I scrambled in my backpack for Ray Bans.

'Bit busy at the moment, Maria.'

'If you could just pop in for half an hour.'

Her voice was pleading.

If it had been anything else, I would have offered to be there for her.

'Or for lunch. My shout,' she added.

It's sad, but I fell for the free lunch. The chance to practise my alleged second language was also tempting. I used to study Spanish, until Diana Luna broke off our relationship; if you could call it that. Since then I'd quit the classes, lost my motivation. Hey, I thought, why not practise on a killer?

2

TRUCKS TOWERED OVER MY VW AS I POWERED PAST THE DOCKS INTO THE city. I rounded the Flagstaff Gardens and turned into the Queen Victoria Market car park.

The market was closed, which was a plus since the parking was cheaper. I frowned at the needle on my fuel gauge, which had plummeted into the red zone; a reminder that the $13 in my purse would need to stretch to payday. I needed to ask Maria for an advance. If I accepted the job, I told myself. If.

It was a short stroll from the market to Maria's law firm in Queen Street. Her office was in a drab grey building, with pretentious columns out front. It wasn't clear if they were structural or made to intimidate us plebs. A Christmas tree with flashing lights towered in a corner of the foyer, brightening the atmosphere. The office was a block away from all the courts – Magistrates', County and Supreme – perfect for Maria's work.

Maria materialised through glass doors and gathered me into an almighty hug, like it had been years since we'd caught up.

She slipped her arm through mine as we entered the café next door. Her mauve fingernails matched her glasses and stood out against her black dress. Maria embodied the Italian sense of style; her taste was excellent and whatever she wore looked stunning. Her girlfriend was a lucky woman.

At the counter, I ordered while Maria grilled a waiter. I left her to it and found a spare table amongst the suits.

'Just wanted to make sure the soup wasn't out of a tin,' she explained when she joined me. 'I made a delicious osso buco last night. You must come 'round for dinner.'

'I scored a double pass to the movies, if you're up for it?' It had been ages since Maria and I had hung out, apart from a quick business lunch. Maria and her girlfriend had become inseparable since they'd moved in together.

'I haven't seen a movie for ages,' she said.

'Here's your chance.'

'Thanks for the offer, *bella*. Might have to be after Christmas. I'll talk to Kristin.'

'They expire in a week.'

'Might be better to see if someone else can go then.'

'I'll choose from the queue outside my front door.' I ditched the oily schnitzel sandwich. My stomach was rebelling.

'Don't be like that.' She plonked her spoon in the bowl and created a mini-tsunami. I felt like I was about to be sentenced to 30 Hail Marys.

'Like what?'

'Any luck online?'

I had to shut her up before she went into another diatribe about my relationship flops, the most recent being Diana, who I believed was… I was going to say "the one", but that's not in my lexicon. I thought she was going to hang around for a while, and we'd, like, maybe move in together.

'I thought we were here to talk about your murderer.'

Maria raised a thin, dark eyebrow. 'Let's wait until I have the file in front of me.'

I was relieved when Maria sipped her last mouthful. After she paid the bill, I followed as she strutted out of the café in her black high heels, her calves accentuated by the angle of the shoes.

Her office was spacious with a floor-to-ceiling window. Opposite, a skyscraper with reflective glass windows loomed, with a slice of blue sky visible above it.

Maria extracted a file from a silver cabinet in the corner and positioned it on her immaculate desk. The only items adorning the desk were a computer, writing pad and black-trimmed silver pen. I plonked my backpack on the carpet, and mobile and sunnies on my side of the desk.

Maria made a note in her elegant handwriting that she was handing the file to me on Tuesday 4 December at 1.38pm.

She slid the file across the desk towards me and launched into the details of the case.

'Earlier this year, a sex worker was allegedly stabbed to death in a brothel by the accused, Ricardo Lopez, who I'm representing.'

I opened the file. There was a mug shot of Ricardo. He had the same colouring as Diana: raven black hair, deep brown eyes and a round face. They could have been siblings. It was disconcerting.

'According to Ricardo, the woman was attacked by an "Asian-looking man" as Ricardo was leaving. The Asian man has been identified as Ju-Long Wang and appears to be a driver for the brothel.'

She leaned back in her executive chair and stared at me over the top of her glasses.

'But Ricardo's story doesn't add up – what I can extract of my client's version, that is. He's hardly talking to me and he's definitely not giving me enough to build a case, so...'

'Can't imagine why you think he's going to open up to me,' I interrupted.

'For one thing, you have a gift for making people say more than they want, plus you speak Spanish. I'm sure that will make him feel more comfortable.'

I rolled my eyes. My life goal was to make murderers feel at home.

'More importantly,' Maria continued, 'the witness statements are inconsistent.'

Her voice lost its warmth. I'd seen Maria in her occasional Magistrates' Court appearances and there was a whole other side to her. In that arena, she took on the advocate persona. It made sense, but it was weird watching her morph in front of me.

She spun her silver pen around in a circle on top of the notepad. It clunked as it landed on its clip after each rotation. I tried to ignore it.

'The witnesses agree they saw Ricardo holding a knife – that Ricardo was trying to kidnap the sex worker, and when she wouldn't cooperate he stabbed her.'

Maria clicked her pen rapidly. 'The timing is hazy. Not unusual.'

I was about to tell her how annoying the noise was, when she laid the pen on top of the notepad, jabbing the pad with her forefinger instead.

'Imagine this. Ricardo and the sex worker walk into reception together. Did he have the knife then, did anyone see it? We need to find out the exact moment he produced the knife, if he did – and more importantly, we need to find out why.'

I casually opened the file; an action that should have come with a warning. Pinned to the inside cover was a crime scene photo: a gruesome image of the murdered woman with her throat cut, lying in a pool of dark red blood that oozed from her neck and covered her chest.

I flipped the page. I wanted to erase the image from my brain; I focused on Maria's words.

'More concerning is the physical evidence,' I heard Maria say. 'Only his fingerprints were found on the knife, which he reported wasn't his. Have a quick read and take a copy of the statements. By the way, Ricardo has agreed to talk to you.'

'Wow, I'm flattered,' I said.

Maria hitched an eyebrow.

The more Maria told me, the more freaked out I became. When I'd enrolled in the PI course, dealing with murderers was last on my list.

'Sounds cut and dried, Maria. I don't get why you need me.'

Maria cupped her upper lip with her lower lip and frowned. 'In order to represent him, I need him to give a full and complete account of what happened. I need every detail.'

I clapped the file shut. 'You want me to find a way to get the bastard's sentence reduced.'

'We don't know he's guilty. Stop diving to conclusions.' Her eyebrows closed in on each other. 'There's more.'

I couldn't wait for the next instalment. 'What?'

'Ricardo is a suspect in a disappearance,' she confessed.

'You're joking.'

Maria shook her head and her dark bob swivelled. 'His fiancée disappeared 15 months ago – never been found. Ricardo is a key suspect but the police haven't been able to find a *particle* of evidence, and there are no leads as to where she or her body might be.'

If my lack of money hadn't been such an issue right now, I would have waved *adiós amiga*.

'And you reckon I'm jumping to conclusions.'

'He's innocent until proven guilty. All I'm asking is that you have a conversation with him, not sell your soul,' insisted Maria.

I grabbed my backpack.

'I'll pay you with Vatican jewels,' she cajoled. She dashed to the door, blocking my escape, impressively fast on her high heels. 'You saw how young the victim was. She was a girl. Think about her parents. We need to give her justice.'

I flung the backpack on my shoulder. 'As if that's what the so-called justice system does. Gives victims justice. Let's be honest.'

'Do it for me then,' she said.

She stared at me, and I felt like a rat in a cage. She had a habit of looking at me like that.

She wrapped her hands around my wrists and squeezed gently. 'You'd be making a difference to my workload. Seriously.'

'No need to get sentimental.'

She laughed, a deep throaty laugh. 'Fabulous. See what you can find out from Ricardo. I'm sure you'll have more luck than me. Check with his family, work.'

My face must have given the game away.

'Of course. I don't need to tell you. If you need anything.'

'Really?' I joked.

'Within reason,' she laughed. 'I'll arrange for you to meet Ricardo. Feel free to read the files in the meeting room or get my secretary to photocopy.' Her mobile rang. 'Sorry, I need to take this.'

Out in the hallway, I remembered the advance I was going to ask for. The sound of Maria's strained voice through the closed door deterred me from disturbing her.

I flicked through the file, though I skipped over the photo. Lee Wu, the young woman who was murdered, was only 18. At least it had been quick. Her carotid artery had been severed, resulting in a massive bleed. She would have been unconscious within 60 seconds and dead within a couple of minutes.

I should have been pleased that the police had taken the murder of a sex worker seriously. I would have been, if I'd been on the other side, nailing the bastard who did it.

After a few deep breaths to ground myself, I popped into Maria's secretary's office. She was young and always smiley. Her blonde hair was cut long on one side, shaved on the other. It almost worked.

'Hey Sandi. Haven't seen you in a while.' She gave me one of those radiant smiles.

'Yeah, it's been too long. How have you survived?'

She laughed, a thunderbolt laugh that belted around the office.

'Maria said–'

'Already done.' She held up an envelope with my name on it.

'Special treatment for me?'

She swivelled her chair from side to side. 'Sweet to catch up. See you next time.'

There was no way I was going to work from home that afternoon and miss one of the five perfect days a year that Melbourne gifted. Winter had been extra-cold and spring had been windy and wet. I'd spent six months holed up in my flat. I was desperate to be outside, soaking up the summer sun.

I meandered down to the local park, avoiding the whining brakes and the stench of diesel that dominated the major truck routes in the neighbourhood.

Despite the general lack of green nearby, some patches existed and my destination, Yarraville Gardens, was one of them. It even had one of the best views in the suburb. Past the shipping containers and cranes, you could see the city skyscrapers.

Once I hit the gardens I realised school was out. Rowdy kids swarmed the playground, while tired mums flagged on park benches.

I strolled to a quieter section, near a cluster of blue gums, and found a spot, half in and half out of the shade. I reluctantly withdrew the police file from my backpack.

I flicked through it again and stopped at the photocopied version of the crime scene photo. The sight of Lee Wu's body was less confronting now she and her blood were in black and white. Her throat looked flat, the sense of texture and movement of the coloured version absent. The unnerving part was that the only image of Lee was with her throat cut.

The post-mortem report described Lee as 155cm in height and 45kg in weight. She had long, carefully manicured fingernails that had recently been painted magenta. Her hair was black and long, her eyes chocolate-brown. I tried to form a picture of her alive, but the dead version dominated.

I turned the page and read the statement of the Colombian guy, Ricardo Lopez, charged with her murder.

At five o'clock when I finished work, I went to the brothel, Club 96. It was the first time in my life I had been to a brothel.

That assertion seemed dubious.

I extracted my phone and searched the internet. Number 96 was the street number. Google Maps revealed a basic fibro house with metal window shutters and red terracotta roof tiles. Club 96 customers were clearly more focused on the service than the architecture.

The accused man's "story" continued, claiming he hadn't attacked the sex worker, who he called Petal, and had in fact tried to protect her.

I could see why Maria was struggling to find a way to defend Ricardo. His statement was a farce.

A couple of rainbow lorikeets screeched past. Their raucous excitement was infectious and I smiled despite the subject matter. I lay down with my head on my backpack, held the file up above my face and continued reading.

Ricardo had told the cops that three others were present at the time of the murder: the Asian man who Ricardo had accused of attacking the sex worker, a "boss lady", and another sex worker, who he described as tall and blonde.

I skimmed to the witness statements. A sex worker fitting that description had denied being present. The "boss lady" Qiao Zeng, the madam of the brothel, reported that Ricardo had visited the brothel before. My suspicion was confirmed.

The police evidence was my next focus. One point stood out. Ricardo had apparently bought a new phone – even though he was still using the one he'd had for a couple of years – that he claimed to have then lost. During the three weeks before Lee's murder, Ricardo had been making regular calls from his old mobile to the new one, with conversations lasting up to half an hour. This second phone, according to phone records, just happened to be pinging off a tower in the vicinity of Club 96. Strangely, however, it vanished on the day of Lee's death.

Had he been sweet-talking Lee before he tried to kidnap her? Maria hadn't mentioned the phone. My guess was she didn't want to add to the list of damning evidence she'd provided me before I agreed to take on the case.

As Maria had told me earlier, only Ricardo's fingerprints were found on the knife. And the forensic pathologist had found traces of blood on his T-shirt and jeans, despite him having tried to wash it out.

I shook my head. The cops would be thrilled by his ineptness.

What about his fiancée? I found that information at the back of the file.

Valentina Rojas was also from Colombia and worked as a Spanish teacher. She and Ricardo had been engaged for some time until she'd disappeared 15 months ago. She left work one day and allegedly never went or made it home.

The cops found her passport at her house, but there was no evidence of phone, internet or bank account activity from the day she vanished. While a family member reported that Ricardo and Valentina had a spat three days before she went missing, he had an alibi for the time of her disappearance.

I did an internet search for the case and found a newspaper article with a photo of a cute woman with an elf-shaped face and cheeky smile, and the heading:

Police fear missing fiancée may have met with foul play
Valentina Rojas was last seen leaving work in High Street, Northcote at 8.30pm on Wednesday. Detective Inspector Shane McIlroy says police are speaking to a person of interest.

I was flooded with an overwhelming sense of regret. Why had I let myself get hoodwinked by Maria into taking on this case? I was helping defend a serial killer. Two women had been murdered by this bastard.

Hang on. Keep an open mind. Of all the reasons Lopez might invent to explain his fiancée's disappearance, I predicted it would be the obvious: that Valentina was having an affair and must have disappeared with the new bloke.

A text from Maria pinged. She'd organised a meeting with Ricardo the next morning at the remand centre.

I texted Maria back and asked if she'd received any phone records from the police.

Not at this stage, came her reply.

In my notebook, I scribbled interview questions and checked my translation app for key terms in Spanish, including "witness", "charges" and "statement". Words I hadn't needed to learn before.

Without anything else pressing to do, I lay back on the grass and watched soft clouds crawl across the baby blue sky…and tried to distance myself from the gruesome crime.

I texted my bestie, Stewart Wright.

Hey Stew, what you up to? Come for dinner?

Not that I had any food to speak of, but Stew didn't eat much anyway. White bread with mounds of honey was his main diet. I exaggerate; he liked pizza as well, and lots of liquid. Beer was his regular go-to and whisky was his treat, and if needed, he could drink anything else available.

At work. Will come at 8.30?

Great, see you then.

I considered doing some exercise, but I was too relaxed. The sun warmed my skin; vitamin D was soaking in.

Next thing I knew, I was shivering, my phone was yelling at me and the sun was setting. A cool wind had crept up. I was completely in shadow and the park was deserted.

I scrambled to my feet and answered my phone. 'Stew.'

'Where the hell are you?'

'I'll be there soon.'

I grabbed my gear, relieved it hadn't walked. My legs took a while to get going. I pushed through the initial muscle burn and jogged up Somerville Road. Truck curfew had kicked in for the night and only a couple of cars, with their headlights on, cruised past me. I turned right into my street, sprinting past apartment blocks and under plane trees. The streetlights came on as I ran into my driveway.

My lanky friend was perched on the stairs to my flat, his head jigging to music only he could hear. He extracted white earphones, brushed blond hair from his blue eyes and coveted long eyelashes, and stood to peck me on the cheek.

'Sorry, Stew; that was weird, I fell asleep in the park,' I puffed. 'Come on up. How was work?'

Stewart now worked in a bar in Fitzroy, though I'd met him four years ago, in a large noisy pub where he'd been bartending. I'd gone there for a friend's birthday but spent the night sitting on a stool chatting to Stewart. We hit it off straight away and had been close friends ever since.

'Oh my God, too busy. I've been standing for eight hours straight – well, apart from driving here. I need to take over your couch for a while.'

'Feel free.'

I unlocked the front door and Stewart headed straight to the three-seater green vinyl couch in the centre of my living room. He took off his shoes and made himself horizontal. I was pleased to see he'd brought a six-pack.

Flicker, my tortoiseshell cat, greeted us with her loud mewing which continued until I picked her up and stroked her firmly along her back. Her muscles rippled in response.

'Hungry?' I asked Stew.

'Starving.'

'Don't think I'm going to have anything you might want.'

'Pizza?' he said.

I loved how predictable he was. 'Can you get this one, and I'll pay next time.' We were always negotiating payment depending on our minimal bank balances.

The beer can whistled as he pulled the tab. He handed it to me and opened one for himself.

Stewart grabbed his mobile and ordered a large pizza, half-vegetarian and half-Hawaiian, while I went into my pint-sized kitchen to stow the rest of the beer in the fridge and feed Flicker.

Stewart shifted his legs when I returned so I could fit next to him on the couch, then plonked his feet, in white sport socks, on my lap. After her dinner and a quick wash, Flicker hopped up to join us, or rather Stewart, who she loved as he'd absently pat her and scratch behind her ears for hours.

I filled him in on my new case, skipping the gory details. Stewart had a weak stomach, probably because he'd never eaten any real food. I had never seen anything green, apart from marijuana, pass his lips.

'How's Ben?' I asked.

'Oh, good.' Stewart's tone contradicted the words. 'He's adorable.' He sat up and swung his right leg across his left, taking care to move Flicker with him. 'Don't know how I got so lucky. Only problem is,' he sighed, 'same story: the *open relationship* He's doing his own thing so often. Like tonight. I think he's going out more without me now. I don't know what to think. When we're together it's fantastic. We have fun, amazing sex.'

'Lucky you.' I raised my can to him.

'I know, I know. Sometimes it feels too good to be true, but when he makes out with other guys... He was up front with me from the beginning, that's what he wanted. I agreed. He has never lied about it, so I have to be okay with that. I guess.'

Stewart deposited Flicker on the couch and paced around my lounge, a whole three steps in each direction.

'But whenever he's out without me, I know he's screwing some guy and I just can't take my mind off it; imagining who he's with, what they're doing, what an amazing time he's having. It's driving me crazy. He says it's nothing to him. Doesn't feel like that to me.'

Stewart's relationships were like the Mardi Gras Parade, brief and full of pizzazz. Mine, on the other hand, started well and then sourly plummeted.

Monogamy, or lack of it, had been an ongoing issue for Stewart. His partners never wanted to settle down into an exclusive couple. My buddy had always wanted just that. Most of the guys vamoosed after a month or two before it even came to discussing something "more". Although the record had been broken with Ben. They'd been together nearly four months and Ben really seemed to care about Stew, unlike his other exes.

Much as I was keen to offer my great relationship wisdom to Stew, I thought it might have been wasted on him.

He smiled wanly at me. His dimple, on the left side, made him look boyish.

I scratched my head. 'Do you want to end it?'

Stewart vigorously shook his head. 'Ben's the best thing that's happened to me.'

The pizza arrived and we made ourselves comfortable again on the couch. Nothing like Hawaiian pizza to lift your mood.

'Met anyone?' he asked.

I wished I hadn't shared my plan to use a dating app. I'd signed up then shied away. At the moment no-one was going to match Diana.

'I'll let you know the moment I discover Ms Perfectly Good Enough.'

Stewart nodded, his movements birdlike, as if he were pecking at something. 'Isn't it Showtime sweetie? Escape from our dramaramas?'

We gobbled pizza, opened another beer and watched one of our favourite *Game of Thrones* episodes for the 10th time. We arranged ourselves over each other and settled in for some fantasy. A good dose of scheming psychopaths, knights skewering each other and a dragon whisperer shoved my minor lust issues under the couch.

3

FLICKER WOKE ME BEFORE DAWN WITH HER SIGNATURE CALL, A MIAOW THAT sounded like she was being strangled. She nudged my chin with her orange-coloured nose, demanding a pre-brekkie cuddle. It was early, even for her. Given Stewart had stayed late, the only greeting she received was grumbled swear words. I fed her a handful of dry food and crawled back to bed.

Despite my tiredness, thoughts about the upcoming interview kept me awake until after a fight with sheets and pillows, I must have fallen back to sleep, because my alarm's high-pitched beep snapped me out of a dream. I indulged in a long shower, then grabbed a takeaway coffee from my local to fortify me for the drive out west to the remand centre. The West Gate Freeway and the Ring Road were clogged with peak hour congestion. As soon as I could, I escaped onto side streets. I was in a foul mood for the farcical meeting with the Colombian, who seemed to have zilch chance of dodging murder charges.

The scenery was as colourless as my attitude – dry brown grass, punctuated only by transmission towers and warehouses. The complex was stuck in the wasteland of Ravenhall, hidden from public view. I managed to nab a spot under a gum, in the packed visitor's car park. Shadows of struggling leaves trembled on the dashboard as I killed the engine. I sank the last of the latte and forced myself out of the car. A cold wind drove through my thin jacket and dark clouds hovered above.

The angular design of the remand centre screamed brutality. The silver roof was a sword, the black walls were shields. High fences, covered in unscaleable metal cylinders, surrounded the perimeter.

I shivered and not just because of the weather. The thought of having my every action controlled by prison guards and being confined to a cell the size of my kitchen made my chest constrict. Confined spaces freaked me out.

A short guy in a black suit, carrying a leather folder, beat me to the entrance. Half-dead plants in giant grey pots welcomed us. Inside the foyer, an enormous papier-mâché clown failed in its attempt to create a child-friendly atmosphere.

Maria had arranged for me to visit as her legal assistant. I presumed she'd already arrived and could verify that fact if need be. I approached the tinsel decorated counter, staffed by six burly guards and surrendered my mobile phone and keys to a distracted officer. Behind him colleagues joked together.

A series of procedures awaited: visitor identification, a photograph of my face and eye, metal and drug detection. I held my arms out to my side, as a droopy-lipped officer in a blue uniform scanned my chest. I resented the intrusion, even though he hadn't touched me.

I was escorted through thick security doors, across a path and into the Visitor's Centre, where a combination of sweat and disinfectant assaulted my nostrils.

A guard showed me into a small interview room with two occupants. Maria gesticulated towards the sullen man slumped opposite her, Ricardo Lopez.

I froze; my comprehension jarring. Ricardo's features were a mirror image of my ex-girlfriend's. His photo in the police file bore a resemblance, but this was uncanny. His brown upturned eyes were identical to hers. His colouring was like a deep summer tan, his nose small and symmetrical.

I was staring at a man accused of murder, who resembled Diana so much they could have been siblings.

Diana had hurricaned into my life six months ago – gorgeous, witty and consuming. When I was with her, my neglected friends faded into the background. After she'd broken it off with her girlfriend, she swore they wouldn't get back together. She'd whispered her promise as she enchanted me with her intense brown eyes, lying on top of me, naked, her tender accent stroking my heart.

The memory of the break-up constricted my throat.

I snapped back to the man opposite and studied him further. The rest of his face differed from Diana's. His furrowed chin was covered in stubble, his lips were thin.

Ricardo glared at me. His attitude was a combination of tough and defeated. Annoyance with him absorbed the painful memories his likeness had produced.

'You're here.' Maria glanced at her silver watch and introduced us.

I plonked myself next to her. After a nod to Ricardo, I turned to Maria. *Focus, focus*, I ordered myself.

Maria blinked through mascara-drenched eyelashes. She tapped the table with mauve fingernails. 'Ricardo, you need to cooperate with Sandi.' Her tone was forceful and didn't leave room for a "no".

'I have another client to interview while I'm here,' she said to me. 'I'll be back.'

We waited in silence for the guard to release her. Maria's tight dress highlighted every Italian curve she had. I noticed Ricardo's eyes following her. I could tell he was as impressed as I was. Anger filled my belly as he ogled her.

I took a moment to gather myself by wriggling my backside into a more comfortable position on the chair.

'*Hola, Ricardo. Hablo un poco de español.*'

I was kicking goals here; Spanish 101.

His expression was either surprised or cynical. I shoved aside thoughts of Diana, not wanting her image tainted by this man.

'*Estoy aquí para ayudarte.*' "I'm here to help you." I hoped I got that right.

Ricardo mumbled something. I asked him to repeat, to speak slowly.

'*Nadie me puede ayudar,*' he said. "No-one can help me."

At least I thought that was what he said. He was hard to understand. I hoped I'd adjust to his accent as the interview progressed.

'*Es inútil.*' "It's useless." He challenged me with his stare.

I was inclined to agree.

I was too tired to think of something ironic to say; anyway, I probably couldn't have translated it. The latte had failed to file an edge off my weariness.

Ricardo Lopez slumped in his chair, his cheeks hidden in his hands.

I forced a smile. I'd been told it was my best asset, so I made the most of it. 'You worked in an auto mechanics'?'

He nodded.

'I drive an old VW Golf,' I offered.

A tendril of interest emerged.

'What sort of car do you have?' I asked.

Ricardo swallowed, his Adam's apple sliding down and up. He squinted as though he wasn't sure whether to answer or not, whether it was a trick question. I realised I'd used the Spanish word for car, and maybe he wasn't familiar with that word.

I asked the question again. '*Qué tipo de carro tienes?*'

He hesitated, but then answered, 'Commodore VF.'

I knew the answer already. The details were in the police report: after the sex worker was murdered, Ricardo had driven home in his red Commodore. On the way, he'd stopped at public toilets in a park, to wash the blood out of his clothes.

I heard what sounded like rain on the roof, but there were no external windows to confirm. It was unnerving being confined by concrete bricks. I forced myself to ignore the walls closing in on me and dragged my attention back to Ricardo.

'Did you like your job?'

'I worked long hours for years. As soon as the police arrived, the boss, he told me to leave. That day. That hour. You know what he said? He said, "We don't want your type here".'

Ricardo's eyes smouldered. The question had prompted more than a one-word response.

'In that moment he took away my *org…*' His raised hand was clenched like a claw.

'Took away your what?'

'*Orgullo,*' he repeated.

'Job?' I guessed.

Ricardo shook his head fiercely.

The Colombian tried explaining, but I didn't get it. He slapped his chest. I was guessing *orgullo* meant pride.

'He took away my pride. I worked hard. The others would have a long lunch when the boss was away. People expect that we take long breaks because we're from Latin America, but in Colombia we don't do that. We Colombians work very hard.'

Ricardo's hands were in constant motion as he told his story.

'If there was a complex electrical problem, I would spend extra time working on it. My boss knew that. But when the police came, all my hard work meant nothing. And now I'm trapped here.'

While he was wallowing, I zoomed in on the opportunity. 'Tell me exactly what happened. I've read your statement, but I want to hear it from you.'

He grimaced.

'The more you tell me, the better the outcome for you.' I kept my voice soft and soothing, easy in Spanish. 'Maria is an excellent solicitor. You're lucky to have her working on your case. You help me and that will help Maria.'

His furrowed brow suggested he was thinking about it. 'Okay.'

I had him. Luckily my Spanish was flowing, though I was sure I was making grammatical mistakes. Ricardo understood me, that was the main thing.

'Who did you live with in Heidelberg?'

'My sister, my young nephew and niece. And my brother-in-law.'

'What do the kids like to do? Listen to music, play sport?'

'My niece, she likes to draw and my nephew plays football. He is very good.' His eyes lit up.

Even murderers have a soft spot.

'AFL?' I asked.

'No, *fútbol*.' He emphasised each syllable as he hitched his lip. 'Soccer,' he added derisively.

'What position does he play?'

Ricardo smirked. 'Centre forward.'

'So, an attacker.'

He seemed surprised that I knew the terminology.

Ricardo nodded. 'He's not tall, but he's very quick; that's perfect for a centre forward. Same as me. In the past, when I was young.'

'You barrack for Colombia?' I was guessing the country had a national team.

'*La Selección Colombia*.' He pumped his fist as he mentioned his team.

The interview process is like a long-distance swim. You have to judge the waves, the distance, the amount of energy it's going to take and the speed, so you can get the result you want. I decided I'd done enough to grease him up; it was time and he was ready.

I double-checked the list of questions I'd prepared. As I glanced up, a face peered through the glass panelled door: a guard checking I was still alive. As I turned back to Ricardo, I kept my face open and friendly.

'I need to ask you questions that will help Maria defend you.

Some of them are personal, but they're important. You understand?'

Ricardo nodded.

'In your statement you say that the day in question was the first time you'd been to a brothel.'

'*Sí*,' he said. 'The first time.'

'One of the witnesses said you'd been there before.'

Ricardo fidgeted with a gold cross on a fine necklace. I'd obviously hit a nerve.

'Not me. Must have been someone who looked like me.'

I decided to let that go for the time being.

'The sex worker you'd spent time with came to the front door to say goodbye. That's what you told the police.'

Ricardo nodded.

'Why would she do that, when you'd met for the first time?'

'She liked me.'

I resisted a snigger. No doubt he'd fallen for her flattery. 'It was more than a job for her? Is that right?'

Ricardo bit a ragged fingernail.

'Did you two talk together? She was your friend? Perhaps that was more important to you than having sex.'

Ricardo's dark eyes darted from me to his stubby hands. 'We had sex.'

I rubbed my hand across the soft cover of my moleskin notebook then flicked to a free ivory-coloured page where I wrote the date.

'Tell me about the sex.'

Ricardo recoiled, perhaps stunned a woman would ask such a question.

'I've heard it all before.' I nodded, encouraging him. 'Nothing's going to shock me.'

I had to find a way to talk about this casually, like how doctors give you a pap smear and make it seem as innocent as checking your tonsils. Thanks to the translation app on my iPhone, I'd memorised specific terms so I could get down to the nitty-gritty. Most of the words were similar to English; easy to remember.

'Oral, anal? Everything?'

Ricardo kept his eyes lowered.

'Since you hadn't been to a brothel before, I guess you might have been a bit nervous. Didn't know what was expected?'

The concrete surrounding us was as impenetrable as Ricardo. My chest was tight in the hot, airless room. As I slid off my jacket and draped it across the back of my chair, I slowed my breathing to maintain my calm.

'Start from the beginning. How did you choose this brothel?'

'It was near my work.'

'Where did you find out about it?'

'The internet.'

'What attracted you to the brothel?'

'It was near my work,' he repeated.

'All right, so when you got to the brothel you…' I indicated for him to continue.

On the surface, Ricardo was embarrassed. A deeper emotion eluded me.

'I went to Club 96 after work. It was the first time I'd been. The ladies, they came out one by one. I said, "I like her. The one called Petal." I went to her room. She took off her clothes. I got on top of her.'

His voice was flat, it was too rehearsed.

'All right, what happened then?'

Ricardo angled away from me, and we listened to rain on the roof for a moment.

'I tried to kiss her. She said, "No kissing". I had sex with her. I got dressed. Then she said she would see me out.'

It was definitely a rehearsed story.

'What kind of sex did you have?'

He covered his face with his hands. I was frustrated that the conversation wasn't flowing. I couldn't seem to loosen him up.

'You know all this will be talked about in court. It'll be tougher than this. Have you been in court before?' My tone was terse.

After a quick shake of his head, Ricardo stared at the scarred table, no doubt wishing he could be anywhere else but in this room. I placed myself in his position. In prison, I thought, it would be dangerous to open up, express vulnerability.

I softened my voice. 'What kind of sex?'

He raised his hands as if to heaven. 'Normal.'

'You mean vaginal sex?'

He looked puzzled. I wondered if it was my incorrect use of Spanish.

'Maybe blow job too.'

'Maybe? Why are you changing your story? I don't get it.' My voice rasped with frustration.

Ricardo stunk of sweat. A V-shaped wet patch on his T-shirt had changed from light to dark green. Was he hot, nervous or both?

'I don't think you had sex at all.'

'We did, we did have sex.' He raised his voice. 'Normal sex, that's all.'

I unclenched my legs under the table. My foot had gone to sleep, so I stamped it on the floor. My head was full of possible scenarios. Was he embarrassed that he didn't have sex with her? Had he been there so often he couldn't remember the details of that instance or had they performed some kink he was too ashamed to admit? I fought the urge to grill him further. I knew I needed to change tack.

'All right, normal sex that took half an hour.' I emphasised the time frame. 'Right?'

Ricardo nodded slowly, as if he wanted me to tell him the right answer. He leaned forward. 'Okay. We talked a little too.'

'Before or after?'

'After.' One of his thick eyebrows had developed a hitch. He was uneasy about where the conversation was heading.

'What did you talk about?' I asked casually.

'Her work.'

'Her work?' A drop of surprise leaked out in my response.

'A little,' he admitted.

'What did she tell you about her work?'

He wiped sweat from his forehead with the back of his hand.

He hadn't said anything about this in his statement – that they talked. Was that why he was worried?

I repeated my question.

He buried his head in his hands.

'She was on a student visa. Did she tell you that?'

'Student?' He suddenly straightened.

'She was studying here in Australia.'

Ricardo appeared confused. Although I was curious about why that fact had thrown him, I wanted to put his distraction to good use.

'The police have evidence that you rang someone in the brothel, over the three weeks before Petal was killed. They know you bought a second mobile, gave it to someone in the brothel and rang them. Often.'

Ricardo banged the table with his fist. 'The first time I went to Club 96, I sat outside in my car for a long time. I went to the front door, but didn't go in. I must have dropped the phone then. I bought a new one, and rang to find out who had my phone.'

I hesitated. Thought it through. 'You've got it the wrong way. You say you were ringing from the new phone to find out where your old phone was; the phone records show you were calling the new phone from the original phone.'

He refused to make eye contact with me.

'Why did you buy the second phone?'

Ricardo nibbled his ragged nails. He was a poor liar and we both knew it.

'Do you realise how many years you'll be locked up if you're found guilty? The evidence is all against you: the witnesses, your fingerprints, the phone.'

'It's useless,' he mumbled.

I totally agreed. Normally, I had no trouble getting people, even criminals, to open up to me. But Ricardo was a clam. I was having trouble working out if I'd lost my touch, if it was a language issue or if the man was hard core.

'Forget it. Just forget it.' His voice rose in decibels.

I forced myself to control my anger, which wasn't my strong point at the best of times. Before reacting, I made my shoulders relax.

'Look, don't worry about the phone. What's important is what happened when you were leaving. In your statement, you say Petal said goodbye to you at the front door when another man attacked her?'

'Sí. Petal opened the front door for me. A big Asian man grabbed her. I heard her scream. I ran back in – to help her.' His voice faltered. 'The Asian man had the knife. Blood went everywhere.'

Ricardo leaped up. 'Too much blood. Petal was lying there, not moving.'

He dropped to his knees, gritted his teeth. Ricardo was acting out the scene. He was either a good actor or he was doing it from body memory.

I stood up so I could see. He rubbed his hand along the steel-blue lino floor.

'The boss lady knelt down next to me. She wrapped a towel over

Petal's neck, and it turned red with blood. The boss lady screamed, "She's dead, she's dead!"'

Ricardo rocked back on his legs; his eyes were unfocused. 'Then the big Asian man punched me in the face.'

Ricardo clutched his jaw. 'I ran out the door and drove off before he could catch me.'

I made him repeat what happened. His story remained the same. It was like he was seeing it happening. That was the first time during the interview I believed anything he'd said, apart from who he barracked for.

'Why did you try and help Petal?'

'I– I...' said Ricardo.

The door suddenly swung open.

A tough-looking female guard with wrinkles like sand ridges yelled, 'Back on your seat, Lopez!'

Ricardo sprang to his feet.

'Now.'

Ricardo dropped to his chair.

The guard eyed me.

'I'm fine,' I answered the unasked question.

The guard backed out the door, her fierce blue eyes focused on Ricardo. Once she was outside, I said, 'You were saying why you were helping Petal.'

'I don't know.'

'You saw the Asian man with the knife?'

Ricardo raised his hands like I'd stated the obvious.

'Yes or no?'

'Yes.' Ricardo voice was a growl.

'What did he do with the knife?'

'Isn't that obvious?'

'In your statement you say he "stabbed her in the neck".'

'You have your answer.'

'Why do you think he stabbed her?'

Ricardo shook his head. I was annoyed that the guard had broken the flow. We were back where we started.

'You stated there was another witness there, apart from the Asian man and the boss lady.'

'Yes, yes, another prostitute.' He hesitated and swallowed. 'Blonde lady.'

'She says she wasn't there, didn't see anything.'

'That's a lie!' he said.

I was surprised by his sudden passion. I tucked it away for future reference.

'All right, you witnessed the murder and then you ran out the door after the Asian man punched you. One thing I'm confused about. Why didn't you call the police when Petal died?'

He stared at me like I was an idiot and laughed sarcastically.

'People normally call the police if someone's murdered,' I stated.

He gazed up at the ceiling where the fluorescent lights created a harsh glare. 'Not in Colombia. Not in my country. The police work with drug lords. They don't work for you or for me.'

Diana had told me about Colombia, explaining why she'd immigrated to Australia. Drug lords dominated the country, corrupt police facilitating their illegal trade. In 1985, the notorious Pablo Escobar recruited a Marxist guerrilla group to invade the Supreme Court and burn Escobar's records, in his brazen attempt to avoid extradition. Over a hundred people were killed in the court siege, including judges. Even though that had happened so long ago, Diana said it permanently scarred Colombia. Apparently, following the siege the government had attempted to eradicate the drug traffickers' grip on the country. Ricardo seemed to be implying that had either failed or corruption had become pervasive.

'What did they do to you?' I asked.

'Not me. A friend of mine was killed by the police.'

Ricardo studied his fingernails. I waited. The silence lingered.

'How? What happened to your friend, Ricardo?'

'You know nothing here in Australia. Nothing.'

'So, teach me.'

Ricardo sighed. 'One day my friend was driving his car through Bogotá. There was a roadblock in his way. He was stopped by two policemen. They told him, *Get out of your car and leave the keys.* He refused to get out of the car, so they shot him.'

I must have been frowning, because he said, 'These things happen all the time in Colombia. In this country, you don't hear about it. You expect me to call the police? I don't trust them.'

I thought about arguing the point, but decided I had more important questions.

'There is an issue with the knife used to kill Petal. Only your fingerprints were found on it. Was it your knife?'

'No.'

'How did your fingerprints come to be on the weapon?'

'I picked up the knife after Petal was hurt.'

Ricardo stared at the door. There was no face at the window, no movement of the handle.

'Why did you pick up the knife?'

'It wasn't my knife,' he insisted.

'Whose knife was it?'

He clamped into a solid muscular knot, refusing to answer. There was no point prodding him on that subject. I flipped a page in my notebook and switched to my final topic.

'What about your fiancée, Valentina?' I asked. 'What happened to her?'

His voice exploded. 'Why do you have to bring that up? I was at work when she went missing.'

Ricardo glanced at the window. The guard's face was absent. His chest heaved and he sprang from his chair and actually snarled and bared his teeth. He lifted his fist, slowly and intentionally as he stared down at me.

I leaped to my feet, my nerves jangling as my body slipped automatically into aikido mode.

'Hey, Ricardo, I'm on your side, remember?' I spoke calmly despite fear yelling at me to do the opposite.

His eyes were pinpoints, like he'd snapped.

'I'm here to help you. We can work this out.'

I kept up my calming chatter. Gradually, Ricardo morphed from a pit bull to a mastiff. Energy seeped out of his body until he doubled over, with his hands on his knees.

My heart was still pumping. The danger seemed to have passed, but I didn't trust him. I remained standing.

Ricardo the killer – was that what I'd witnessed? It had been so sudden, the change from a calm and dejected man, to one ready to assault me, with relatively little prodding. Was it a result of being imprisoned or his natural inclination?

I weighed up whether to call it quits, when Ricardo raised his head.

'I didn't hurt Valentina.' Ricardo punctuated each word with a punch to his forehead. 'I'd never hurt her.'

'All right, that's clear, Ricardo.'

He squeezed his hands together. '*Es inútil.*' It's useless. His mantra.

I noticed a face at the window. So did Ricardo. He rapped on the door and when the guard opened it, he was led away. I spotted Maria on the other side and wondered how long she'd been there.

After Ricardo's outburst and being cooped up in a tiny room, I was jittery and couldn't wait to escape. An officer escorted us out of the Visitor's Centre and back into the reception area. I grabbed my mobile and keys and rushed outside.

'I thought I had him.' I slipped into my jacket. 'When I turned up the heat he shut down like a Spanish siesta. No way should he be allowed to testify, Maria. His story is like a spinning prize wheel. You never know where it's going to land.' I shook my head. 'He doesn't deserve you representing him. I'll have to work out another way to find the info you need.'

'I'm sure you got further than I did, Sandi. Let me know where your investigation leads.' Maria regarded me with warm brown eyes. 'Hey, are you free to come to dinner with Kristin and me on Sunday?'

'Sure.' I gave up on the idea of having her to myself.

The icy wind made us dash for our cars. I thought about going home back to bed, but I was wide awake. Amazing how adrenaline boosted your energy levels. I was determined to uncover Ricardo's story and there was only one way to find out.

4

I'D BEEN BIDING MY TIME OUTSIDE CLUB 96 IN PRESTON, WAITING FOR THE right moment. A metal fence half-hid the cacky-coloured fibro brothel. I'd parked diagonally opposite, next to a large park with a playground, where I had a clear view of the front door via the driveway entrance.

My meeting at the remand centre had made my head swirl. The only facts I'd driven away with were that Ricardo had talked to Lee, or Petal as he'd called her, and he had the capacity for violence – or the threat of it.

But I believe all of us in the "wrong" circumstances have that in us; and if propelled we could kill – at least in self-defence or to protect someone we love. I also knew from my childhood that men in particular could hurt the ones they claim to love.

As I'd driven across town from the remand centre, a strategy for gaining insight into the details of Lee's murder crystallised. I doubted Maria would have approved but she never needed to know the specifics.

I'd decided on the target for my plan – a guy wearing a blue T-shirt and beige pants who'd already gone inside – and was hoping the next punter would arrive soon. The steady flow of customers suggested I wouldn't have to wait long and, sure enough, a suited john in designer sunglasses locked his Volvo, crossed the road and darted into the building, with me close on his tail.

I was wearing a woollen jumper, beret and thick black glasses. My car boot was full of such useful gear.

Inside the front door, the stench of acrid sweat lingered. Mood-lighting emanated from a couple of red bulbs in a bronze lampshade on the reception desk. The décor was an improvement on the frontage, though the colour scheme was predictable. A couple of crimson arm chairs stood vacant. Off-white walls with crimson trimming glowed as if they'd received a recent coat of paint. At least they stopped the asbestos seeping out.

I was already at the door leading into the inner sanctum of the brothel before the receptionist – dressed of course in an indigo corset with matching coloured eye shadow – realised I'd snuck in with a punter. I twisted the old-fashioned handle. The door remained firmly shut. Shoving my shoulder against it, I tried again and then banged on the door with my fist.

'You bastard,' I yelled, 'get your arse out here.'

'Wait, please,' the receptionist said firmly to the suited john, who was snug up against the counter.

The receptionist sped to my side. The front door slammed. The john had disappeared. I guessed his urge must have shrivelled up.

'No entry. Please, what do you want?' The receptionist's voice was high-pitched and strained.

Although her high heels gave her a lift, she was still a head shorter than me.

'I want my cheating, good-for-nothing husband to get his arse out here!' I thumped the crimson door.

The receptionist blinked. Her enormous black eyelashes were too heavy for her delicate brown eyes.

'No, your husband isn't here.' She shook her head vigorously, her long black hair swinging like a horse's tail.

'He bloody well is!' I blasted back. 'I followed him here.'

'His name?'

'It doesn't matter what his name is, I bet he'll bloody lie about it anyway.'

I described the man I'd seen coming into Club 96. He was solid, hairy and sweaty, and wore a blue T-shirt and dirty beige work pants. I imagined he'd be shoved into a shower quicker than a galloping greyhound.

Up close, the receptionist was older than I'd first thought. Thick foundation was unable to conceal the wrinkles that branched out from her eyes like the lines of a shell.

I was guessing she might have been Qiao, not just receptionist but the madam of Club 96 and one of the witnesses to Lee's murder. I tapped the invisible shutter button on the arm of my black-rimmed glasses.

I'd had an idea of the space where Lee was murdered but the

reception area was smaller than I'd imagined. I was recalculating when Qiao said, 'Please wait outside. This is a good club, no trouble.'

'No trouble! What about that prostitute who was murdered here? *Good club*! What a load of hogwash.'

I stepped away from the locked door. On the wall hung a photo display of women dressed in lingerie. None of their faces were visible, either because of the angle or the Photoshopping.

One image, taken from above, was of 'Plum' crouched on black sheets, with her knees spread and her physical details listed: Size – 6, Eyes – Brown, Hair – Black, Bust – B.

A slim "Snow" wore white lingerie and an unbuttoned white shirt; her index finger plucked at her panties. An olive-skinned "Rose" revealed wide hips and plentiful cheeks either side of a hot-pink G-string. Equal opportunity was on offer: the business catered for all backgrounds, shapes and sizes.

I had a friend who got herself through uni by doing sex work. She said that men go to sex workers like women go to counsellors. Most of the job was listening to the punter's problems. When she started it was to pay the bond on a new house, but she found she didn't mind the work. It paid the rent for a couple of years. It was definitely not what I'd want to be doing, but then I'd never been interested in pleasing men.

I studied the photos again and thought Snow might be the sex worker that Ricardo named as a witness to Lee's murder. She was the only blonde employee on display. I tapped my glasses to snap all the sex workers.

Qiao picked up the phone and spoke in what sounded like Chinese.

When she hung up she said, 'Your husband, he'll come soon.'

'He'd better get his arse out here real quick, or he's done for. I don't care if I have to march in and drag him off the top of one of your girls.'

As I was ranting, the crimson door through to the brothel interior swung open. A man as wide as the doorway filled the gap. He was built like a sumo wrestler, although was thankfully dressed in a black suit and purple shirt.

I tugged my beret firmly onto my head and angled towards him, so I could photograph his face.

He lurched towards me. I dodged and steered past him through the still-open doorway into the interior of the brothel.

'Stop.' Sumo's voice was full of gritty authority.

I hesitated for a moment before striding down the long corridor. A woman in pink lingerie emerged from a crimson door to my right.

A large hand grabbed my wrist and dragged me backwards. I turned and twisted out of the hold by pushing Sumo's thumb in a direction it shouldn't go. Once free, I ducked past him, back towards reception.

Sumo, who was light on his feet for a big man, was quick enough to head me off.

Qiao yelled something in Chinese.

Sumo spread his arms so I couldn't dodge past him into the corridor. He corralled me towards the wall and into the crimson-upholstered chair under the photo board. His aftershave was overpowering and made my nose twinge.

I was guessing he was Ju-Long, the other witness to Lee's murder and the "large Asian man" that had punched Ricardo. In her statement, Qiao had described him as a driver for Club 96, but he was clearly the resident bouncer as well.

'Wait here,' ordered Ju-Long. 'I'll get the man for you.'

Ju-Long lunged back through the locked door. A red mark circled my wrist. I rubbed my arm, feigning more pain than I felt.

There was a buzzing noise. Another punter dressed in a brown T-shirt and a cap was let in and Qiao swiftly escorted him through the locked door. I considered barging through with them, but decided there was more I could learn in the reception area. She was back in a few seconds, pulling the door shut behind her.

'What sort of man is he, to treat a lady like that?' I held my arm and blew on my red wrist.

Qiao adjusted her corset then tiptoed back to the counter as if she was walking over rough ground.

'I'm trying to save my marriage.'

She glided over to me and wrapped my hand in her delicate fingers. Her touch was gentle. 'You'll be okay.'

'You seem like a lovely lady; wouldn't you do the same as me?'

Qiao sighed. 'Ju-Long keeps us safe, but sometimes. Sometimes he's too strong.'

My question was answered. 'Men, hey.'

She patted the back of my hand.

'We need them, but they're trouble,' I said.

There was a flash of a smile from Qiao.

A tall blonde woman with double-D breasts that were bulging out of her white lace bra appeared through the crimson door. This must be Snow.

Qiao joined her behind the counter, held her shoulder and whispered in her ear.

Surrounded by all this lingerie, I was beginning to feel overdressed and warm. I used the cover of removing my jumper, making sure the beret stayed put, to edge nonchalantly towards the reception desk.

'Out of curiosity, where did she die, that girl?' I asked. 'There's blood, I can see it, right here.'

Qiao leaned over the counter. 'Where's the blood? No, there's no blood.'

I indicated a dark stain on the carpet. 'There's definitely still blood there. Is this where she was killed, by that man? From Colombia, wasn't he? What was his name? Mario?'

'Ricardo,' they replied in unison.

'Ricardo, that's right. They say he was trying to kidnap her.'

Qiao squeezed her lips together. 'Terrible,' she said in a quivering voice. 'She was like a daughter to me. She came from China too. We're all family here.'

Qiao fetched a tissue with her indigo-manicured fingernails, and dabbed it beneath her eyes.

Snow extended her skinny arm, revealing a hot pink butterfly tattoo, around Qiao's shoulder.

'Did he murder that girl right here?' I pointed to the floor.

'Yes yes, that man killed Petal. My poor Petal.'

Qiao covered her mouth with her hand, to muffle a cry. Meanwhile Snow's index finger was pointing at the front door. The two women appeared to have different ideas about the exact location of the crime.

'Ricardo had a knife?' I said.

'Yes, in his coat,' Qiao replied.

'But why did he kill her? Do you know?'

'That man, Ricardo, always liked Petal. He liked her too much. He wanted her to go with him. Poor Petal. She was a good girl, the best girl and he killed her. He tried to kill Ju-Long too.'

Snow leaned up against the wall behind the counter.

I glanced at Snow. 'Did you know Ricardo too?'

Snow hadn't said a word the whole time she'd been there and now just gave the slightest nod. When Qiao twisted her head to look behind at the working girl, Snow covered her mouth, as if she'd exposed a major secret.

A dark-haired sex worker opened the internal crimson door and held it for a bald-headed punter wearing khaki shorts and a ragged T-shirt.

'All okay. No problem.' Qiao smiled, her ultra-red lips stretching apart.

The bald guy slipped out the front, peering at me suspiciously. Qiao followed the woman but even before the door closed behind her Qiao was screaming at the working girl; her all-caring facade had fizzled.

I smiled broadly at Snow. I hoped I had enough time to wheedle information from her, before Qiao or Ju-Long returned with my "husband".

'Did you see what happened to that poor girl?'

Snow's blue eyes darted from side to side, obviously uncomfortable with the question.

'That Ricardo is a wicked man trying to kidnap and then kill Petal.'

Snow gave the whiff of a nod.

'Did he ever hurt you?'

Snow wrinkled her nose. 'He only ever wanted Petal.' Her tone was unimpressed.

'Fussy?'

'She did whatever he wanted.' I picked up her accent as eastern European.

'She never said no to anything.' I played along.

'She tried to please everybody. She had no self-respect, that one.'

Snow had betrayed her colleague with no more than a nudge. I wondered if that was how she normally operated or if she despised Petal.

Qiao, with Ju-Long on her heels, returned to the reception area. The bouncer and Snow exchanged looks before she disappeared back into the interior of the brothel.

Ju-Long propped himself in front of the door like a sentry, with his arms crossed.

I stepped into character. 'What's taking so long? Where's my husband? He's done this before and he's not getting away with it this time.'

The crimson door swung open again and Ju-Long stepped aside to let my cheating husband through. His face red and sweaty, the hairy guy with the dirty beige pants was still adjusting his T-shirt, and he was understandably confused about why the hell he'd been summoned.

'What? Who's this? You look a bit like my Bruce, but you're not Bruce. Where is Bruce?' I hoped I sounded suitably het-up. 'Anyhow, you should be ashamed of yourself, coming in here. What would your mother think?

'I know Bruce comes here. He always says he's going to Bunnings, but he never comes home with anything, doesn't answer his phone. I know what he's up to.'

The man who was not Bruce yelled, 'What the hell are you doing, you bitch? Go fuck yourself.'

Qiao started yelling and Ju-Long charged towards me as I backed towards the front door saying, 'You tell my husband, next time he comes, I know what he's doing.'

I cleared out before either of the guys decided to throttle me.

In any case, I had a meeting with someone from my past I was keen to keep.

5

The lane, off Smith Street in Fitzroy, was ridden with deserted warehouses splashed with graffiti. Bent bars protecting windows, evidence of failed squatters. The stains and stench of men's piss infected the footpath. At the end, a dimly lit café emerged.

A tangle of emotions vied for supremacy as I spied Cassy Joynson, her back to me.

She was focused on a newspaper article, her familiar cropped haircut exposing the snake tattoo winding behind her ear. Of all her tattoos, the black snake was the stunner.

I hesitated, my hand on the cool metal handle; I pulled my shoulders back and shoved open the door to the crowded café.

I was next to the table before Cassy noticed me. She sprang out of her chair.

'Sandi, it's been too long.'

She kissed me on the cheek. Well almost; she didn't quite make contact. There was a puff of air instead.

'Surprised to hear from you,' I said.

My chair scraped on the concrete as I dragged it towards the table. Cassy's gaze returned to the newspaper, as though she couldn't bear to be drawn away from it, then she closed it, neatened the edges and slid it to the wall. Her nose ring glinted in the wedge of sunshine seeping through the front window.

'Can't believe you've set up a detective business. Congratulations. Sounds perfect,' she said.

'Private Investigator,' I corrected. 'Word's getting out there, so it's slowly building up.'

'Does Facebook bring in much business?'

'I don't really use it to promote my work.'

I wondered where this was heading. The lack of a "what have you been doing the last seven years?/sorry I dumped you without an explanation" was kind of curious.

'Facebook can be useful. It was great to find you, but it's a serious problem.'

Cassy always did have a suspicious take on everyday activities.

I ordered a latte, as the waitress delivered my companion a cappuccino. Cassy destroyed the Rosetta pattern with her teaspoon. She glanced up.

'Criminal gangs exploit social media,' she said, proving my thought. 'It's completely changed the face of crime. Especially pornography.'

Cassy's intense green eyes lured me. My cheeks were hot despite air-conditioning. I felt an old tug and a new wariness.

I changed topics. 'What are you up to these days?'

'Based at the Fair Sex Coalition now.'

I knew the organisation she was talking about. The Fair Sex Coalition exposed the bastards who trafficked women for the sex trade. It didn't surprise me that Cassy worked there. Her commitment to the underdog had always been zealous, a trait I admired.

'One of our callers is a young woman who's being held prisoner in a brothel, here in Melbourne,' she whispered. 'She was lucky. One of her customers bought her a mobile, so she was able to contact us.'

I focused on Cassy's ruby lips, so I could catch her quiet words.

'It's taken ages, but gradually she's revealed more and more details. She wants to escape.' Cassy caught me with a stern stare. 'She needs your help.'

'My help?' I chuckled, focusing on the exposed brick wall. Cassy had an odd way of asking for assistance.

'You're perfect for this job, Sandi. That's absolutely clear. You're capable, courageous, smart. We've got funding, we can pay you. Jae's mentioned that other women have been severely punished for trying to leave. It's so difficult to escape. That's why we need you.'

She stopped abruptly, dabbed her mouth with a serviette.

'Jae,' I said.

'Jae Shin's her real name, not her brothel name. She's from South Korea. She's been here four months, trying to work off a so-called debt of $80,000. Her spirit's beginning to flag. We've got to get her out before she goes under. It's taken weeks to build up her trust. She hasn't told me where she is yet, but she's about to, for sure. Imagine, Sandi; you can help her escape from slavery.'

It was weird and unappealing that Cassy's case also involved a sex worker, and this one trafficked. Besides, I was dubious about working for Cassy; she liked to be in control.

'I've got enough work at the moment. Anyway, I think it's a job for the cops.' I needed the money, but not the drama.

Cassy's emerald eyes skewered me. 'We've promised Jae there'll be no police involvement. She's terrified about what might happen – talk of kicking her out of the country, threats to her family – the owners have scared her to death.'

My jaw clenched in an effort to stop myself forming a picture of Jae.

'Usually we meet with women, if they can get out alone. Some are allowed to go to the local shops; sometimes we can go into the brothel with an information kit. Jae's situation sounds horrendous. The women are constantly monitored.'

It was time for me to escape, before I committed to something I might regret.

'Well, thanks for considering me. I'll give it some thought.' I nudged my chair back. 'I need to head off, but I'll be in touch.'

'Okay,' she said firmly, 'We'll talk tomorrow about next steps.'

'I said I'll be in touch. No promises.'

Cassy dropped the volume down a notch. 'Look Sandi, sorry if you feel this has been sprung on you. The way we finished, it wasn't – and we've only just caught up again, so no hard feelings if you decide not to, but you'd be making a difference. Everyone at the Coalition is counting on you.'

Before Cassy had time to follow me, I scurried down the laneway and drove straight home to the oasis of my flat.

I grabbed a beer from the fridge and slamming cupboard doors, prepared dinner.

Ricardo's case had me longing for the clichéd client whose boyfriend was cheating on him. This insane request from Cassy felt too much of the same – with a dollop of organised crime thrown in. Breaking a woman out of a slave brothel! Cassy was delusional. This wasn't a job for a PI. I knew I should ring her immediately and say I wasn't interested. In more ways than one.

As I cut the fat off a steak, Flicker rubbed against my legs and mewed loudly. I fed her tinned food as the meat sizzled under the grill.

Had I really expected an apology from Cassy?

A long overdue catch up with no ulterior motive would have been the next best thing. But that had never been Cassy's style. Instead I'd ended up with a request to be a pawn in a "Cassy to the Rescue" drama, with the potential of my arse on the line.

All right, maybe I was overreacting.

We *were* young when we were an item and I know I wasn't without fault either. And really, the only risky moment I'd had with Cassy was when we went camping at Wilson's Prom. She'd goaded me into an impromptu hike that took five hours instead of three. We'd been caught in hail and without raincoats were soaked within seconds. Then the sun had set. We'd had to trudge back, shivering in the dark, taking turns to use the torches in our mobiles, so the batteries didn't die. Luckily the track was wide and easy to follow. Nothing bad had happened, apart from me catching a cold and the whole experience made for a great pub story.

Another memory floated to the surface. Skinny dipping in a moonlit pool. Cassy had somehow scored free resort accommodation for us in Port Douglas. I was disappointed we couldn't swim in the open ocean for fear of stingers, but strolling through the rainforest hand in hand in search of a cassowary, and making out in the blue resort pool under the glow of a full moon, made up for it.

With dinner in hand, I pushed cups and books aside to make room for my plate on the coffee table in the living room. Flicker perched and purred, as I settled on the couch and turned on the TV. The news was predictable: accidents, murders and political deceptions. I cut a generous slice of steak for her. Spoilt cat.

I turned on my laptop and re-read the Facebook message from Cassy that had led to our meeting today.

Sandy, is it really you? Where have you been? Be so great to catch up after all this time. When can we meet? Is tomorrow too soon?

My misspelt name was annoying. More infuriating was the way she acted as if we were old friends who'd accidentally lost contact. Another beer was not a great idea, but it beckoned.

I checked out the Fair Sex Coalition website. As I read the facts, I

44

cringed. I knew that women were trafficked for sex. What was shocking was the extent of the crime – in our own backyard. The website claimed that about 1000 women were trafficked into Australia each year.

I thought about Jae making the tough decision to leave her home, her country, just to survive. Then her "dream job" of working in a bar was a hoax – God, worse than a hoax – and now she was living in a nightmare, a prostituted slave. No money. No escape. No hope.

My phone pinged. A text from Cassy. It was almost like she'd been reading my mind.

Great to see you again. We'd really appreciate your assistance with this one. Thought you might like to know more details. When Jae was 13, her father died in a car accident. She left school and started working to support her 4 younger siblings. Her brother was also about to quit school, to help keep the family afloat, when Jae was promised this lucrative job here in Australia. Now she knows that her brother's hopes of finishing school are dashed. Hope you have time to assist. It'd be amazing to work closely with you to help Jae.

Bloody hell! Bloody Cassy. My gut became a knotted mix of fury with Cassy and sadness for Jae. I couldn't help wondering if Jae's family knew where she was or if they thought she was dead. Would they have searched for her? Reported her missing?

I slapped my thighs. *Enough.*

I was about to change into shorts and a T-shirt and head out to practise aikido in the local park when Flicker decided we should have a night in. She nudged my hand with her mottled nose and dug her claws into my thigh. I let her settle on one half of my lap as I stroked her thick coat with one hand and opened an episode of *RuPaul's Drag Race* with the other.

I hoped a decision about Cassy's mad-cap scheme would leap off the screen like the charismatic contestants. Otherwise, it would have to wait until morning.

6

I spun left onto The Esplanade in St Kilda, and passed the Espy Hotel, where I'd spent long nights as a student drunkenly dancing to my favourite bands, instead of studying tedious torts. The venue had been renovated and cleaned up, like the rest of the suburb. The white-coated building glowed. Down the end of the street loomed the monster mouth entrance to Luna Park.

I scored a park facing the bay and took in the green sea, past the palm trees. The day was stunning; blue sky domed above. Twisting the rear vision mirror towards myself, I licked my finger tips and re-spiked my bleached fringe. I hopped out of the car and breathed in the salty sea breeze. As I poured coins stashed in my VW's ashtray into the parking meter, a tram clunked past.

It was a fabulous view but was it foolish being here?

I'd woken that morning to another text from Cassy.

Jae told me where she's working. Come to mine?

The second text was Cassy's address. She'd always been insistent.

Over Vegemite toast I shared with Flicker, I'd toyed with the idea of knocking back the job; working for one ex-lover was complicated enough, without taking on Cassy as well as Maria. Sure I'd feel bad about Jae, even though I hadn't even met her, and it'd be stupid to pass up the income, especially when rent was due in a couple of days and car rego next week.

Was I worried about Cassy bullying me into taking on risky tasks? Given I'd been in the game a while, I should be able to keep her in check. I'd accepted and refused all kinds of bizarre requests, like one old woman who'd wanted me to camp in her ceiling because she was sure spies were videoing her each night. Compared to some clients, Cassy would be a short swim in a calm ocean.

So here I was outside Cassy's 1930s art deco apartment block. A prime real estate address, with expansive views of the bay; quite a step up from the crumbling St Kilda East share house she lived in when we were together.

I pressed the intercom button for apartment three, heard Cassy's fuzzy voice, and the buzz that opened the gate. Meandering around the back, I spied a gold arrow pointing up to Cassy's place.

'Hi,' I called through the open front door.

'Down the hallway, Sandi.'

In the loungeroom at the end of the hall, Cassy was propped up against red cushions on a black leather couch, a laptop perched on her knees. The room was dark despite glass doors leading to a balcony.

The walls were a gallery of paintings and photos, all of them female nudes. Two small bronze statues occupied corner stands diagonally opposite each other. One statue beckoned and my fingers outlined her curves. When I tipped her sideways, I discovered Jean Patou's flourishing signature on the base.

'Quite a collection,' I said. 'With a little help from your folks?' Cassy's surgeon father had always been financially generous.

I twinged with envy, but there was no way I'd have wanted a scrap of support from my father. He'd acquired a new family when I was 12, and we were relieved when he dumped his old one.

Cassy's neck blotched with shades of pink, clearly from embarrassment. She closed her laptop. 'It's the only decent thing he's done for me, buying me this place.' She looked at me sideways.

In fact, Cassy's father had destroyed her childhood. Was the apartment recompense? Not that I wanted to ask at that moment.

She sprang off the couch. 'Something to drink. Come with me.'

I followed her down the hall, through a walkway then into an old kitchen, with scarred wooden floorboards and rough benches. The green gas stove was outdated. Either Cassy revelled in the rustic décor or her father's money had dried up.

We carried glasses of mineral water, adorned with wedges of lime, back down the hallway. As we passed closed doors, I wondered which one was her bedroom. I resisted the urge to "need the loo" so I could snoop and check if she was seeing someone. *Don't go there!*

Cassy led me back through the lounge room and onto a small balcony overlooking Port Phillip Bay, where the green sea met blue horizon. A rainbow of power kites punctuated the sky in amongst puffy white clouds. Apart from small white breakers near the shore, the water hardly rippled. The expanse of cream sand was dotted with sunbakers. The brilliant view certainly made up for the ancient kitchen.

Cassy dropped onto one of two padded cane chairs.

I turned on an angle towards her, without tearing myself away from the sights. 'Ever get tired of the view?'

She frowned.

I wondered if she even noticed it.

'Jae called me again, yesterday,' Cassy hugged her knees. 'This time, she told me where the brothel is. Well, she gave enough information to work out the address. She told me she's been sick, sounds like the flu. One day, she couldn't get up. They dragged her out of bed, ripped off her nighty and forced her into her work gear. When she cried and begged them to give her the day off, one of them punched her in the stomach.'

As I sat down next to Cassy, I wondered how she coped listening to stories like this, probably on a daily basis. I had to stop myself from imagining what it would be like to be forced to have sex even when you felt like shit.

'She was crying and speaking so quietly, it was hard to understand her. She's so scared. But she gave us what we need,' continued Cassy.

I noticed the use of "we" and wondered if she meant me and her, or her colleagues at the Coalition.

Cassy squeezed my thigh gently and left her hand there, the warmth of her palm seeping through my jeans.

'She's working about 15 minutes' drive from the city, near a tram route. She said the brothel is double storey, in a side street, and close to a McDonald's,' stated Cassy.

'I could find out where she is, Cassy, and check it out, but this is really a job for the cops. If she's in danger–'

Cassy whipped her hand away. 'Traffickers cover their tracks by bribing crooked police, lawyers, migration agents. Here on our doorstep. When women report to authorities they're not believed – same as any sort of sexual abuse – or it's impossible to *prove* what's happened. We worked with a woman from Thailand who got mixed up about dates and times. For God's sake she'd been in the brothel for months, being raped constantly, how was she going to remember what bloody day it was, let alone the date. The police dumped her because they said they didn't have enough evidence. You wouldn't believe how often that happens. Jae needs to disappear quietly. We have to help her.'

'Doesn't your Coalition have, like, a procedure or something?'

Cassy clicked her tongue. 'Every case is unique.'

I stared at the bay, where the freedom of the kite boarders jarred with Jae's nightmare.

When I turned back and set my empty glass on a Frida Kahlo drink coaster, I realised Cassy hadn't taken her eyes off me.

'All right. I'll find out where the brothel is, what their routines are, suggest some options,' I said firmly.

Cassy beamed at me. 'That's fabulous.'

She leaned over and pecked me on the lips. I was surprised by the jolt of pleasure it gave me, and by my sudden urge for more. Diana's rejection had left me feeling unwanted, undesirable. Like I had an inherent fault that would doom me to a single life. Cassy's mouth on mine had woken in me all the old passion we'd once shared. But before I could return the kiss, Cassy bounced out of her chair. 'Right! We have to get organised.'

She dived back inside the apartment and reappeared with the laptop.

'What're you doing?'

'Seeing where the McDonald's might be.'

'It's all right, I'll do the research and get back to you. It's what you're paying me for.' I hesitated. 'Before I head off though, what about a walk down the beach?'

'Sure. First things first. How much do you charge?'

We discussed payment and she agreed to pay the first instalment within 24 hours. While she was so focused on the screen, I lounged in the chair, soaking up the sun, pretending it was a tropical resort.

Finally she looked up. 'There are 12 McDonald's Jae could be near.'

'Brilliant. Email me the link. Now how's about the beach?'

'Okay, but when do you think you'll get onto it? Can you give me an update tomorrow?'

Really? I considered giving Cassy a lesson in investigative processes but decided to keep it light.

'Not much point in that. The only thing I'll be able to tell you is that I'm on the job. Happy to send you a blow-by-blow description of the culinary delights I consume on reconnaissance, though they're predictable: muesli bars, trail mix, maybe an apple.'

Cassy's expression remained serious. I remembered she often missed my attempts at humour.

Grabbing my mobile, I consulted the calendar. 'Give me a week. I need to find the brothel first then check out their routine, scope what the options are and then–'

'No, it's not safe to wait that long.' Cassy wriggled in her chair. 'Jae's worried they're going to find out she's been ringing me. Her handlers are thugs. Let's catch up in two days, early on Saturday and try to get her out on the weekend.'

'I have no idea if that's remotely possible yet.'

'You could start now.' Cassy's voice was hard. Her eyes were like daggers.

Geez, the job had hardly begun and she was acting like my old school principal.

'It's been too nice, all this reacquainting chitchat.' I stood up smartly and snapped up my backpack.

Cassy rubbed her hands up and down her thighs, then lightly slapped her legs. 'Jae's been worrying me.'

I laughed. 'No kidding.'

Cassy had a history of over-involvement. When she was working on the Sexual Assault phone line, she spoke to a young woman who was still living with her abusive father and didn't want to report it to the cops. Cassy told me she planned to rescue the woman. After a lot of convincing, Cassy agreed there might be other ways to help the woman out.

This was how she felt about Jae, that it was all her responsibility.

I risked a hand on her shoulder, hoping to rekindle that earlier moment of physical connection. When she didn't resist, I used both hands to massage knotted muscles and stroke the snake tattoo. Cassy rolled her neck in response.

'I just need an hour in the sun. If you want to join me, feel free.'

Cassy stood up and rocked from foot to foot. 'You're right. An hour or so. It's too good a day. Let's head down to Acland Street. There's a café with delicious Black Forest cake.'

She smiled at me, tipped her head to one side. The cute look.

I patted my stomach. 'I've just had a massive breakfast. It's the beach that's calling me.'

We jogged across the Esplanade and down the stairs. After darting across the crazy commuter bike path, we finally reached the sand where we kicked off our shoes.

Rolling up my jeans, I ambled down to the water. Small waves rolled over my ankles, my toes twinging in reaction to the cold. The water was a dull green, typical for the bay. I stared out to the horizon towards the Heads. Even though I knew Point Lonsdale and Point Nepean almost touched, it looked like an expanse of clear sea from this vantage point. A summer full of swimming in the sea rather than being submerged in chlorinated pools awaited me.

I turned back to find Cassy watching me braving the high seas.

'Come on,' I called.

She shook her head. 'You know that water comes straight from Antarctica.'

'Oh, you wuss,' I teased.

She parked herself away from the waterline and filtered sand through her fingers.

When I'd had enough, I joined her, the sand scouring my tender soles. We strolled along the beach and out along St Kilda Pier. A couple of kids on bikes weaved around us and an old man straddling an esky, fishing line in hand, gave a friendly nod.

'Remember that guy who used to start every meeting with a theory lesson about Marx?' asked Cassy.

I remembered it clearly. That's where Cassy and I met, at a Socialist Party meeting in our early twenties.

'Yeah, and everyone would be yawning and shuffling papers while he was crapping on.'

We laughed and she linked her arm through mine. The breeze picked up as we continued along the pier. At the end, the St Kilda Pier kiosk glimmered in the sunlight, its second storey resembling a two-tiered cake. We skipped up the three steps towards the weatherboard building, painted a brighter shade of straw.

The scent of burgers wafted from inside the rust coloured door. Through the hobbit-house-shaped window, a family perched on stools gobbling fish and chips.

We lingered out the front of the kiosk and watched boats bobbing on the water, before ambling back to her apartment block.

When we arrived at my car, the parking meter still had seven minutes left.

'Thanks for getting onto this so fast, it's really appreciated,' said Cassy.

I leaned against my VW, keys hooked over my index finger.

Cassy stepped towards me and kissed me, long and soft, her body merging with mine. Our tongues delved. Prepared to hang out as long as she liked, even cop a parking fine if she wanted to retreat inside, I was disappointed when she extracted herself from my arms and with a wave vanished through her gate.

Awash with desire, I drove off dreaming of further possibilities with Cassy, but as my mind turned to the job ahead, I started to freak out.

Why the hell had I agreed to take on a case involving organised crime?

7

AFTER A DRIVE-BY OF POSSIBLE BROTHELS, I DOUBLED BACK TO A SEMI-residential area of Richmond, away from the Vietnamese shopping hub and factory outlets.

Amsterdam Angels, a freestanding Victorian terrace with a black, cast-iron balcony, fitted Jae's description: double storey, in a side street and a couple of doors down from Macca's. This section of Coppin Street lacked trees, except outside the brothel where a spindly sapling begged for a drink. Two surveillance cameras were positioned on the north and south corners of Amsterdam Angels. Around the corner ran the bustling Swan Street, full of flashy shopfronts beneath shabby second storeys. A few businesses had spilled over into this end of Coppin Street.

I parked opposite the brothel, outside a furniture shop that had a steady flow of customers and shifted into the passenger seat so I could lean against the door and look back at my target.

The first to part the red plastic tassels that hung over the brothel's front door, and sprint down the street and around the corner as if his wife was chasing him – or a PI watching him – was a man in a brown suit and dark glasses.

Surveillance gigs were always ultra-boring, so I entertained myself by timing how long the punters spent inside. In the first hour there were 10 guys with an average stay of 26 minutes.

There was no sign of anyone fitting Jae's description; in fact, not a single woman had entered or exited the premises.

The punters came in all shapes and sizes though; an older man dressed in a white suit (he'd taken an hour), a couple of guys in jeans, one in grey trackies (so suave), and a guy in Lycra (yuck), though his bike was nowhere to be seen. Most were subtly disguised in sunglasses.

I wondered who their partners were, the lies they told, the money they squandered.

Reminded that rent was due in two days, I checked my bank account balance. The deposit from Cassy had already landed. Same day. That was a relief. I'd been putting off asking friends for a loan.

I returned my attention to the task at hand. Not surprisingly the brothel's downstairs windows wore dark heavy sunshades; but it was odd that the upstairs windows seemed to be blacked out with paint. Someone with a bit of Christmas spirit had threaded red and green tinsel through the wrought iron lace work from one side of the off-cream building to the other. Only three more weeks until Christmas, though the spirit was yet to grab me.

The empty block next door was surrounded by a spray-painted wooden fence, a yellow and green hamburger the only colourful artwork. Next to the hamburger, a black-lettered tag identified the artist. I wondered if it was a social comment about the dominance of the fast-food chain or just the artist's favourite snack.

Dog walkers passed, oblivious to what might be happening inside the two-storey house. When I took a quick stroll down the street, I realised there was a park with a playground only a minute away over an old railway bridge. A mother with twin preschoolers pushed one of them on a swing, while the other screeched for attention up the top of a slide. I thought about helping out, but I couldn't afford to miss any brothel action and headed back to the car.

After a couple more hours, my legs became restless. I relocated to the corner of the McDonald's car park, where I could view the rear of the brothel. More cameras were positioned at the back and sides of the establishment. Talk about security conscious. Were they worried about police raids or nefarious dealings outside their business?

I popped on my own clever disguise – baseball cap and sunnies – and got out of the car to peer over the fence. A rectangular shape that used to be a window had been plastered over with the same stucco as the rest of the back wall. And there was no back door. Only one exit in the entire building? There was a municipal violation right there, not to mention they'd have been stuffed if there was a fire. I tossed around the idea of reporting them to the council. I tucked that idea away for later.

'Hey, you.' A hoarse male voice boomed from behind me.

I was caught with my red hands clutching the top of the jagged wooden fence. It wasn't the first time; and sometimes I'd been in the backyard, not just poking my nose over the fence.

The thought of facing a mobster was unpleasant, but my major concern was I'd blown my chance to remain incognito. I lowered my heels to the concrete, ready to defend myself if need be, putting on my innocent face as I turned.

'That your car?' A bloke wearing a high-vis vest stepped his steel cap boots towards me.

'There a problem, mate?'

'Can't open my door.' He tipped his chin towards his white van.

'No worries, I'll move.'

I reversed into another spot, laughing at myself for assuming the worst. I snapped shots of the rear of the brothel with my almost-new DSLR Canon camera with telephoto lens, vital equipment for a PI that, in this case, came courtesy of a recent client – a gay photographer, who earned six figures a year and so could afford to donate his discards.

Nipping into Maccas to use the loo, I then joined the queue behind excited kids and construction workers for a cheap and quick carb fix.

I drove back to my spot near the furniture shop and demolished my survival rations; the crispy fries, coated in salt, satisfied me for a whole five minutes. I scrunched up copious amounts of packaging and stuffed it into an overflowing rubbish bag, wrapped around the gearstick. Using a tissue, I mopped up thick shake drops from the dark blue upholstery on the driver's seat.

The day dragged. And then dragged some more. With nothing specific to concentrate on, the memory of Cassy's kiss lingered on my lips.

I didn't need to remind myself she was trouble. On the cusp of recovery from Diana, I was considering putting myself out there again, definite I was going to avoid past mistakes. And getting back with an ex was on that list.

To keep myself alert, Instagram photos copped loads of loves, my moleskin notebook recorded pointless doodles, and nuts filled my belly.

I called Cassy. No answer. I left her a voicemail telling her I'd probably worked out where Jae must be. An hour later when she hadn't rung back, I texted her. No response.

The more the boring day crawled on, the more pissed off I got at her lack of response. What the heck was she playing at? She was the one so desperate to rescue Jae and now couldn't be bothered getting back to me.

I shoved Cassy to the back of my mind and forced myself to focus on Maria's defence of Ricardo Lopez, as much as I could while stuck in a car. I downloaded the photos of Ju-Long, Qiao and Snow I'd taken with my faux reading glasses at Club 96 and mulled over the shots.

The images were grainy, but adequate for the purpose of getting Ricardo to identify the people in them. What had drawn Lee Wu to work at Club 96? Cultural connection? Qiao had seemed genuinely upset at her murder. 'We're all family,' she'd said.

An internet search for footprints of the players showed no sign of Ju-Long, Qiao or Snow that I could locate. Ricardo had a Facebook page, but it lacked even a profile photo. His sister Luz Aitken, on the other hand, had endless snaps of fiestas. Her Facebook albums held old photos of Ricardo and his fiancée Valentina all smiley and romantic, wrapped around each other. It seemed there had there been a time when they were happy before she'd disappeared.

I kept one eye on the brothel and by 7pm I reckoned over 100 punters had paid a visit to Amsterdam Angels. Profitable business, especially if you had minimal salary overheads.

For a change of scenery, I took a possie on a metal bench at the tram stop on the corner of Swan Street, which still had a good view of the brothel. It was unlikely their cameras could pick me up from that distance.

The smell of exhaust fumes increased as cars took off from the lights. Behind shopfronts, the sun was vanishing and while the clouds weren't threatening, they were gathering. Opposite me, a grand old three-story pub painted in viridian green advertised Parma on Thursdays.

I made room for a woman with shopping bags and her toddler asleep in a stroller and we chatted as she waited. When a tram arrived, I helped her lift the stroller up. Her bench spot was taken by an old woman in a floral dress and cap, with a glistening gold-teeth smile. I knew she regarded me as a captive audience.

'I'm 83,' she shouted. 'Have 15 grandchildren.'

'Good for you.'

'Don't see them much.'

'Ah, that's a shame.'

'Going to church now to pray for grandchildren to have good jobs, get married, have children.'

I lost my companion to the next tram as a cool breeze cut through my blouse. Resisting the temptation to go home, I forced myself back into the car.

Red lights flooded the upstairs balcony, the black of the cast iron lacework and painted windows stark against their glow. Two doors away, Maccas glared back at the incongruity.

I sang along to the radio to distract myself. When I was a teenager, my older sister humiliated me in front of her friends during a karaoke party at our house, so now I only sing alone.

After 11pm, the punters started to converge like a piranha feeding frenzy, now camouflaged by darkness. I tried not to think about how many men each woman had to "service" in a day.

A tangle of drunken blokes swaggered into Amsterdam Angels. One re-emerged a second later and threw up in the gutter, wiped his mouth on his sweater and re-joined his mates. Geez, another treat the women had to put up with.

My eyelids started to droop and my legs ached like after a half marathon. I shook them, massaged them, thumped them, but my calf muscles had seized up.

Close to losing my mind completely, I realised I hadn't heard a tram for ages. In fact, the street was quiet. I checked my mobile: 2.33am.

The last three men I'd seen go in emerged one at a time over the next twenty minutes. As the last punter strolled towards the corner, a large dark van cruised past me, did a U-turn, and pulled up right in front of the brothel. The driver disappeared inside before I had time to clock his face.

Within seconds, a line of scantily-dressed women streamed out of Amsterdam Terrace. Pale faces emerged as slightly-built women shifted into the light of the doorway. I snapped photos, hoping they'd pick up what I couldn't. The whole process took less than 30 seconds for 14 women to pile into the van. I checked the time: 3.15am.

These women were definitely prisoners. Why else would they be escorted so closely? It could be a drop-off service to keep them safe, but that seemed far-fetched. I'd had my doubts about Cassy's story, but not anymore. Her phone calls with Jae had to be real.

The balcony lights snapped off. The driver, a man with short black hair, jumped back into the van before I could take a photo.

I turned the key in my ignition. Nothing but a splutter.

'For Christ's sake, come on.'

The van's headlights flashed on and it headed towards the corner, its left indicator on.

God, I needed a new car. I tried again. There was a hideous metallic scream and it coughed to life. I spun into a U-turn, chucked a lefty, ignoring the red light in front of me, and sped down Swan Street. The van, which I could now see was dark green, was crossing through the next intersection. The traffic signal ahead flashed red. As I reached the intersection a horde of taxis passed through, blocking my view of the van and stopping me from running a red.

'Hurry up!' I yelled at the lights.

Green. I slammed my foot on the accelerator and careered down the tramline to overtake three yellow taxis that ambled along like cows in the middle of a dirt road.

Too late. I reached Hoddle Street, but the van had vanished.

'Shit!' I punched the driver's window.

My bet was they were heading into the city. How else would Jae have calculated the car trip to Richmond? I drove past the Tennis Centre, over the Yarra River, through the city, but there was no sign of the van.

I'd spent 16 hours outside the Amsterdam Angels dump, my body aching from tiredness, my head thumping from caffeine withdrawal, and I'd missed the moment. My meeting with Cassy was going to scream success.

8

ANOTHER AFTERNOON SPENT WATCHING CREEPS COME AND GO, AS intermittently as the showers dousing the street, made me seethe. No decent plan for rescuing Jae had emerged from the hours trapped in my car. Lame ideas – like what if Stewart infiltrated the brothel as a sex worker, I pretended to be a cop and took the traffickers into custody, or we ignited a fire out front – tumbled into an uncreative pit. My mood sank another notch. I had to work out a plan to get Jae out. A real plan. The meeting with Cassy was looming.

The image of the women as they traipsed through the red tassels of the brothel last night kept replaying in my mind. I wanted to orchestrate Jae's rescue, but now I was worried about all the women trapped inside. That was overwhelming.

I decided to give surveillance a rest. Nothing was going to happen at Amsterdam Angels, I knew, until late at night, and I needed a break. Sleep or be active. That was the choice. I'd missed my aikido class the day before and my body was desperate for some movement.

I drove through Clifton Hill and up High Street to my old neighbourhood, Thornbury, passing the cosy vegan café, Crunch, where my friend Kat liked to hang out. If she hadn't been in New York, I would have texted and seen if I could pop around for a quick cuppa after class. Around the corner was my favourite shopping haunt on the north side, Psarakos, featuring massive tins of olive oil and a deli rivalling the Vic Markets'.

I was nostalgic about the days when I lived in a share house off High Street. If I dug deeper, that time was dotted with a few heady moments in amongst long and fraught periods of dealing with a housemate's emerging mental illness. Some of my friends said it was drug induced. Who knew the truth? I'd heard she'd become a psychologist.

During that time, I'd joined the nearby aikido dojo. I'd been with the same school for four years. These days, I went two to three times a week, depending on cash flow, as well as social and PI demands. The instructors had the right combination of discipline and encouragement, so I continued to trek across town after I'd moved suburbs. Well, apart from the excuse to visit old friends. All, bar Kat, thought crossing to the western suburbs required taking leave from work, packing a suitcase and working up an itinerary. It was up to me to make the 16 kilometre trek through 45 minutes of mundane traffic to visit them.

I changed into the thick white uniform and tied the brown belt around my waist in the change rooms. In the side pocket of my backpack, I checked the asthma puffer was still there. It had been ages since I'd had an exercise-induced attack, but when I did, it flipped me out. Better to be prepared.

The Fast and Furious class were already sitting on their heels in two rows by the time I arrived. The floor was blanketed with interlacing blue mats. Silence permeated the room as I padded in and took a position at the end of the second row.

Sensei Kobayashi entered and glided to the front. After the formalities, we swiftly moved into warm-up exercises. The instructor's deep voice led us through a series of stretches.

'Bend forwards and backwards.'

We followed the movements. The sensei was ridiculously flexible. If only my back bent like his.

'Twist the hips.'

As we lay on our backs, rolling our legs over our heads, my body embraced the movement, the stretches. I could feel my spine engaging with the floor and was aware of each vertebra.

This was exactly what I'd hungered for, after slouching in a car for two days. I released tension as I breathed, counted and stretched. A sense of calm flowed through me and with it the belief that I could devise a plan to liberate Jae. I just had to resist Cassy's time pressure.

Sensei Kobayashi moved us onto throws and locks technique practice. My partner was the sensei, a real bonus. He was my height, strong and centred and, of course, highly experienced.

We bowed to each other. At first, I'd thought the bowing was pretentious, but it had grown on me and I saw it as a sign of mutual respect. It was strange what you could adapt to, and what felt normal – more than normal: right. Maybe I was really just a girl who wanted to fit in. Maybe I deluded myself that I was living on the fringe. Whatever the truth was, I needed this discipline and skill – for my health and my job. Facing crims was easier if you knew you could immobilise them.

'Imagine your arm as a sword,' the sensei instructed.

I straightened my arm and attacked him, swiping my hand towards his neck. He grabbed my wrist and dropped me to the floor in a swift throw. He kept me lying prone by bending my wrist back. Even the smallest twist of a joint in the wrong direction could be agony. I smacked the mat and he released.

When we swapped, I could sense the power of his sword-like arm. We stood far enough apart for our hands not to touch. His body was angled towards me, with one foot behind the other, his balance centred. I matched his stance. I wanted to ensure I threw him first go. In the New Year, I planned to go for my black belt and I needed to perfect the technique.

The sensei approached me, his arm slicing down towards my head, and I sidestepped using my toes to turn.

'Don't receive the attack on this angle; you may hurt your back,' he said.

I was annoyed I'd stuffed up.

'Common mistake,' said my instructor, as if he'd read my thoughts.

After years of training small adjustments were still needed. I thought about my encounter with Ricardo at the remand centre. Even if I had laid him on his face, I might have been injured, not because of his attack, but because I hadn't turned a couple of centimetres enough to the left. Aikido required concentration, precision and compliance. The latter wasn't my best suit.

The sensei stepped back and demonstrated the position that was necessary in that scenario. I copied. He attacked me again in slow motion. I adjusted my angle slightly and threw him to the floor, locking his wrist in my hand.

As he patted the pads with his free hand he said, 'Better.'

That was praise enough; improvement was the aim.

My reactions became sharper as we progressed through different scenarios. As he and I took a breather, I checked out my fellow students' routines. Shouts of "Kiai!" filled the room as others threw their partners to the floor.

After class, I grabbed some prawn and pork rice paper rolls on my way back through Richmond.

With my body and mind satiated, I settled back into surveying Amsterdam Angels.

Visibility out my car windows plummeted as it started pouring. I'd learnt the hard way that using the windscreen wipers chewed up my car battery, so I hung out under the verandah of the then-closed furniture business. I huddled in a dark corner, hugging my jacket around my chest. My clothes weren't cutting it against the Antarctic wind. I scrounged around in my boot for something warmer, yanked a wool jumper over my head and returned to the protection of my car.

The rain petered out, stars appeared in the slice of visible sky, and the lights of the brothel glowed. As if a switch had been flicked, punters reappeared in droves. I forced myself to stay awake by getting out and doing stretches and push-ups, against the car.

A bit after 1am, back in my car seat, the dark green van pulled up. The thump of a subwoofer sound system died with the engine. A guy built like an over-supplemented gym jock emerged and lit up a cigarette. His features were concealed by a thick, dark beard and moustache. Long hair draped over his cheeks and forehead. I whipped out my camera and studied him through the telephoto lens. His arms were littered with swirling tattoos, where primary colours merged like an abandoned palette. He wore a Destruction band T-shirt sporting an image of a desperate orange hand reaching up towards a shattered black skull with purple liquid pouring out of its orifices.

Once skull-man flung his butt into the gutter, he strode inside as though it was his second home, shoving the red plastic strips aside. I started the car, wondering if the women would have an early night. After twenty minutes, I turned the engine off.

At 3am I did a U-turn to be ready when the van loaded up its exhausted women, after their twelve-hour plus shift. At 3.15am, as the last punter came out, I turned on the ignition again. After 18 minutes of wasting petrol, the thin line of women appeared briefly outside through the door before disappearing into the van, the skull-man in his Destruction T-shirt escorting them.

He took off quickly. This time I was close behind. He sped down Swan Street, now devoid of cars, except for a couple of taxis. I ignored a red light, hoping for no cameras. The van swung around the Melbourne Cricket Ground towards the city. I allowed a taxi in between us and pulled back until the next set of traffic lights neared. A couple of doglegs later, we were in the city. The van turned into Lonsdale Street, close to the Greek Precinct – home to a strip of Greek shops and restaurants, one of which served the most mouth-watering moussaka I'd ever tasted – and disappeared into a car park below an office building.

I slammed my foot on the accelerator to beat the wire mesh gate that had started to grate downwards as soon as the van was through. I managed to squeeze under; no scraping of the paintwork on my car roof that I could hear. Within seconds the gate hit the concrete behind me. The van turned left down a ramp and I drove straight ahead; certain the driver would have noticed me up his backside. I stopped my car and lowered the front windows.

From the floor below, there was a slam of a car door. I reversed towards the entrance, edging my way down the ramp, following the noise.

When I reached the basement, the van was already parked. I caught sight of a few women shuffling towards the entrance to the lifts. I spun into a vacant spot, cut the engine, flung the door open, and sprinted towards them. Too late. The doors to both lifts were sealed.

One of the lifts was heading up. It stopped at the eighth floor. When the other lift arrived at the basement, I jumped in and pressed eight. No light. No movement. *Damn.*

I noticed a key fob sensor. That could restrict my movement in the building. As I hopped out, I spotted a fire exit next to the lift. The door opened from my side, stairs heading upwards, but depending on security arrangements, I knew I may not be able to get back from another floor.

After shifting my VW to a more concealed spot, I rummaged in my boot for some small rectangles of wood. I stuck the first of them in between the fire door and the door jamb in the basement before jogging up two sets of steps. Annoyingly, that staircase went no higher. As I stepped into the lobby, I inserted another piece of wood to hold that door ajar.

In the lobby, the name of the building was revealed – Lonsdale Heights Apartments – with numbers of the apartments listed, though no residents' names. On the other side of the lifts was another emergency door that failed to open when I pulled on the handle. I pressed the button for the lift, and when it arrived pressed all other buttons. It wouldn't let me travel up or down.

Back in the lobby, I considered ringing all ten apartments on the eighth floor, though even if someone answered at this hour, it was doubtful I could determine where the sex workers were being kept, let alone rescue them.

After making sure the wooden pieces were firmly in place, I strode back to my car, mentally preparing for an all-nighter. Surrounded by concrete, and ablaze with fluorescent light, the basement was freezing. I grabbed a coat out of the boot, before adjusting the car seat back. Staying awake was the plan, but I was too exhausted to sit upright.

I woke with a start, wondering where I was, then remembered how I'd crazily decided to head underground following the van. I had to stop sleeping in random places. My neck twinged as I straightened my head. My fingers were stiff and sore. I breathed on them then stuck them in my pockets.

The car park was silent and eerie, the van still in the same spot. I checked my phone. It was 5am and my battery was under 10 per cent. I turned the car on for the heat and the charger.

My shoulders twinged as the gate upstairs screeched and car wheels squealed. A Honda sped down the ramp to the basement, the driver clumsily reversing into a spot nearby. She managed to park it without incident. Her passenger flicked open his door and jabbed the car next to him. The couple struggled out and clutched each other as they zigzagged towards the lifts. Within seconds, I joined them.

A lift opened immediately.

The woman tapped her fob against the card reader and pressed five. I followed them inside, tapped eight and was gratified when the number lit up.

The woman examined me. She seemed to be trying to work out whether she recognised me, whether I was legit.

'Good night?' I asked.

'Do you live here?' Her slurred question hung.

I smiled enthusiastically. 'Yeah, haven't bumped into you before.'

Before she had time to challenge me further, we arrived at the fifth floor and the couple stumbled out of the lift.

Up on the eighth floor, I stepped into a silent corridor. There were no obvious lights under any of the doors. It was early, or late, depending on which way you looked at it, to be randomly knocking on doors.

I chose the apartment closest to the lifts. A bleary-eyed man wearing a navy dressing gown responded to my rapping. His hair was grey, receding and askew.

'I'm looking for a friend of mine, Charlotte. Is she here by any chance? She buzzed me up, but I've forgotten her apartment number.'

The man shook his head and squinted at me.

'Do you know which apartment it is? She lives with a whole lot of other girls.'

'Do you know what time it is?' He had an old-man frail voice, and I had a snippet of guilt for waking him up.

'I'm sorry, but I don't think you could miss them, a group of girls living together? Mostly Asian.'

The man was tall and stooped. He seemed to have trouble turning his neck. He twisted his whole torso and pointed down the hallway on the opposite side of the corridor.

'At the end?' I queried.

'Yes. Now goodnight.' He shut the door firmly.

I knocked on the door of apartment 810 and stepped to the side to avoid being seen through the peephole. When nothing happened, I banged harder. The sound echoed down the corridor.

'What?' came an unwelcoming voice from the other side.

'Oh, hi, I'm just wondering if my friend Charlotte is here. She buzzed me up, but I've forgotten her room number.'

'Nah, no Charlotte here.'

'Do you know which apartment Charlotte does live in?'

'No fucking idea, so fuck off.'

The slam of a door, a second male voice and women's whispers slithered from inside.

'Shut up,' I heard their guard yell.

I was in the right place, though staging a rescue mission immediately was impossible. Reluctantly, I caught the lift back down to the lobby.

As I stepped out to take the stairs to the basement, some graffiti on the side of the lift caught my eye. I bent down to get a closer look. Letters had been etched into the metal wall. Although half the "p" was missing, the word "help" popped.

9

THE FAIR SEX COALITION'S OFFICE WAS HOUSED IN A DETERIORATING single-fronted terrace in Gore Street, Collingwood, made more drab by being stuck between two brightly renovated copies. As I opened the squeaking wrought iron gate, the spiderweb of cracks in the stucco became more obvious. I stood on a threadbare welcome mat in amongst broken tiles, prodding the doorbell as rain sliced at my ankles.

When the door opened, black hair and one green eye appeared around it. Cassy stared past me to check if I'd brought a party of thugs. Without bothering to wipe my feet on the soaked mat, I tussled with Cassy to open the door wide enough so I could make it through.

As she forced the swollen door shut, I waited for her in the dark hallway. A smell of musty soil seeped up through the floor. Off to my right a sizable room, presumably the previous master bedroom, was stuffed with desks. A woman dressed in clashing colours, holding a handset to her ear, glared at me. I guess that line of work breeds suspicion.

I had no plan to get Jae out and was pissed off Cassy had ignored my calls *and* texts.

Cassy strode past me and I reluctantly followed. She ushered me into a large room with high ceilings. A clunky desk positioned at one end near a window failed to let in any light.

'Your office?' I said.

'Most of us hot-desk upstairs.'

She'd prepared her laptop for action on a scratched wooden table. I slumped on a plastic chair opposite her, with my back to the wall.

A feminist poster, blu-tacked to the wall opposite, attempted to hide a gaping crack in the plaster. The slogan *The strongest fabric, women supporting women* outlined four women drawn in primary colours. They held their joined hands high.

'What's the plan?'

'I left you a message,' I said.

Cassy's eye contact was unflinching. I studied the emerald speckles in her eyes. She dropped her gaze and her fingertips tapped the keyboard. 'Things got hectic and there wasn't a chance to call, but we're here now.'

That was typical of Cassy; never taking responsibility.

She laughed. It was her nervous laugh, stilted and falsetto. She smiled at me but her lips were tight. 'Just got a lot going on at the moment.'

I crossed my arms, unwilling to easily excuse her.

Cassy held her right hand out, over the table. The lines on her palm were deep and long. Her heart line was chain shaped. Once, I went to a palm reader, her wild hair stereotypically witch-like, who told me I would meet a man when I was travelling in Africa, get married and have three kids. Suffice to say, I had no faith.

'There was a media flurry yesterday. Did you read the paper?'

'Strangely, I was a bit preoccupied working on your case,' I said.

She blinked, as though uncertain at how to respond. 'A major illegal brothel in Sydney has been exposed. We all had to drop what we were doing and focus on finding survivors willing to be interviewed. You know how the media is.'

Small movements of her fingers punctuated her spiel. Her fingers were slender and long, elegant compared to mine.

'You should read the article,' she said, 'it's hard-hitting.'

She tapped on the keyboard. I wondered what she was typing. Perhaps she was doing something completely unrelated, creating a shopping list for all I knew.

'Have you worked out a plan to rescue Jae?'

The room lacked a visible heater. I watched as rain attacked the window. It sounded like the gutters were overflowing as water pounded onto the ground.

I shoved my hands into my jeans pockets to seek some warmth. 'No, I've just been sitting on my butt watching the complete box set of *Buffy*.'

Cassy's eyes flicked to one side. *Buffy* had been one of our favourites when we were an item. 'Sandi!'

I traced my forefinger along a deep scratch in the table. 'Jae's working in a brothel in Richmond and sleeping briefly in an apartment in the city.'

'Yes, you messaged about Amsterdam Angels.'

I loved Cassy's small talk. I waited for more from her. Some acknowledgement would have been nice. Four hours sleep after my all-nighter and no time to grab a coffee was making me resentful.

'I know I'm being paid, but for Christ's sake, you could at least offer me a cup of frigging tea.'

Cassy's expression resembled a dog's, when it hasn't a clue what it's expected to do. 'Tea?'

'You know, the leaves you make a hot drink with.'

'Jae's depending on us.'

'Are all the staff at the Coalition this welcoming?'

Cassy frowned.

I gave up trying to make any connection and told her all I knew. My voice was flat, my enthusiasm waning. My report became a list of facts: the guy in the Destruction T-shirt being taxi driver and minder; the addresses of the brothel and apartment; the hours they finished work; the etched sign in the lift. She seemed silently interested in the call for help.

Her neck strained towards me as I showed her the photos. Outside, the wind howled.

'The plan?' she said again.

'We could report them to council. They've got dodgy plaster covering the back windows.'

'Don't be ridiculous,' Cassy huffed.

We scowled at each other.

'I need more time,' I said.

She raised her hands like bookends. 'Why will that make any difference? We were going to get her out this weekend.'

Under the table I clenched my fists and tried to dissuade the snarl in my voice. 'How much surveillance have you done in your life, Cassy? It's not something that provides instant answers. Time and patience are what's needed. If that's not all right with you, we can call it quits – doesn't worry me. Call the cops. Get your co-workers to storm the brothel.'

Being treated like a lackey was way more than I'd signed up for. What having to scrape together the rent had reduced me to.

'Your colleague looks like she's totally up for nights in cold cars, watching paint dry. Go for it.' I pointed my thumb towards the voice owned by Ms Clashing Colours in the next room.

Cassy flinched as a door slammed. She dragged her laptop towards her, causing a sound like sandpaper as it scraped across the uneven surface of the table.

We both turned our heads as the handle of the office door creaked.

A short woman with shoulder-length black hair entered, a briefcase in one hand and a golf umbrella in the other.

'Bani.' Suddenly Cassy whizzed to her feet. She snapped the laptop shut and tucked it under her arm. 'We weren't expecting you.'

Bani's hair swayed as she propped the dripping umbrella near the window and deposited her briefcase on the desk. 'No problem, sorry to have to kick you out. I've dropped in to do some follow-up work from the media frenzy yesterday. Another article was published today. Hopefully, it'll generate more income.' Her voice undulated.

Bani focused on me while she unloaded her briefcase. Drops of water slid down the dark-green umbrella and gathered on the speckled beige carpet. Cassy edged towards the door, clutching her laptop. I decided to make up for Cassy's ineptness and crossed the room to introduce myself.

Cassy skulked closer to us. 'Bani Anand is the Director of the Fair Sex Coalition. Sandi's helping out at the moment.'

Bani's smile was genuine. 'Oh, yes. Very good to have your assistance.'

'We were winding up anyway. There's work to do upstairs. Congratulations on the article.' Cassy sped to the door, tipped her chin up towards me.

'Good to meet you, Bani. I hope I can–'

'Sandi.' Cassy gripped the doorjamb.

I zipped up my backpack, taking my time.

Once we were out in the corridor, Cassy herded me down the hall. She hissed, 'We'll have to talk later.'

I jerked myself away from her. 'What the hell?'

Outside, Cassy dragged the front door closed and stood staring at me. I balanced on the edge of the narrow porch. The rain battered the verandah roof and pelted at my legs.

Cassy raised her hand as if to cup my arm. I backed down onto the stairs, preferring to get soaked.

Cassy stared down at me. 'Normally, Bani's room is out of bounds. You know, confidential information. The others said it would be fine, but she can be prickly about that sort of thing. She's totally great about you doing this, but we probably overstepped the boundary.'

'Jesus Christ, Cassy.'

'Hopefully Jae will ring on my shift. You need to get back on the job anyway. We'll be in touch.'

Cassy had recovered from whatever nerves her boss sparked off.

'Jae's lucky to have you on her case,' I quipped.

Cassy blinked, trying to work out if I was being sincere.

Without a goodbye, Cassy turned and disappeared inside. I almost slipped as I ran down the remaining steps and sprinted to the car.

10

Preoccupied with guzzling a take-away latte, I hardly noticed the fifteen-minute drive back to Richmond.

As I hung outside Amsterdam Angels in my VW, the memory of the women being herded into the van in the early hours of the morning pierced my chest. I had no idea how to get Jae out of brothel and wondered about the wisdom of continuing to park opposite, potentially drawing the trafficker's attention to the fact that someone was watching them.

Cassy's disdain at my lack of progress made me squirm. I silently yelled obscenities at her and berated myself for caring about her opinion.

The coffee had only taken away a slice of my exhaustion. I had an hour or so before I was due at Ricardo's sister's in Heidelberg and I craved a sugar hit. I ended up back in what had become my favourite fast-food joint, the McDonald's on the corner of Swan Street.

As I sucked up the last of a chocolate thickshake, I spotted a group of skinny young women totter across the bitumen car park from the direction of Amsterdam Angels. They were dressed in short skirts and high heels but were definitely not a group of friends gathering for a high-school reunion. My fingertips tingled like icy extremities thawing. My God, after all my surveillance and they'd landed right in front of me at Maccas.

The breeze made the women clutch their skirts and flick long hair out of their eyes. A tall woman struggled to open the McDonald's glass door against the force of the wind. Despite heavy make-up, most of them looked like teenagers, especially the ones with smaller Asian builds. Inside, the women rearranged their outfits and hair, before huddling together in the queue.

I jumped up ready to convince them to flee and squeeze them all into my VW. My plan was thwarted when the door to my left was flung open and their guard stomped up behind the young women. He wore shorts and his Destruction T-shirt with the shattered black skull again. The women tensed as he muscled into their midst. When it was their turn at the counter, they spoke in broken English, ordering burgers, fries and soft drinks. One woman broke ranks and ordered a salad. Once he'd sorted the bill, Skull-man stomped outside. He raised his boot heel against the window and lit a cigarette.

I pretended to text while taking photos on my phone. Trays filled with food and drinks and the eight women moved like ants to two adjacent lime-green booths. They all seem hunched and tiny, apart from the taller woman with big cheekbones who doled out their meals. I presumed she had a role in keeping them in line.

My mind was working harder than in a Torts exam. If this was a regular visit by the trafficked women to Maccas, Cassy could organise for Jae to subtly vamoose out the other exit of the restaurant, while Skull was having a ciggy.

I wondered if Jae was there. My gaze shifted from a woman with delicate features and half-closed eyes to another with a round face who flinched at every sound: when beeping noises pinged from behind the counter or a baby squawked. She picked up a thin chip and forgot to eat it. Of them all, she seemed the most terrified. Her brown eyes were wide and alert.

Outside, Skull sucked in his cheeks and inhaled. He spun around to come inside, flicking the burning butt into the car park.

Cassy would have five minutes max. It was tight, but possible, if Jae acted quickly.

As the minder approached one of the booths, the tall woman nudged her companion. They squeezed together to make room for him. On the other side, the one with delicate features continued whispering to the woman beside her. Their minder towered over her. She'd become the centre of attention at their booth. As she realised they were all watching her, she turned in slow motion towards the minder, her mouth agape. He bared his teeth and raised an open hand. She cowered and hid her face in her fingers. She shuffled along the seat and he plonked next to her, ripped off the wrapping to a burger and sunk his teeth into it.

I leaped to my feet. He'd threatened a woman in broad daylight without a qualm. What the hell happened behind closed doors? I scanned the restaurant. Everyone else seemed oblivious. My instant reaction was to confront him. As I stood primed for action, I considered what was in the women's best interests. It was like intervening in a domestic violence incident in a public place by having a go at the bloke. You knew he'd go back home and take it out on her.

As I was contemplating how to respond, Skull, with a mouthful of chips, bolted towards me. The decision had been taken out of my hands. I centred my weight and prepared to throw him to the floor. He hitched his lip and clenched his hands. He pounded straight past me towards the counter. He bumped a preschooler in a pink tutu. She wobbled, only keeping upright by clutching her mother's pleated dress.

He beat his fist on the counter. 'Where the fuck's my Coke?'

'Coke?' said a pimply-faced attendant.

The minder raised his hands as though he was about to strangle the boy. The arteries in his neck bulged. 'Yeah, I paid and you didn't give it.' His voice bellowed out over the piped music.

All the sex workers in the booths were fixated on their minder. One had her hamburger raised towards her mouth, oblivious to the red sauce dripping onto the table. The restaurant was packed, but apart from a kid screeching, all the customers were silent, tuned in to the commotion. I thought about kneeing Skull, but at that moment it seemed a Coke could save the day.

'Of course, sir. Very sorry. I'll get one right away,' said the boy.

The pimply-faced boy retreated to the drink machine and dragged down a large cup, which slipped out of his fingers. It rolled on the floor. He threw a glance over his shoulder at Skull, who was drumming his massive fingers on the counter. The pimply-faced boy managed to fill another cup. As he held the drink out towards the minder, his shaking hand caused some drops of Coke to spill, forming a black puddle on the counter.

Skull snatched the drink out of the kid's hand, splashing more Coke. With his spare hand, he grabbed the boy's shirt, his hairy face centimetres from the kid's pimply one. The boy was dragged half-way across the counter, his top soaking up the spilled liquid.

I found myself next to the minder, who was twice my width and with personal hygiene that I sensed wasn't his strong suit.

'Hey, mate,' I said to him, 'I agree with you. Where's the coffee,' I said to the harassed lad behind the counter, 'I ordered half an hour ago?'

I tapped my fist on the counter, before turning to Skull. 'Good on you for pulling him into line. Can I shake your hand, mate?'

He released the boy's shirt slowly. 'Are you taking the piss?'

Before I could answer, he snatched a straw and returned to his booth. He tipped his chin to the women and they instantly released paper cups and dropped carboard chip packets. He grabbed a burger from the table and scoffed it as he waited for them to scurry out of the door. Half-eaten food and crumpled packaging littered the table. The group disappeared out of sight around the empty lot, back towards the Victorian terrace.

The pimply boy held a coffee out towards me. 'If it's cold, we can make you another one.' His voice quivered.

I smiled. 'Hey, I just said that 'cos I thought you might have had enough of his paws on your chest.'

'Oh,' he said relaxing his hunched shoulders. 'Oh yeah. There you go.'

'Has that guy hassled you before?'

'He's complained, but never like that. Those ladies always have some body-builder with them, though usually the guys wait outside.'

'How often do the women come?'

'Every couple of days, I reckon. Usually about this time.'

Finally, I had a viable plan for Jae's rescue.

11

It was time to attend to my other case, for Maria. My next stop was Heidelberg West, where the athlete's village for the 1956 Olympic Games had been built. The estate had clearly deteriorated since that heady time. I trod down a cracked concrete driveway towards a sad red-brick house, in only slight better nick than its neighbour, which wore old sheets as curtains. The scent of freshly mown grass came from somewhere else, as I stepped onto the porch and knocked on the screen door.

Ricardo Lopez's sister, Luz Aitken, greeted me. Her features resembled her brother's enough that I'd have recognised them as siblings even if I hadn't known. She beamed as she ushered me inside; no hallway, just straight into the lounge room. Luz's red-haired husband, I assumed, lounged in shorts and a white singlet in front of a flat screen, watching cricket. Their dark-haired son was engrossed with an electronic tablet.

I followed Luz through and into the kitchen, where something sweet wafted in the air. A chubby girl of about six years old perched on a swivel stool at the kitchen bench, surrounded by coloured pencils and paper. She was still holding the red pencil she'd used to draw hair on one of five stick figures. Of the two smaller figures, one wore a purple skirt, like hers. Three taller people, two with black hair and her father with the red, completed the family portrait which I assumed included Ricardo.

The girl grinned at me, then used the back of her hand to wipe the white stuff off her mouth. When I spotted *alfajores*, a South American version of yo-yo biscuits, I realised it was icing sugar.

Luz arranged two Christmas-tree-shaped *alfajores* on a plate and presented them to me.

'Eat, eat.' Her smile was generous, her eyes bright.

Plastic bags of groceries covered the laminated bench. Luz careered around the kitchen, packing the shopping away efficiently into the fridge and pantry.

I asked if she'd seen Ricardo recently.

'*Sí, sí,* yesterday. Ricardo said you visited him.'

She said "Ricardo" with the strong Spanish rolled *r*. It made his name sound exotic.

She indicated outside through double-glass doors, towards a weatherboard garage at the end of the back yard. 'He asked if we keep his tools in the garage clean. He loves making things.'

She chortled. Her eyes were crinkly at the corners. I wondered if she was an eternal optimist or if it was a cover for her pain about him being in remand.

I propped myself next to the girl. 'And what's your name?' I asked. The girl, still smiling but suddenly shy, began adding the sun to her picture.

'Blanca,' Luz said. 'And she helps her *mamá*, it's true *mi niña?*'

Luz kissed Blanca on the lips. White specks transferred from daughter to mother, blotching Luz's chilli-red lipstick.

I noticed Blanca had added another stick figure to her masterpiece. This one had spiky yellow hair – it was clearly hard to match my bleached-white. She offered me the pencil case. I chose purple, and when she smiled, I started sketching an image of her on a clean sheet of paper.

'You have questions for me?' asked Luz.

I opened my mouth to ask about Ricardo's fiancée, but Luz didn't wait.

'Ricardo, he is a lovely boy. He goes to mass every week. He loves his family, he loves my children and his grandmother more than the whole world. He does everything for his family. Before, he sent money to our grandmother.'

Although she sounded upbeat, her narrowed eyes gave away her distress. 'There is a problem for him, how do you say, reading and writing.'

I frowned, thinking maybe his schooling was interrupted.

'Dyslexia,' she answered her own question. 'The job with cars was perfect. The boss was nice when Ricardo started, but after, no. Ricardo says that our cousins, they went to the shop. I think our cousins are the problem.'

It was the first I'd heard of any cousins. I scanned my memory for any reference from Maria's legal brief about them. I came up with a blank.

Without me having to prod, Luz had offered more information in a few minutes than Ricardo had in an hour. She was the opposite of him: cheery, chatty and charming. Of course, he might be quite different when not incarcerated for a murder he claimed he didn't commit.

'His cousins? How have they made problems?' I asked.

'The police, they think that Ricardo has done terrible things with our cousins,' she whispered. 'But no, he hasn't done anything bad. I told him, Ricardo, don't see our cousins any more. They are evil people. Terrible to say about our family, but true.'

It was hard to find a space to interrupt, so in the end I made myself speak over the top of Luz.

'What do the police think Ricardo did with his cousins?'

Luz loaded Blanca's plate with more *alfajores*.

'Blanca, take the *alfajores* for your brother and you in the lounge. Ask Papa if he wants more too.'

'But Mama.'

'You go now and see what your brother is doing. After, you can play on the swing. It's a pretty day to be in the garden.'

Blanca slipped awkwardly off her chair, concentrating on balancing the plate.

Luz took over her daughter's stool; her gaze imploring. Although I wanted to pull back, I was drawn by her gentle eyes. So like Diana's…

No, stop. Don't bloody go there! Diana was haunting me. Every time I thought I was over her, the agony I'd endured when she dumped me kept erupting. I locked my breakup back in its vault and focused on Luz.

'I think about Ricardo all the time. All the time. Our *abuela*, she rings me and says, "What are you doing to help Ricardo? Other grandsons do bad things here in Colombia. Ricardo," *mi abuela* says, "he is my best grandson".'

'You were telling me about Ricardo's cousins and the police,' I prompted.

I could sense she was torn. She wanted to tell me but had to admit to a dark secret.

'They think he was working with our cousins to sell drugs,' she whispered. 'Ricardo says our cousins wanted his help, but he always said no.'

Drugs. Fabulous. There was more than alleged murder in his world then.

Luz wanted to save Ricardo, even if he was a lost cause. The more information she gave me the more she was damning Ricardo, even though her intention was the opposite.

'Do you know if any of them have been charged?'

'Charged?'

'Yeah, like having to go to court because of what they've done.'

'Ricardo, no. But the police, they came here and asked questions. So many questions.' Luz squeezed my wrist, plucked a tissue from a box on the bench and wiped her teary eyes without disturbing her mascara.

'So much pain for my brother. His fiancée, too, Valentina. We loved Valentina too much. Ricardo and Valentina met at a fiesta. Valentina and my girlfriend's sister were friends.'

It was like she'd anticipated my questions. If everyone I grilled was as open as her, my job would be as easy as swimming in a pool.

'How did they get on, Valentina and Ricardo?'

'Happy all the time. Now Ricardo is lonely in that place.'

'What was Valentina like?' I gently brought her back to the topic.

'Valentina was clever, friendly. She helped Ricardo to write.'

'They were engaged, weren't they?'

'They loved each other, but also to stay in Australia, Valentina needed to get married.'

Interesting, I thought. Was it a marriage of convenience for Valentina?

'Do you know what happened to her, when she disappeared?'

Luz cringed. I felt uncomfortable, making her go there, but that was my job. Making people talk about shit they'd rather forget.

'Everyone loved Valentina. No-one would hurt her. It's too sad, for me, my brother, her family.'

Luz grinned at me. 'Ricardo says his lawyer, Maria, is a very good lady and you too. You are helping Maria and Ricardo. *Muchas gracias*, Sandi.'

After my futile meeting with Ricardo, I couldn't believe he'd told his sister that I was helping him. Luz was clinging to hope.

'What about the sex worker who was murdered. What happened?'

'Ricardo didn't kill that girl. Ricardo is – *cómo se dice* – *muy amable*… a very kind person. To everyone.' Her voice was flat and quiet. 'It was the first time he went to the *prostituta*.'

I had to tell her the truth. She was going to hear it in court anyway. 'He'd been to the brothel often. He gave the sex worker a mobile and used it to ring her.'

I could sense she didn't want to hear the truth. It corrupted her picture of her sweet, innocent brother.

'Maybe our cousins gave him the phone,' she said.

I pondered that one. She must have noticed my expression. 'To make him do the work with them.'

I didn't know what to make of her comment, so I stored it away and jumped in before she veered off again.

'What happened when Ricardo came home after the sex worker was murdered?'

'When he comes home, always he parks in the garage. Then, he goes to his bedroom.' She pointed outside and I spotted a second door leading to the back section of the house. 'This night Ricardo came to dinner. As always. He didn't talk much, but Ricardo never talks much except about soccer or cars.' She chortled.

Was she hiding something? Her cheeriness jarred now we were talking about Lee's murder.

'Your brother comes home with blood splattered on his clothes and you notice nothing?'

She shook her head vigorously.

An argument had erupted in the lounge.

'Shut up,' I heard her husband say. 'I can't hear the score. For God's sake. Luz!'

Luz vanished into the other room. I heard loud voices in a mixture of Spanish and English.

Luz's husband paced into the kitchen with a plate of crumbled *alfajores*.

I wondered how he and Luz had met and what they had in common. *Another marriage of convenience? Who for?*

'The kids dropped them all over the floor.' His accent was broad Aussie, his tone terse.

He lurched to the bin and threw out the remainder of the *alfajores*. As he dusted his hands, he thrust his chin out at me. 'You with that lawyer?' The empty plate clattered as he plonked it into the sink.

'Yep. I'm doing background work for her.'

'Yeah, well Ricardo bloody needs it. What's a bloke to think, first his fiancée and then that tart. Had a temper, gave me cheek, the little shit. I hope he gets off, but I've gone beyond the call of duty for him. Let him stay in my house since he came here from Colombia. He was here way too long. I told Luz he needed to move out. Never expected he'd end up in the clink, but.'

He crossed his arms over his pot belly.

'Luz takes the kids to visit him. I don't want them hanging out with crims. Geez. I've told the wife, but she's all like, "He's family",' he mimicked her.

I disliked him mocking Luz, whatever the truth was about Ricardo.

'It's him who got himself into this shithole, hanging out with the wrong crowd.' His voice was strident.

'You mean his cousins?' I intervened.

'Hell yeah, are they bad news. They showed up here once – that was once too much – and I swore to Luz that I'd call the cops if they ever rocked up again. You can just tell they're crims; Santo, the ringleader, his sidekicks, Diego and Carlos – wearing sunglasses in my house, like gangsters. Ricardo was hanging out with the wrong crowd and now he's stuffed everything up for us.'

He brushed his large hand down over his walrus-like moustache. The moustache wasn't tamed by his attention.

'How did Ricardo and Valentina get on?' I asked.

'Cute sheila. They had a spat not long before she went missing.'

'What did they argue about?'

'She was bossing him around, telling him to spend more time with her. "Who wears the pants?" I said to him.'

The kids darted through the kitchen, Blanca squealing. They sped through the open sliding doors and into the backyard. Blanca hopped onto the swing and her brother started kicking a soccer ball. Luz returned with a dustpan full of crumbs.

Her husband ambled back into the lounge. 'Bloody hell!' he yelled.

The sound of feverish commentators spilled from the other room. I guessed Australia had lost a wicket.

Luz twitched at the sound of her husband's voice, but when nothing further followed, she emptied the dustpan into the rubbish bin. I wondered if Ricardo was the only one with an anger management issue in this family.

'Can you help my brother? He's dying in prison.'

'I'm doing my best. If you give me the contact details of your cousins and the friend of his fiancée, that would help.'

Luz searched for the friend's number. She explained that she didn't see her cousins anymore; didn't know where they were living or how to get in contact with them.

'It would also help if Ricardo would cooperate.'

'*Qué?*' What?

I clicked my tongue. 'When I went to see him, he...' I thought about how to sum up Ricardo's hostile response. 'He needs to tell me what's really going on.'

'*Por supuesto*. Of course. I'll tell him he has to talk to you. If you have a problem, we'll go together.'

'Mama, Mama,' Blanca called.

Luz scooted out to the backyard. I followed. Low-lying dark clouds punctuated the sky.

'Mama, push me,' sang Blanca.

She kicked her legs as Luz pushed, making the swing wobble.

'Ricardo, he plays with the children all the time, all the time.'

'When is *mi tío* coming home?' Blanca pouted.

'Tomorrow we'll go to see him.'

Blanca's brother was dribbling a soccer ball. 'Yeah, but I won't be able to play soccer with him in there.'

'I'll play with you Nicolás,' said Luz.

'It's not the same. *Mi tío* knows how to play.'

I kicked the soccer ball back to the boy as it strayed my way.

'Luz, I'd like to check out Ricardo's bedroom and in the garage, if that's all right.'

'The police looked in Ricardo's room.'

'That's good. I'd just like to see if it helps us at all.'

She showed me the way and then left me to it. She clearly believed her brother had nothing to hide.

Ricardo's room had enough space for a double bed, wardrobe and bedside table. He had a view out the window of a decaying fence. The off-white walls were a patchwork of posters of cars, soccer stars and images of Jesus.

I opened the doors to the wardrobe. It contained what you'd expect of a wardrobe: clothes and shoes.

I slid open the drawer of the bedside table, which was stuffed with tickets to soccer matches, both in Australia and Colombia; real estate flyers; and photos of Ricardo's niece and nephew, Luz and Valentina. I removed a couple of snaps that I suspected might have been of his cousins.

After having a kick of the ball with Nicolás in the back garden, I entered the garage by a wooden door to the side. It was surprisingly ordered. The wall opposite the door contained shelves stacked with power tools. The wall nearest the door was covered with tools hanging from hooks, each with a black shape drawn to note its spot. I checked out the chisels, feeling the polished wood handles under my fingertips.

On the back wall, with a window looking into the garden where Luz's kids continued to play, a wooden work bench indicated a project in process. A couple of screwdrivers and an electric sander stood next to a pine bench that looked like it just needed a coat of varnish to finish it off, the timber still giving off a fine forest scent.

Under the bench, shelves contained offcuts of wood, paint tins and metal containers filled with screws, nails and bolts sorted by size. Kneeling on a clean rag, I removed every plank of wood, container and paint tin and stacked them on the concrete floor, removing lids and investigating inside. I tapped on a paint tin that sounded empty. Levering the lid off with a sturdy screwdriver, it revealed a tiny layer of white paint.

I stood up and leaned backwards, before giving my neck a stretch. This was no doubt a pointless task, but it helped build a picture of Ricardo, if nothing else.

Back on my knees and underneath a pile of canvas drop sheets, I unearthed a small plastic zipped lunch bag. Inside, in between a blank piece of paper, lay neatly folded toilet paper.

Back on my feet, I carefully removing the squares of paper and slipped them onto the bench. Two sheets had simple, elegant drawings of flowers. My first thought was that Blanca had drawn them, but they were too intricate for a six-year-old. They could have been drawn with thin pastels or soft pencils. One picture was of a black curled stem featuring three carnation-pink blossoms. Perhaps charcoal pencils had been used for the stem and outlines of the blossoms. The pink flowers were of a thicker, sticky looking substance that smelled faintly sweet.

The last square of paper had elegant writing in thick black pen. I smoothed down a crinkled edge. It was an Asian script, maybe Chinese or Vietnamese. I arranged the toilet paper on the bench and took photos.

I found Luz. She confirmed the photo I'd unearthed was of their cousins.

'Do you know who drew these?' I showed her the toilet paper.

'*No sé.*'

'Mind if I take them?'

She shook her head.

I zipped them into the plastic lunch bag.

As I was heading off Luz said, 'You need to ask more questions, you come back, anytime.'

'If you promise more *alfajores*,' I joked.

At the front door, Luz hugged me. Although I had a moment of feeling awkward, I extended my arms around her shoulders. She held onto me for longer than felt comfortable and I broke free.

12

TIME TO CALL IT A DAY. I NEEDED TO GET MY LIFE IN ORDER AND IT *WAS* THE weekend.

Luz must have inspired me. After buying cat food, bread and vegetables at the supermarket, I washed the dishes, vacuumed and put on a load of washing. Beyoncé's *I Am… Sasha Fierce* album set the tempo.

As I was wiping the coffee table, Mum rang. Guilt spiked my up-beat mood, the promised phone call to her forgotten.

'Sandi, been expecting you to ring,' she slurred her words.

I deposited the Wettex back on the kitchen sink. 'Everything all right?'

'Been gardening all day. You?'

'Been coping with ratty kids in my swimming classes,' I offered.

'End of year exhaustion.'

'Yeah, and had a lot of other work on the go, so haven't had a chance to call you.'

'I wanted to sort out Christmas,' she said.

My mood plummeted and not because she'd been drinking. That had been a daily occurrence for a decade. And not because I was a Grinch. In fact, Christmas was the only day I could be sure of catching up with my nieces, an event as rare as a holiday. Problem was that joy involved my sister-created dramas.

'Iris doesn't want to have Christmas at her place. And she says it's too far for her to come here, cos she has to go to her in-laws for dinner that night. Which is fair enough. I just want everyone to be happy,' said Mum in a maudlin tone.

I was torn between knowing it'd be better to work it out when she was sober and not wanting to upset her by suggesting she ring back.

'Can you talk to her?' she pleaded.

My initial reaction was resentment. 'What am I meant to do with my crackpot sister, Mum? If you can't do it, how am I going to convince her?'

'She respects you.'

That was a blatant lie. The first and last time my older sister listened to me was when I was 15 and I threw her to the floor. Who knows what triggered that argument, but I was already taller than her and had no trouble knocking her flat. Soon after, Iris moved out of home. Mum had been upset, but I was relieved.

'I haven't got time today.'

'You're always so busy.'

You're always drunk, I wanted to say, but resisted. I'd tried talking to her once, after seeing her down a cask of white wine by herself. She claimed she only had a couple of glasses a night. I knew it was her way of relaxing. Given what she'd had to deal with, it made sense, but I hated it. She wasn't the smart, competent woman I loved and respected when she was pissed.

'Hey, I'll tell you how I go at lunch next week,' I said.

I wasn't convinced I was going to have time to fit that visit in, but didn't want to disappoint her. Mum seemed satisfied with my promise and we ended the call with our 'Love you,' refrain.

As I was packing away my work gear, I turned on my camera and studied the photos from the toilet paper in Ricardo's garage. On my laptop, I compared Asian languages on the internet. The script on the photos seemed Chinese, as the characters were similarly square and dense.

I searched online for a fast, reasonably priced translator. Maria was always willing to pay for worthwhile additional expenses. After finding a company that fitted my needs, I closed down my computer. Time to party.

After chucking my clothes in the dryer, I changed into my worn but favourite dancing gear – my white shirt, with frayed cuffs and sleek black pants, which had become more grey than black. I drove over to Stewart's house, chewing over ways to get payback on my sister for making family get-togethers a nightmare and for upsetting Mum. Iris always found an excuse to stop her children hanging out with their grandmother. Mum had brought us up by herself, worked full-time in a job she grew to hate, spent every spare cent on us and drove us all over town for sporting events. And this was how Iris repaid her. My sister's attitude was upsetting and ridiculous, but no matter how much I tried, she was impossible to reason with.

When I arrived in Fitzroy North, it took ages to find a park. Stewart's street was full of single-fronted houses with no off-street parking. His home stood out with its rusty red corrugated-iron roof. Inside, it always smelled mouldy. Stewart cared more about the proximity to cafés and music venues than the leaky roof. Mostly I avoided going to his place; his attention to housework was zero and he shared with two other grungy boys.

Stewart answered the door wearing white sports socks, tight-fitting jeans and a bright yellow shirt. His blond hair was spiked and black eyeliner highlighted his blue eyes.

In the lounge room, the stench of stale beer oozed up from the carpet. Every surface was covered with plates, plastic chip packets and beer bottles. Stew shoved stuff down one end of the couch. He indicated for me to sit next to him, but I didn't want to risk it. I flicked a chip packet off a book called *We Should All Be Feminists*, brushed the salt off the orange cover and flicked through the dog-eared pages. Stewart devoured feminist and queer theory. He loved to fill me in, so I was almost as up-to-date with current thinking as he was, without reading a page.

'You should give it a go.' He glanced up at me as he tied yellow shoelaces on blue runners. 'Tough week?'

I suppressed my frown and forced myself to smile. 'All good, but I reckon I deserve a night off after being shoved out in the rain by my ex-girlfriend, mauled by a sumo wrestler and threatened by a murderer. The only light moment was eating *alfajores*.'

'God, that sounds awful.' Stewart's face was pinched. 'Are you okay?'

'Amazingly unscathed,' I joked. 'Now, I've got money in my pocket and am ready for a night out with my bestie.'

'Good-oh. I was counting on it. The black rings under your eyes made me think you might want an early night.'

'You joking,' I replied.

Moments later I had to jog to keep up with Stewart as he loped down the street.

'What's the rush?' I panted.

He waved a hand in the air. 'I'll fill you in over a beer. Ben and work. Can't complain while I'm sober.'

Once we'd hit Brunswick Street proper, Stewart was forced to slow down. The footpaths were buzzing with a mix of hipsters, Goths and queers. A tightness loosened in my shoulders as we strolled through the crowd. We passed packed cafés, live music hotspots and alternative clothes shops before settling on the Provincial Hotel for a pre-club drink.

While I minded a table outside, Stewart went to buy the first round.

I sat facing the city, where the grey housing commission apartment towers dominated the view up the hill, the dull monsters scarring the cityscape.

Stewart reappeared, beers in hand. As soon as he'd deposited mine on the wooden table, he drank half his pot in one go, froth sticking to his upper lip.

I waggled my finger at his face. He slid the back of his hand across his mouth.

'So, man, what's happening with you?'

He did a little shimmy. 'The one thing that's going well in my life is dancing. I love it. Classes are the highlight of my week. I learn so much each lesson and feel my body getting stronger and more flexible. It's amazing.'

I was rapt that Stewart had enrolled in a dance school. It had been his dream, and finally he'd saved enough to pay the fees. Although he was gifted, he lacked formal training. His dad had been adamant no son of his would be a sissy.

'Work, though is a different story,' said Stewart. 'On Thursday I was 15 minutes late. That's all. The boss called me into his office for that minor misdemeanour. Oh my God, do you know what he said? "We won't be able to keep you if things keep going this way." I just about shat myself on the spot. That's never, like *never*, happened before.'

Stewart drained the rest of his beer. 'Another?'

I was only a third of the way through mine. I had the urge to slow him down.

'My shout, but tell me what happened first,' I said.

'It's just tricky for me, what with dancing school and Ben.'

I scratched my chin. 'Yeah, but don't you start work at, like, 4pm or something?'

He tried to get another mouthful out of his glass, but there was only a drop left. 'I know. It's just my body clock. But if it happens again.' Stewart ran his forefinger across his throat and made a sound like a duck quacking.

Stew did have a habit of being late. It seemed the boss's warning would be enough, but I added, 'Yeah, if I'm worried about waking up after a late night, I set multiple alarms.'

'Good idea,' he nodded.

I mooched inside to buy us another beer.

'Ben?' I asked as I returned.

Stewart sighed. 'Yeah well, I haven't seen him for a week. He said he had work in Sydney, but I saw a photo of him that his friend Toby had posted on Instagram at a club that looked like a lot like Zanzibar.'

'Indiscreet,' I commented.

'Why would he do that, if he wasn't trying to piss me off?'

'Hey, don't jump to conclusions. Talk to him.'

Stewart gave me a "der" look. 'He said he was in Sydney the whole time. I'm like, "What about the Instagram photo?" He said Toby must have taken that weeks ago.'

'Do you believe him?'

'Hardly,' said Stewart.

'His word against social media,' I said. 'Who would you trust?'

He waggled his foot and avoided eye contact. I could tell he was considering my point.

We left our dramas behind as we caught a tram into the city. A soft pink and orange sunset glowed through the office towers.

We hit an awesome rooftop bar with views of city lights and a DJ dishing up RnB and Hip Hop. We danced, drank and danced some more. I laughed as Stew spun me around. For a skinny guy, he was ridiculously strong and agile.

A short guy dived in between us and edged close to Stewart. My friend put up with him for a couple of numbers until the guy started grinding into Stew's backside. I was ready to intervene if Stewart wanted me to when he shouted in my ear, 'Let's disappear.' We sped down the stairs and out the door.

We skipped the queue at New Guernica and wandered through narrow lanes to Casablanca. The dance floor was thrumming with Latino and non-Latino dancers. Stewart slid into the throng beckoning me with his index finger. I could manage a basic salsa, especially with Stew leading me, so I followed him.

After a few dances, I stepped aside to watch women gravitating towards Stewart, keen to partner with a guy who could expertly spin them.

The lights grew softer, the music louder, and the crowd more hyper as the morning went on. I offered to buy a drink for a cute woman wearing tight denim jeans. She glared at me as if I'd touched her up and made a point of leaping off the floor into the arms of a lanky dude. My luck was out to sea.

I hung out at the bar and ordered a glass of iced water and suddenly it hit me – the details of how we were going to get Jae out. It was brilliant. I grabbed my phone and clicked on notes.

Stewart appeared next to me.

'Hey Stew, you have to help me free a girl from sex slavery. Are you up for it?' I yelled in his ear.

'Alsolutely,' slurred Stewart. 'Show me where she is.' He surveyed the room, as though trying to spot who I was talking about.

'Not now, you idiot,' I laughed.

Stewart ordered another drink while I tapped furiously, hoping my notes would make sense. The predictive text was an added complication.

'Next week. We'll get her out early next week.'

'How come you're rescuing her?' Stewart jived in front of me.

'Good question. What the hell was I thinking. Forget I said anything.'

'Oh, well, if you need muscle, I'm up for anything.' Stew strutted off to the toilet in a very un-straight line.

I made myself another note that I wasn't getting involved, in case I forgot.

We caught separate Ubers to our separate homes. I couldn't face going back to the mess in Stewart's house, despite my car being there. The streets were devoid of traffic. As the Uber topped the West Gate, the sun rose over the city.

13

After last night's heavy drinking session, this was exactly what I needed: to lie on a banana lounge with a Moon Dog lager on Maria's tiled patio. *Gracias Maria.*

Chopping and stirring noises trickled from inside the house. I would have offered to assist, except it hadn't worked out in the past. Firstly, there wasn't enough room in the kitchen. Secondly, Maria and her partner, Kristin, were gourmet cooks and whenever I'd helped, they'd critiqued the angle of the carrots or the consistency of the avocado.

It was safer for me to stack the dishwasher afterwards.

I caught sight of myself in one of the hexagonal mirrors on the back fence. My lips were pinched. Leaning back, I let my jaw relax. My seediness faded as I lapped up the early evening sun.

Through the glass doors to the kitchen, Maria and Kristin glided around each other like they were dancing the rumba. Their movements were sensual and they caressed each other even when they were doing mundane chores like unloading the dishwasher. The tall, angular-faced Kristin leaned over the voluptuous Maria, her chin on her shoulder, her arm draped across Maria's breasts. The scene unfolded through a glass screen, like a movie. I was entranced and stabbed by their intimacy.

Maria's girlfriend was a lucky woman. I should know, after our fling, when we were studying Torts – the driest subject in the galaxy. During lectures about trespass and negligence, I was distracted by the way Maria let the tip of her tongue appear when writing elegant notes or stroked her chin as she considered the minutiae of case law.

My time with Maria was a brief flame that fizzled before all the candles sparked.

I shook off self-pity and reminded myself how lucky I was to have

Maria in my life. She'd been a steady and generous friend through all my dramas, study, work and relationships.

Maria appeared on the patio, shoes tapping on the floor, a white apron tied over an elegant black dress. 'Sorry I'm neglecting you, *bella*. We're almost done. Another beer?'

I shook my head. 'My week's been nuts, I'm loving doing nothing.'

She stepped closer and kissed me on the forehead before tapping her way back inside.

As I was dozing off in the warm evening sunlight, Maria announced dinner. I idled over to the outside table, which was covered with a white tablecloth and set with silver cutlery.

Maria brought out two large white plates stylishly arranged with Pan-seared Atlantic salmon, quinoa, roasted potatoes and rocket salad.

My stomach rumbled in response to the oily scent of the fish.

'Would you like another one of your beers, or a glass of red?' Kristin asked me, appearing with a bottle of Red Claw Pinot Noir in one hand and her plate in the other. She was born in Denmark and still had a slightly choppy accent.

'Thanks, a red sounds great.'

The wine gurgled as Kristin poured. Maria swished hers around and stuck her nose into the huge wine glass before sipping it.

The couple had a whole rack of wines under the stairs. I'd been privy to their collection and been envious of the sheer number of bottles.

'Nice drop,' said Maria.

'Silky.' Kristin brushed her hand across Maria's shoulder.

I had a taste. It was definitely better than an ultra-cheap bottle, but I didn't know what the fuss was about.

'Sensational,' I said after swallowing a mouthful of succulent fish.

Kristin ate slowly, like she was sticking to the rule of 30 chews to a mouthful. I was almost finished and tried to slow down. Such a delicious dish deserved savouring. Whenever I enjoyed a great home-cooked meal, I promised myself I'd experiment with tasty recipes. My intentions were good.

'How's work?' I asked Kristin.

She worked at the Commonwealth Bank as a financial advisor, which from what I'd gathered involved making more money for already rich people.

'Oh, it's hectic, but satisfying.' Kristin was one of those people who insisted on the glass being half full.

Kristin and Maria beamed at each other.

'Yeah, here's to work,' I said.

We clinked glasses.

'Kristin was promoted, weren't you babe?'

'More money?' I queried.

'A little, but mainly more responsibility.'

I reckoned her pay packet had skyrocketed. A woman I used to swim with, who worked in a bank, said that each time bank managers got a promotion their wage rose by at least another $25,000 a year.

'But worth it, hey?' I nodded.

'Definitely. It's a chance to learn about managing people. It was too good an opportunity to knock back.'

'You're already so well respected,' said Maria. 'All her colleagues rave about her.'

'Thanks, sweetheart. Who knows, one day I might be able to contribute more to the community or the environment movement.'

'Well, we're paying off the mortgage much faster now, so in a few years, babe,' said Maria.

'We'll be able to focus less on earning,' Kristin finished.

They held hands across the table, until Kristin noticed me, and slid long fingers back to her fork. At least Kristin had thought about how couply they were acting, unlike my friend, who seemed oblivious.

Maria was laughing. Relaxed, with the wine, the girlfriend. Meanwhile, my shoulders were as hard as cricket balls. Sipping my red wine, I got up to admire the deep crimson blooms of the climbing roses behind the raised veggie patch in their small garden. I stuck my nose into a rose with a loose cluster of petals, inhaling their sweet scent.

'What are these?'

'Climbing Crimson Glory.'

'Stunning.'

'Yeah, I'm really pleased with how they've taken off,' said Maria.

'Maria has a wonderful way with plants,' said Kristin.

I felt like I'd intruded on a mutual admiration society, which I was glaringly not part of.

'Yep, our Maria, she excels at everything.'

I don't think Kristin noticed my gibe, because she simply kissed Maria on the cheek. Maria's expression was an odd mixture of a snarl for me and a smile for Kristin.

I stacked the empty plates, seeking a moment's respite.

'I'll take them in.' Kristin combed her hands through Maria's hair, then swanned off inside.

As I retreated to the climbing roses, I asked Maria, 'How's things with your folks?'

'Oh fine, except Mum hassles me about having children.'

'She's moved on from praying you'll find a hubby, hey?'

Maria sighed. 'If only my brothers would hurry up. I think Mum's worried she'll be dead before we produce any offspring.'

'Have you thought about having kids?'

Maria twirled her spoon on the table. 'Definitely. You know, hitting thirty, you have to, don't you?'

I nodded as I rubbed the velvety petals of a rose between my fingers.

Maria slid her glass to one side. 'Anyway, how's your investigation going?'

I'd been avoiding giving Maria an update as I hadn't spent as much time on Lee Wu's murder as planned because of the pressure from Cassy to rescue the trafficked woman, Jae Shin.

'Did you know that Ricardo Lopez was a suspect in a drug-dealing ring, with his cousins?'

'Where did you hear that?'

'His sister Luz said the police had questioned Ricardo, but hadn't charged him.'

'That's interesting. Surprising it hasn't been mentioned. Do you know if his cousins have any convictions?'

'Not clear yet. I'm planning on grilling Ricardo further, and that's one of my questions for him. I popped into the brothel, surreptitiously. Remember Ricardo said another sex worker was there when Lee was murdered. Her name – well her working name – is Snow. I'm sure she saw what happened. Don't know why she lied to the cops. She seemed jealous of Lee and something was going on between her and the bouncer, Ju-Long. You wouldn't want to make enemies with him.' I rubbed my wrist, remembering his grip.

Maria raised one thinned black eyebrow. 'Next steps?'

'I'm organising meetings with Ricardo's boss and a friend of his fiancée's.' That was overstating my arrangements, but I was planning on pursuing those connections. I didn't mention the drawings and writing under the drop sheets at Luz's house. First, I wanted to find out if they were relevant. 'And follow up the phone contact that Ricardo had, presumably with Lee.'

'Phone contact?'

'Yeah, I messaged you about it.'

It was surprising she'd forgotten that detail – Maria's memory was phenomenal. I wondered if her case load was so ridiculous, even she couldn't be across all the facts. She would find that excruciating.

'So, you'll give me a report in a couple of days?' Maria's voice was extra strained.

'Yep no problem,' I promised, hoping I could deliver in time.

'I'm in court this coming week, but I've set aside time on Thursday to prepare Ricardo's defence,' she said.

'I've got another case on the go as well. The Fair Sex Coalition? Heard of them?'

Maria tilted her head to one side as if trying to place the organisation.

'It's also to do with a sex worker, strangely,' I said. 'A South Korean woman under lock and key. She's terrified about police involvement, so the Coalition's contracted me to work out an escape plan. I know someone who works there. You remember Cassy. Yeah, she's the one who got me the job.'

Maria glared at me with her dark, intense eyes. 'Excuse me? Oh my God, Sandi.'

I opened my palms. 'What? What?'

'That woman has trouble typed all over her.'

Even though I might have said the same about Cassy, criticising an ex was my prerogative. 'Oh, come on, that's totally over the top.'

Maria stood up and seized the cracked pepper and home-made olive oil dressing. She stared down at me with her signature tight-lipped frown.

I placed my glass back on the table and almost up-ended it. 'She's just a bit headstrong.'

'You've obviously forgotten how you hardly left your house when you two broke up and I brought you over cooked meals because you were too depressed to go shopping.'

Maria's criticism stripped me naked. Here she had achieved the perfect relationship versus me having been deserted by Cassy, dumped by Diana, unable to manage myself.

'Oh bullshit. I might have spent a week or two feeling low, but what crap, unable to make a meal.'

'It's totally true. She's the arch manipulator.'

I squeezed a corner of the tablecloth between my fingers and resisted the urge to yank it off the table and watch all the glasses smash. 'I can handle myself. You're not my fucking mother.'

Inside, Kristin was drying her hands on a paper towel, her torso twisted so she could keep an eye on us.

Maria gripped the back of her chair, her knuckles white. She was superb at winning arguments. I braced myself for the next attack.

Kristin arrived with lemon tart. Maria knew it was one of my favourites, she'd no doubt gone to the trouble of making it for me. My appetite had fizzled like the morning after glimpse of a drunken choice.

Maria marched inside with the condiments and after depositing them, disappeared down the hallway.

As Kristin sliced the lemon tart, she took up the slack. 'Being doing much aikido lately?'

'Been a bit busy with work.' I peered down the hallway, trying to work out if Maria had gone to the loo or upstairs to their bedroom.

Seeing my attention was elsewhere, Kristin turned around to look inside. At that moment, Maria re-joined us, her eyes red. She focused on eating her lemon tart as Kristin squeezed her hand and continued to try and engage me in small talk. My answers were mostly monosyllabic, in between forced mouthfuls of dessert.

After stacking the dishwasher, I feigned exhaustion.

With my toes hard on the accelerator down Rathdowne Street and around the zoo, I wondered if my friendship, as well as my main source of income, was in jeopardy.

14

A PEELING BOB'S MOTORS SIGN MARKED THE ENTRANCE. ON A BUSY TRUCK route in Heidelberg not far from where Ricardo had been living, the mechanics' business was stuck between a plywood factory and a sporting goods clearance centre.

I hurried inside to escape the stench of diesel and the roar of engines.

The entrance led straight into the workshop with a reception area off to the side. When I opened the reception door, no-one was present and there was no bell to attract attention.

I exited and hovered in the entrance to the workshop. It was thick with the smell of grease and petrol and chock-full of cars, mainly Toyotas and Holdens, some with bonnets open, others on hoists. Stepping further in, I noticed three guys leaning over the engine of a red Toyota station wagon. The eldest one noticed me; a man in his early sixties sporting a bushy moustache.

'Hang on a sec,' he said in a raspy voice as he indicated towards the reception. I followed his direction back into the room, bereft of any creature comforts. One hard steel chair was the only option for customers. Behind it, a dirty white blind with a frayed edge half covered frosted windows. The newest item was a poster advertising lubricant.

The older guy appeared from a door leading from the workshop and wiped his worn hands on a rag. It seemed a pointless task given it was a patchwork of black splotches.

'Alrighty, what's up?'

My car had been spluttering as I drove up the hill.

'My VW Golf,' I said. 'I love it, but I think it might be nearly at the end of its life. How long do they last?'

'Depends if you look after 'em. Parts, though.' He tapped the till and winked. His eyes lit up like a medical specialist's when they discover some complex condition that needs to be solved. 'It's out front?'

As we headed outside, we passed an overflowing rubbish bin on an overgrown nature strip, littered with takeaway cups and plastic bags. I popped the bonnet and he propped it open. Together we studied greasy black-covered parts. It seemed filthy even to me. I had a second of embarrassment and wondered how the heck it kept going with the poor attention it received.

The old guy scrunched up his nose. 'Definitely overdue a service,' he said mildly. 'How long since the last one?'

'Left it a bit long, I know.'

'The sooner the better, love.' The mechanic's voice beefed up as a road train of trucks clanked past.

'Next pay packet,' I agreed.

'You want to book it in?'

'There's another reason for my visit.'

'Yeah, what's that then?' He clutched the metal rod holding up the bonnet.

'You the owner here? Bob?'

'That's right,' he straightened up.

'I wanted to ask you a few questions about Ricardo Lopez.'

Bob's eyes became slits. 'Rick. That scumbag. What about him?'

'I've been employed by his solicitor to get some background.'

I was hoping that was still true after my tiff with Maria the night before.

Bob yanked the metal rod out of its socket and slammed my bonnet shut. He marched back into the business entrance. He had a limp I hadn't noticed earlier and favoured his right leg. I had to stride to keep up despite that handicap.

It seemed he was going to disappear back into the workshop without a word, when he swivelled back around towards me. 'I'm busy.'

'You could save time by answering a couple of questions now, instead of being subpoenaed.'

Bob's face wrinkled. 'That a threat?'

'Just a fact, Bob. Be easier to deal with this here and now. I can see how hectic you guys are. Don't want to drag you away, if we don't have to.'

'What a load of bullshit,' said Bob. 'Rick deserves what he gets, lazy little shit. Excuse my French. Was about to sack him anyway, even before the cops called. Always knew he was dodgy.'

'Wasn't up for employee of the year?'

'Employee of the year my arse. Kept taking time off, always on the phone, and when he did decide to show up, he was late. I put up with his Mexican siesta ideas for too long. After all my patience with him and his ways, I finally told him where to go, when I knew what he'd done. He was off to jail anyhow.'

Bob slapped his grease-covered hands past each other. 'Out the bloody door.'

'When did he finish up?' I pulled out my ocean-blue notebook.

'I can tell you the exact date.'

Bob stomped back into the reception area, behind the counter. Pages snapped as he flicked through a day-to-a-page diary. 'March the twelfth. Good bloody riddance.'

He stabbed the spot with his oily finger, smudging the white-lined page with black stains, then slammed the book shut.

Lee Wu had been murdered on 11 March. I made a note and underlined the date Ricardo was sacked.

'You believe he murdered the sex worker?'

'Bloody oath. Shady as. Him and his cousins. They used to drop in. I told him to keep 'em out of my sight. Those thugs wanted their cars serviced here. There was no way I was gonna have their filthy business.'

Saliva formed at the edges of his mouth. 'Rick as thick as a fart in the dark with them.' His lip became a snarl. 'One day his cousins drive up in a black Holden Malibu. Park in the driveway here, blocking the entrance to the workshop.'

Bob nodded towards the concreted driveway. 'Two blokes jump out and pose like bodyguards, while another two bolt in here wearing Gucci sunglasses, and when I ask them to move their car, they totally ignore me. Couldn't see their eyes. Never trust a bloke if you can't see the whites of his eyes.'

Bob pointed at his own bloodshot eyes. 'They aren't big bastards but they act tough you know, wearing leather jackets that I'd bet me bottom dollar are hiding guns. They say they need to talk to Rick. So I say, "Leave me your number and I'll get him to ring you." Suddenly Rick's at my side. Tells me their grandmother's in hospital. He just needs to talk to his cousins to find out if she's all right. "Not on my time," I tell him.'

Bob banged the counter and the diary ricocheted. 'Rick bloody ignores me and starts scheming with those thugs.'

A zinging noise from a bolt-tightening machine in the workshop peppered his words.

'They don't go anywhere, sit in the Malibu for ages, Rick and his cousins. I'm sick to death of this caper and decide to call the cops, but just as I pick up the phone Rick appears. I'm a tolerant man, but not that bloody tolerant. I don't like being used and I don't take kindly to him bringing thugs onto the premises. Final straw came soon after. I wasn't gobsmacked one bit, when I heard he'd stabbed—'

The phone interrupted his diatribe.

Bob opened the diary and flicked pages. 'Tuesday, yep, that's fine, mate. Lucky, just before Chrissie. But I can squeeze you in. 8am, yep, see you then.'

He hung up and wrote in the diary before making eye contact with me. 'When I told those cousins where to go, Rick threatens me, "Don't say that to them. They can hurt you".'

The truck route outside competed with Bob for dominance.

'I know about drug cartels, and stuff. I know he was mixed up in all that.'

The phone rang again.

'Look, love much as I'd like to kill time hanging shit on that drug lord, I've a bloody business to run.'

Bob turned away to answer. 'I'll give you a tingle back in five,' he said into the handset.

'You still here?' he asked me as he hung up.

'I need to talk to his co-workers,' I stated.

'No bloody way you're going to waste their time as well as mine. That little prick has cost me enough without you comin' in here taking up space as well. Disappear before I get real annoyed.' His raspy voice had turned into a growling dog. A thick black forefinger indicated the way out.

'No worries, thanks for your help. By the way, you wouldn't have happened to get the number plate of the cousins, would you?'

Bob's eyes slide sideways. 'Nup.'

'They sound like the kind of guys you'd like to see locked up.'

Bob grunted. 'Too right.'

I saw myself out. The old VW would have to wait for some decent attention. As I started the engine, I steeled myself for my next meeting, with Cassy.

15

I STOMPED DOWN A BLUESTONE LANEWAY IN AMONGST COMMERCIAL RUBBISH bins and air-conditioning units near Melbourne Central in the city. Set back from the lane, gold coloured doors with spear-shaped handles interrupted the pattern. Cassy's choice of rendezvous didn't surprise me. Escaping the whoosh of exhaust fans and the stench of rotting meat, I entered the cavernous café, far removed from my cosy local.

A waiter indicated the only free table for two and I perched on a stool, waiting.

Cassy appeared in the doorway in a sleeveless T-shirt, a spiderweb tattoo on her upper arm fully visible. She navigated between customers to join me and squeezed my wrist.

'Sandi, good to see you again.'

I grunted in response.

After we'd ordered coffee, I launched straight into business. Whatever payment I could negotiate would have to suffice.

I laid out a series of photos across the table, as Cassy extricated her laptop from a Frida Kahlo bag. The photos were superior to my plan to rescue the trafficked woman, Jae Shin. What seemed flawless when drunk became substandard when sober. I braced myself against the inevitable: Cassy ripping my idea to shreds.

I cleared my throat. 'I've cased out the brothel and there's no access apart from the front door.'

As I pointed to where the windows had been blacked out and external cameras positioned, I compared my chipped turquoise nail polish to Cassy's professionally manicured jade-green fingernails. 'Obviously, storming through the front door isn't an option, unless you can hire some muscle. If not, no go at Amsterdam Angels.'

Cassy rolled her hand, indicating for me to keep going.

'I've also checked out the apartment in the city, where the young women get taken after their shift. I followed them at 3.30am one night. You can't get in there without the minders giving you permission. God help anyone who tries. Those guys would make my aikido teacher quiver.'

Cassy shot me a questioning look.

'The solution I've come up with is to get Jae out through the takeaway joint next door.' I hoped Cassy missed the hesitation in my voice.

I tapped the hard copy photos of McDonald's, its car park, the drive-through and the interior. 'The women get to visit Macca's regularly. Major treat for them. They're always accompanied by a minder who usually waits outside.'

Apart from my single encounter with Skull, this whole plan was based on what a McDonald's employee reported about their routine. Geez I hoped he was right.

Pointing to a photo that showed the counter, toilets and exits, I said, 'My advice is: next time Jae contacts you, tell her to text you when they're going to Macca's. Get her to make an excuse to need the bathroom. Meet her there, give her a coat and hat, or whatever, to disguise her. The minder will be out the front. You head out the back. Take her to a safe house. I'm presuming you have that bit sorted.'

To brace myself, I settled both feet firmly on the concrete floor. 'It'd be better if you had someone in the car with you, engine running. One of your colleagues.' I linked my hands behind my head. 'Thoughts?'

Cassy had been furiously taking notes, the tendons pulsating on the backs of her hands.

This plan needed to be sorted before Cassy hooked me into anything more. Maria's words about Cassy having "trouble typed all over her" replayed in my head.

Cassy clapped the laptop shut. 'Thanks for all your work, but it's not ideal.'

'Is that right?' I couldn't stop a half laugh, half grunt escaping.

'There are lots of risks in this scenario.'

'Hey, Cassy, as well as finding a solution, I've provided a detailed plan. Of course, it's going to be risky.'

'Not for me. For Jae. It might mean having to wait days. That's too long.'

I packed away the photos.

'We have to get her out now. We can't wait until tomorrow. Jae rang me yesterday. She was desperate. Tonight, there must be a way, with or without extra help, some way to get her out.'

Cassy's emerald eyes appeared genuinely scared, her normally olive skin pale. 'She's terrified they're going to kill her. Maybe they suspect she's been talking out-of-school.'

An image filled my mind of the women following their minder like dogs with tails between their legs. Their scared eyes, the call for help in the lift.

Another image replaced it of my mother's eyes – absent and frozen, long before we left.

Suddenly, the front door to the café slammed and without warning, I was back in the terror of my childhood.

Like a tape replaying, I heard the slam of my parent's door and an agonising scream. In the next room, my eight-year old self huddled under the safety of a single doona, shaking uncontrollably.

'Sandi.'

Cassy's voice sounded distant. I could see the dark timber of the table. I dragged my palms back and forward on the hard surface and focused on the smoothness of the wood. My thighs shook. I breathed deeply, trying to force my legs to be still. Cassy squeezed my hand. I turned mine under Cassy's and folded my fingers over hers.

The jitters started to fade. I withdrew my hand and slapped my legs. It was still as terrifying as it had always been. The last flashback I'd experienced was years ago. I thought I was over it.

'You okay?' she asked. 'It never disappears does it?'

Cassy's face had transformed from a tight, anxious knot into a warm caring face. 'It's hard for Jae too. You get what she's going through.'

It was all too clear. Cassy got it too; she always had.

'Let's find a way to get her out now Sandi. The owners are mongrels.'

'It's not just the owners.' My voice was still shaky. 'I'm working on this other case where a punter murdered a sex worker. She was an overseas student making ends meet with a bit of sex work on the side, and had her throat cut by a customer.'

'Where was she from?'

'China.'

'You sure she wasn't trafficked?'

'Nah, she was on a student visa.'

'Yes, but traffickers often organise student visas to cover what's really going on. Then the trafficked women can stay in Australia up to five years,' said Cassy.

'What about the study requirements?'

'Once they're here, it doesn't matter. They're not at the address on their application, so they can't be traced.' Cassy fiddled with one of the silver studs in her ear. 'Traffickers have so many options open to them: bribing corrupt officials or changing the visa status. They keep the women's passports so they can't escape.'

I was shocked at the idea that Lee could have been a sex slave.

Cassy smiled. 'The other day, what happened – it's just my boss Bani is such a micro-manager, she makes me nervous.'

'No kidding?' I laughed.

Cassy tipped her head to the side, obviously perplexed by my amusement.

'We really appreciate all your work on this. You don't know how much,' she continued as she slid her stool next to mine and kissed me on the lips. Her hand caressed my neck. My body tingled.

'Come off it, Cassy,' I managed to say just as she landed another kiss, her soft lips getting through my guard.

My mouth responded. *Don't do this*, I thought. My hands were on her hips, ready to push her away, but instead I wrapped my arms around her back. She didn't resist. We kissed until we snapped into awareness of our surroundings and finally drew breath. A teenager at a table nearby was staring at us. I grinned back at her.

'When this is all sorted.' Cassy caressed my fingers.

'Why wait?'

'Business and pleasure,' she justified.

I held her hand, stroking her smooth skin. 'I've never had a problem mixing the two.'

She pecked me on the lips. 'Where to from here?'

If only I could have had some distance from her. While my body ached to dissolve into Cassy's, my brain yelled at me to stop before I leaped back into bed with the woman who'd ditched me. I should have left and gathered my thoughts there and then.

'Can we work out how to help Jae escape first?'

'I thought we had,' I answered.

'There are a couple of hurdles. Our resources are stretched at the moment, with all the media coverage, more sex workers are calling, which is terrific.'

Cassy stared at the metal beam above us. 'There's more, Sandi. Last night when Jae called, she sounded suicidal. The traffickers supply the women with drugs so they're spaced out enough to do the job. Jae's been stashing heroin away. She said she wanted to sleep and not wake up. After we talked, she promised not to do anything yet. Now, you can see why it's urgent. If you could sit with me in the car while we're waiting. That's all.'

I must have been frowning.

'What?' Cassy's face was a picture of innocence.

'Come on. We agreed I'd work out a plan, which I've delivered on. I'm not getting paid enough to risk my arse out there. Thanks for the invite, but it's over to you now.'

'We can organise more money if that's your concern. Easy. This plan is risky enough. Please come, just as a lookout in case anything goes wrong. Jae has to get out. Tomorrow, preferably.'

I sighed.

'You've no idea how much it would mean to me. You're the perfect person because you've developed the plan, you know the layout,' said Cassy.

'A minute ago you thought the plan was a load of crap.'

'After thinking it through, it's the best – the only – option.'

I wanted to say no, but I was having trouble forcing that word out.

'I'm busy tomorrow and the minder has already spotted me. If it's the same one, I'll be recognised,' I justified.

'You're the mistress of disguise, aren't you?' She gave me the cute look, a mix of coy and cheeky. 'Wednesday then.'

We strolled through city crowds to the sloping lawn outside the State Library. Cassy flopped onto the grass and after a moment, I joined her. I'd never been good at sacrificing pleasure for the sake of a sensible decision. Her cute smile was too hard to resist. Cassy's thoughts about keeping business and pleasure separate had obviously taken a back seat too, because she propped herself on an elbow and kissed me, deep and long. After lazing in the sun, we went our separate ways.

It was on the train, heading home, that a ball of anxiety invaded my gut.

16

I RETURNED TO REMAND AND WAS GREETED BY A BASKETBALL-TALL GUARD. Perhaps he'd had some good news, maybe a win at the pokies, because he grinned and joked as he escorted me to the Visitor's Centre. My attitude was the opposite. I cringed at the prospect of facing Ricardo again, though this time I was prepared to quash any outbursts.

The guard led me to an empty, windowless interview room, next to the room we'd been in the week before. I positioned an envelope on the chair next to me and made sure the photos taken with my black-rimmed glasses were in order.

A guard opened the door, and Ricardo entered the room kneading his hands.

'*Hola Sandi.*' His smile was forced.

I was sceptical about the sudden change. Maybe his sister, Luz, had convinced him to cooperate.

'*Hola Ricardo, qué tal?*' 'How's it going?' As soon as I asked the question, I realised it was a mistake. What good news stories would he have to share from his prison cell?

'I met your niece and nephew,' I said in Spanish, without waiting for a reply. 'Blanca drew a picture of the family, you included.'

'One day she will be an artist,' Ricardo responded with a genuine smile.

He cared for the kids and they loved him. Whatever he'd done, some humanity existed within him.

'I don't have much time today,' he said, 'I have a job in the metal workshop.'

Perhaps that was why he was more positive.

'I've brought photos.' I placed the envelope on the mission-brown table between us.

When Ricardo reached towards it, I slid it back towards my side of the table.

'First, I have a few questions. Luz told me about your cousins, Santo, Carlos and Diego.'

A worried expression glazed his face. This was more like the Ricardo I'd met before.

'Did you work for them?'

'I had a job. Remember?' he scoffed.

'Tempted by a top-up?'

Ricardo's body closed in. I'd hit a wall as hard as the concrete behind him.

What had happened with his cousins? I'd seen it before, how people took a few steps into the ocean and were suddenly caught in a rip.

The silence in the room became uncomfortable. It was as claustrophobic as the last time, even though I was prepared. If we could have taken a stroll along the beach and had this discussion, it would be easier – on both of us.

'Have any of your cousins ended up in prison?'

'My cousin, Carlos, punched a man in a bar. He gets into fights. I'm not sure what happened but I don't think he went to jail.'

'Were your cousins involved with Lee's death?'

Ricardo shook his head. He wiped the table as if sweeping away grime but the dark stains were ingrained, there was no way to erase them.

'Have they got some hold over you?'

He sneered. 'I never want to see them again in my life.'

Ricardo stood up and I knew I was about to lose him again. When I held up the A4 envelope, he begrudgingly sat back down.

My follow-up questions about his cousins went nowhere, so I took out the photos, bar two, and laid them in front of Ricardo.

'*Es ella*. It's her.' He stabbed the photo of Lee's colleague, Snow. 'She was there.'

'She witnessed Lee's murder?'

'Yes,' he insisted. 'She knows everything.' It was interesting how fired up Ricardo was about Snow.

I asked about the other photos. He confirmed the identities of the large Asian man and the boss lady.

'Ju-Long and Qiao,' I said.

'Yes, they were there.'

'Snow saw Ju-Long attack Lee?'

'Yes, that's true.' His voice wavered.

'Is that right, Ricardo?'

'Yes,' he growled.

I reached into the envelope and drew out a photo. 'By the way, did Lee Wu draw this picture for you?' I flourished the image of the pink blossoms drawn on toilet paper in front of Ricardo.

He jabbed his elbows into his sides as if bracing himself. 'Where did you get that?'

'Did she give it to you?'

He shifted in his chair and refused to make eye contact.

I held the final glossy paper by the corner, still hidden in the envelope.

His body became an agitated tangle. He knew what was coming.

'Do you know what the poem says?'

'What poem?' he asked.

I handed him a printed document with the verse in Spanish. After receiving an English version from the translator, I'd converted it into Spanish, with one click on the internet. A qualified translator could have done a better job, but it would suffice for this purpose.

'Recognise this?' I asked.

His torso collapsed as he clasped the photo.

I recited the Spanish version to Ricardo.

I'm saddened by the thought that my mother's cheeks are lost
When sunlight fades, I'll vanish like footprints of an ant
My bed will be the coffin of the next crushed girl
Eternal sleep awaits, dreamless of earth's cruel curse.

As soon as I started reading, Ricardo's eyes doubled in size. By the second line, he'd hidden his face in his hands. At the end, Ricardo exploded out of his chair. He raised his fist and punched the concrete wall.

'Stop. Back on your chair Lopez,' I ordered in English.

He spun towards me, his knuckles red and raw, skin hanging from his fingers. Trails of blood trickled down the wall.

'Sit down,' I ordered again.

Ricardo blinked as though confused about who I was, what role I played.

The door flew open.

'Back to your cell,' the female guard commanded.

Head lowered, Ricardo silently left the room. Those guards certainly had a way, perhaps a job as prison officer would have been better training than aikido.

'He might need a dab of betadine,' I suggested to the retreating guard.

Was Ricardo's outburst a sign of guilt or was he upset because he'd been caught? Had Lee been terrified of Ricardo or someone else? I left the compound more determined to uncover the truth.

On the drive home in the airconditioned comfort of my car, I mulled over Ricardo's cousins. They seemed to be the key to this case, but it wasn't clear how. I planned the phone calls I needed to make. One was top of my list.

Alice Brodie was my go-to for all police intel. She always offered me tidbits without getting herself caught. We'd met playing basketball with the Space Jammers team. When she first 'fessed up to being a cop, I was totally sus. My trust in cops had vanished the night they barged into my childhood house and, ignoring Mum's black eye, decided that our poor father was the one who had been putting up with a nagging wife. But cop Alice had won me over with her infectious laugh and stories of working with sexual assault victims to actually nail the perpetrators.

Walking through the door to my flat, I dumped my backpack, sank onto the couch and rang Alice. She answered on the third ring. Raucous voices in the background made me reduce the phone volume a notch.

'Hey Sandi, miss our chinwags. What's up?'

'I'll come watch your next round, goalie queen. Meanwhile, thought I'd fill you in on my latest case and ask you a quick question.'

'I'm out of town at the mo'. Up for a friend's 30th in Sydney – harbour cruise tonight, pretty cool, but I have a sec in between stuffing my face and throwing back cocktails.' Alice's voice was like a cool summer breeze, always refreshing.

'I'm working with a solicitor to build a defence case for a Ricardo Lopez. He's been charged with the murder of a sex worker. Seems he might also be involved in drug dealing with his cousins Santo, Carlos and Diego Perez.' I emphasised their names.

'Perez. Got it.'

'Also, Ricardo was a suspect in his fiancée's disappearance, Valentina Rojas.'

'Interesting. And the quick question?'

'There's evidence that Ricardo had been ringing the woman he's been accused of murdering, but last I heard the police informant hadn't supplied any call details.'

'Maybe they're still investigating and don't have any more evidence yet. After an accused is charged there's an ongoing duty to disclose anything relevant to the case as it arises whether is supports the prosecution or the defence.'

'All right thanks, I'll double check if we've received anything.'

'That'd be my next move. Okay, gotta go now. Be back next weekend. Guessing you've got the Space Jammer's fixtures.' She signed off. Alice preferred being circumspect over the phone. Fair enough; it was her job on the line.

My next call was to Maria's secretary.

She bubbled, 'Perfect timing. I was going to get in touch with you, Sandi. We received a new notice yesterday that the police have details of Ricardo Lopez's call records. You'll need to request the full records from the OPP.'

'You're a star.' I imagined her wide smile as she swivelled on her office chair.

Next, I dialled the Office of Public Prosecutions and was put straight through to an efficient sounding legal support officer.

'Hi there, Sandi Kent here on behalf of Maria Luisetto. I'm hoping you can help me out. I'm requesting additional evidence, which we've been informed the OPP have.'

'Representing?' she asked in a no-nonsense tone.

'Ricardo Lopez.'

I heard rapid tapping. 'What specific information do you require?'

'Firstly, the content of the text and voice mail messages, the full call-detail record from Ricardo Lopez's two mobile phones and copies of any voicemail between the phones.'

'You'll need to put that in writing and once we receive your email, we'll ensure we supply your office the transcripts.'

'How quickly will you be able to do that?'

'I'll be able to follow up this afternoon or tomorrow at the latest.'

'We do need it asap,' I insisted.

'Certainly,' was the curt answer. A red End appeared on my mobile.

I fired off an email to the OPP, CCing Maria's office into the communique, in case there was any question about my legitimacy.

Flicker had dragged herself out of the bedroom to greet me. As I sat on the couch, she sprang onto my lap. After a couple of pats, she decided better of it; neither of us needed the extra heat it generated. In fact, I had to rip off my jeans. From my chest of drawers, I unearthed white shorts that hadn't seen the light since last summer.

Back on the couch, I put in a call to Valentina's friend, Erica García. She was hesitant, but agreed to talk to me. Though as she was working all week, we arranged to meet on the weekend. That would completely throw Maria's plans to wind up her work on this case quickly. Gawd, another sin for Maria to add to her tally.

That made the next phone call even more of a challenge but essential. Maria had left three messages, and in the last one she'd sounded exasperated. I'd needed a couple of days to calm down after her interference in my life and to steel myself against her wrath.

Maria's phone immediately kicked into voice mail. I put aside my remaining shard of irritation and left an upbeat message.

Within a minute, my mobile rang.

'Sandi, at last.' She sounded relieved.

'Been hectic,' I explained.

'Everything okay?'

'I met with Ricardo again and think we're getting somewhere.'

'Excellent.' She cleared her throat.

I wiped sweat from my forehead. When I spread my hand on the flyscreen of the window a burst of hot air tickled my fingers. The north wind swept through the plane trees lining the road.

'How about lunch one day soon?' Her voice rose to a pitch, as if she was worried I might refuse. 'You can fill me in on all the gory details then.'

'Can't wait.'

We hung up and I wondered if guilt had motived Maria's calls. That was all right with me. Her deadline for my report seemed to have sunk to the seabed.

The sun pouring into my flat turned it into an oven. I yanked the window closed and tugged the blind down to stop the radiating heat.

After extracting the electric fan from the broom cupboard and setting it up on the coffee table, I lounged on the couch with a long glass of iced water.

Later that afternoon, I drove my car over to Ricardo's local brothel in Preston, Club 96. The content in the police file and the snippets from Ricardo were a sliver of the story, like staring through a keyhole. How had he ended up with a poem from Lee? Was Cassy right about Lee being trafficked or did Cassy's job cause her to see trafficked women everywhere?

I slouched in my VW with the windows open as a steady flow of punters parked in front of the pastel-coloured playground and then dashed across the road to the asbestos-riddled brothel. In the park, the swings and monkey bars buzzed with kids, but as dinner time arrived, their numbers dwindled.

Despite the sun retreating, the heat was stifling in my tin can and my T-shirt clung to my chest. The joys of Melbourne's constantly changing weather. For a break, I headed into the park and flopped on a bench. The breeze, although hot, made it easier to breath. That angle provided an excellent view of comings and goings from the front door of Club 96, past the metal fence. I took photos and noted down the registration of a silver Mitsubishi SUV parked in the driveway.

To the warble of magpies, I stretched stiff muscles before weaving back through gum trees and resuming my surveillance position in my car.

As a burnt-orange sunset swept across the western sky, the river of customers slowed. Streetlights came on at the same moment the SUV in the brothel's driveway beeped and began reversing out.

Making a quick decision to pursue the car, I twisted the key in my VW's ignition and, for once, it started first go.

The SUV took off towards the CBD, where a river of cars kept me hidden behind it.

A couple of intersections later, we were hightailing it up Bell Street, past the turn off to Ricardo's house. Distracted by looking in the wrong direction, I lost sight of the SUV for a second, then spotted it turning right. I spun across two lanes, darting in front of a semi-trailer and ran a red to follow.

Keen to make up ground, I accelerated towards my quarry just as my mobile rang: Cassy. *Not now.*

Turning my attention back to the road, the traffic lights ahead were red and I was suddenly up the SUV's bum. I jammed on the brakes, hoping to hell the driver – hidden from view by dark tinted windows and high seats – wouldn't notice. I double checked the car doors were locked in case a thug leaped out.

As I wiped perspiration from my forehead with the back of my hand, the lights turned green and the SUV took off.

Rattled by my inattention, I backed off as we headed down the now quiet shopping strip of leafy Ivanhoe, the upper-crust suburb of the north, dotted with boutique clothes shops and French bakeries.

When the car veered off into The Boulevard, memories flew back of a visit to this very street one Christmas Eve, when Mum drove my sister and me all the way across town to the "show". Every mansion in the street was covered with flashing Christmas lights and long gardens were decked with life-sized decorations – kangaroos with red hats, reindeers on roofs and swaying Father Christmases sticking out of neat lawns. That night was one of the few times that my sister and I were so engrossed we forgot to fight.

As I trailed at a distance, giant ghostly gums looming on one side, the SUV pulled into the driveway of a modern three-storey house where double garage doors automatically opened. A small woman in high heels, who I recognised immediately, emerged and trotted up the long external staircase. On the balcony overlooking the street, a guy sitting, wine glass in hand, waved to her. As I drove past, Madam Qiao let herself into the property and the guy swanned inside the house.

Further up the road, I did a U-turn and then drove off the bitumen onto the gravel shoulder. It was tricky judging precisely where the road disappeared into the dense bush below. *Phew. No mishaps.*

When I opened the driver's door, camera in hand, a dose of eucalyptus oil filled my nostrils and the gums whistled eerily in the wind. Suddenly, headlights from a car rounding the curve captured me in their spotlight. I automatically hid the camera behind my back before the car disappeared around the bend. Perhaps I was becoming jittery, but some folk might consider my decision to stalk Qiao outside my brief. I'd discovered years ago that results were rarely achieved by strict adherence to rules.

I sprinted to the house and took some snaps. A tennis court abutted the property. Spotting a different mansion behind the tennis court, I realised it must be the neighbour's. It seemed Qiao wouldn't be out there first thing then, in runners and whites.

Before leaving, I slipped past the silver letterbox and discovered Alistair Payne had two letters he'd been too busy to come down and claim.

What was Qiao Zeng doing with this Alistair Payne in leafy suburbia? That line of enquiry would have to wait. I needed to sleep. The plans for the following day required me to be clear-headed.

17

From the passenger seat of Cassy's Subaru, I stared at branches of a tree on Swan Street flapping in the north wind.

'Only suggesting an alternative.' Cassy's nose ring glimmered in the sunshine.

'Can't you give it a rest? I've said I'll go inside instead of you. This shitty plan isn't going to get any better by tweaking it.'

'Okay, okay, okay.' Cassy's voice pierced my eardrum.

I silently hummed *Cell Block Tango*.

Cassy and I had been hanging outside Maccas since 9am – a repeat of yesterday – parked with a line of sight from one side of Maccas to the other, through glass windows. My emotions had been flying between desire, panic and exasperation. Cassy had been harassing me about my "flawed" plan for what seemed like hours. I couldn't deal with her anxiety; my nerves were frayed enough. So many factors needed to align for this operation to succeed: the trafficked women coming at all; the minder going outside; Jae having been properly prepped by Cassy and having the guts to follow through… the list went on.

As I chided myself for becoming over-involved, a cluster of women dressed in short skirts and skimpy tops appeared in the car park on the other side of the building. *Finally.* My body became a tangled root system of contracting muscles.

Their usual minder, Skull, herded them like a fierce cattle dog. When the only Caucasian woman amongst them lagged behind, he gave her a shove. She started running, teetering small steps in flimsy high heels and almost tripped in her rush to keep up with the others. The group slunk into the fast food joint, followed by their minder.

'I thought you said he'd wait outside.' Cassy's mouth was so tight there were wrinkles above her upper lip.

'He'll pay for their food first.'

This whole plan was predicated on him having a smoke, like last time. I crossed my fingers: desperate measures.

We watched them order, a slow process with so many of them. Skull flicked cash money at the attendant as he arranged hamburgers, chips and soft drink on plastic trays.

Cassy was in my ear again. 'All this and now it's ruined.'

My throat was so tight, I didn't think my voice would emerge. 'Just wait.'

The eight women carried the food to two adjacent booths. The terrified one with the sweet round face and mocha-coloured eyes, who I thought might be Jae, ended up stuck in the middle next to the tall woman, who'd also been there the time before. If the scared one was Jae, why hadn't she positioned herself on the end? Maybe Jae was the other one with the delicate features who was in the right spot to escape.

Stop second guessing.

As Skull unwrapped his burger, the women in the booth nearest him shuffled closer together to make room. Maybe Jae was right and they suspected something, given he remained inside. He scanned the Macca's clientele as he demolished his bun. In Cassy's car, we spontaneously sank lower into our seats as his gaze skimmed towards us.

His attention back on his charges, he picked up a packet of chips, scoffed a couple then strode out the door.

'See.' A hiss of air escaped my chest.

The next move was Jae's, but no-one was moving.

'What exactly did you tell her to do?' I asked.

'She'll go any second.' Cassy frantically tapped the steering wheel. 'I know it.'

The scared woman in the middle stood up, extricating herself and scurried in between tables before disappearing into the corridor leading to the bathrooms. As swiftly and calmly as my body allowed, I grabbed the green shopping bag next to me and jumped out of the Subaru. I raced towards the building, tugging at my cap and keeping my head down.

As I opened the Macca's door nearest to us, the stench of fried food and the blare of music accosted my senses. On the opposite side of the building, I spied Skull, lighting up a smoke as he stood on one leg, with the sole of his other boot forming a black pattern on the window.

In the bathroom, Jae shrank in the corner between a hand dryer and a white basin. She shuddered, her almond-shaped eyes wide. I smelt her fear; sweat coated in cheap perfume.

'It's all right,' I whispered. 'You're safe now.'

'Cassy?' she asked.

'I'm Sandi. Cassy's outside waiting.'

Jae heaved as if she was about to throw up. We had no time.

With nervous fingers, I whisked out a cotton scarf, arranged it over Jae's head and tied it under her chin. Next, I offered her a cheap pair of sunglasses. As she reached for them, they fell, clattering on the black and white tiled floor. She flinched as if I was about to strike her.

I forced myself to smile as I retrieved the glasses and slipped them over the ridge of her nose. Up close, baby blue eye shadow partially hid a black eye. Without commenting, I eased a black trench coat over her bony back for comfort as much as camouflage. It was way too big. She was probably a size eight, not a 12, but there was no alternative.

Outside the women's bathroom, heavy footsteps echoed. *Had Skull discovered us?* I edged open the door to the corridor as a construction worker entered the men's bathroom. The door croaked and groaned as it automatically shut behind him.

Turning back to tell Jae the way was clear, I found she'd retreated into a toilet cubicle, the door still ajar.

As if she was one of my swimming students, I said with gusto, 'We're right now.'

She didn't look reassured, but took a step forward anyway.

Taking her hand, I peered down the empty corridor. As we crept towards the exit, I edged Jae in front of me with my palm on her upper back.

As we snuck outside, Cassy catapulted out of the car to open the back-passenger door. Jae hoisted herself up, as I turned in search of the minder. He took a last deep drag and flicked his butt into the car park. At the booth, the tall woman was on her feet. We locked gazes.

I pelted towards the driver's door and sprang inside. 'Get in Cassy.'

'Jae's lost her shoe.'

'They've seen us,' I hissed.

The tall woman had joined the minder out the front. His face as fierce as an orc, Skull whipped around and eyeballed me.

As soon as Cassy dived in the back with Jae and her shoe, I lurched out of the car park, keeping an eye on the rear vision mirror. Spinning into Swan Street, I expected Skull to leap in front of the car any second, but as we passed the intersection leading to the brothel, I spotted him jumping into his van outside Amsterdam Angels.

'Fuck.'

'Calm down.' Cassy's voice was low and hushed.

Ahead red lights halted a line of traffic.

'Hold on.' I shot past stationary vehicles and waited, revving the engine on the wrong side of the road. A turning car almost collected us, but swerved in time, missing our driver's side mirror by a centimetre.

As soon as the lights flicked to green, I burned rubber to swerve in front of the line of cars and return to the correct side of the road. Ignoring a battering of car horns, we sped away across the Yarra River.

Through the rear vision mirror, I caught sight of the top of the van two cars behind us. I spun into the next side street and flew down a winding road. With the van 100 metres behind, I chucked a leftie and was forced to slam on the breaks, a barrage of cars blocking our way. Skull was up my bum; he flung open the driver's door.

'Help.' Jae squeaked.

'Quick.' Cassy yelled.

Squeezing into a minor gap, I turned right, left, right, racking my brain to work out which way to go. The major roads were familiar, but not the backstreets; the wealthy eastern suburbs weren't my territory.

It seemed we'd lost him and Cassy clapped, ready to celebrate, when the van appeared again, gaining ground. My foot slammed down on the accelerator. Jae screamed as we thumped over a median strip and took out a keep left sign, metal on metal squealing.

A familiar road appeared that led to the freeway. I belted down it, overtaking wherever possible without crashing into an oncoming car.

We hit the freeway and after a few kilometres, it straightened and the traffic thinned with no sign of the van. Though none of us said a word, a collective sigh of relief eased the tension in the Subaru.

Signs to Frankston appeared. We must have lost him, I thought, though I kept vigilant, glancing into the rear-view mirror every few seconds like a nervous tic. Meanwhile Cassy's chatter returned to normal as she filled Jae in about the beach near the safe house. Jae was silent, her body hunched. She declined the shrimp-flavoured crackers Cassy offered. How was Jae processing this journey out of bondage?

As soon as the freeway ended at Frankston and slowed our progress, I became jittery again.

'Come on,' I growled at a red light.

Opposite, a grey-walled shopping complex loomed, reminiscent of the remand centre.

More traffic lights barred our way and forty-kilometre speed restrictions at a primary school, plus the added congestion of parents picking up kids, made us crawl through the seaside suburb.

Finally, we turned onto Nepean Highway and my heart rate eased. 'What street?'

Cassy had her arm around Jae's shoulder. 'You'll be safe there.'

'Thank you,' said Jae. 'I'm so lucky.'

Cassy had told me the safe house was on the Mornington Peninsula. She'd avoided telling me the exact address, which I'd assumed was about top-secret Coalition business.

'We're nearly there,' Cassy said in an overly chirpy voice.

We rounded Oliver's Hill, where you're usually rewarded with a view across the bay to Williamstown, on my side of town, but today the sky was hazy and the sea grey and choppy.

'Turn here,' said Cassy, as we passed the sign to Mount Eliza.

I was trying to work out what sort of a safe house it could be as we passed mansion after mansion shielded by giant trees and high fences, when Cassy said, 'This is it.'

From a cul-de-sac, we entered a tree-lined driveway and parked beside a fountain circled with sculptured hedges. In front of us towered a columned entranceway to a palatial two-storey residence. As soon as we'd turned off to Mount Eliza, I should have twigged. My nerves had clouded my focus.

'What the hell?'

'It'll be fine,' said Cassy.

'What's wrong?' asked Jae.

Cassy bounded out of the Subaru and sprinted around the car. I scrambled out and grabbed her wrist before Jae had time to emerge.

'Are you mad? It's too dangerous, especially now they've seen your car,' I whispered. 'I thought you'd organised somewhere real. What the hell are you playing at?'

Cassy tried to twist out of my grip. 'It'll be completely safe; it's all been carefully arranged. We'll find somewhere else for tomorrow.'

'Now,' I demanded.

'Let's just go inside. You're scaring Jae.'

Jae looked like she was about to shrivel up, but I refused to let go of Cassy's wrist.

'Come on, Sandi. This is the last place they'd think of. That's what makes it so perfect. My boss Bani thought it was a brilliant idea.'

Her wrist remained locked in my hold.

Cassy relented. 'I'll ring Bani and see what she says.'

She indicated the front fence. Although I resented her bossing me around, I released her and stomped down the driveway to shut the elaborate metal gates: a flimsy defence if Skull found us.

Joining Cassy and Jae at the entrance, the doorbell chimed like a church bell. A sprightly grey-haired woman sporting a bright floral scarf and a perfect blow wave opened the door.

'This must be Jae and—' Her voice was elite private school, even more than Cassy's.

'Sandi,' piped in Cassy.

'Of course,' Cassy's mother said, 'your old—'

'Friend.'

'I'm Beatrice.' She introduced herself to Jae.

She kissed us all on the cheek, in the same way Cassy did, with a whisper of air. Beatrice's eyes were a haunted and paler version of her daughter's.

I couldn't believe Cassy had involved her mother in this scheme. Surely the Coalition owned a safe house, or had access to women's refuges – something less risky than relying on family members. The only time I'd met Beatrice before, at a restaurant celebrating Cassy's birthday, she'd struck me as extremely conservative, so it was surprising she'd even agreed to such a plan; or maybe Cassy had hidden the details from her.

We padded down a hallway lined with original artworks and antique cabinets, past a room containing a billiard table and bar. Beatrice led the way into a massive open-plan living area where floor-to-ceiling windows offered a view of a 25 metre in-ground pool and spa.

Geez, I'd known Cassy came from Mount Eliza, but I was gobsmacked at the plushness.

'The kettle has just boiled, so I'll make a pot of tea. I'm sure you all need a drink after that long trip.'

A nourishing meal might have been more beneficial for Jae.

Beatrice invited us to sit at a 12-seater dining table. Jae clutched the coat she still wore from her escape. Luckily, an air conditioner dispatched cool air.

I reluctantly plonked myself opposite Jae, though my body yelled at me to get the hell out of that house and drag Jae with me. Outside, blackbirds sang as if all was right in the world.

The whole scene was bizarre. We'd rescued a sex slave from traffickers and here we were languishing around a mahogany dining-room table being offered pots of tea by a woman who spoke like she'd sailed in from Westminster.

Beatrice poured black tea into green Wedgewood cups. Jae perched on the edge of a straight-backed chair and clutched the delicate cup between both hands.

'Beatrice, has Cassy told you that—'

Cassy shoved a silver milk jug in front of me. 'Mum is perfectly aware.'

'Including how we were chased?'

'What's that, dear?'

'Oh, it's nothing, Mum, just have to check in with work about next steps.' Cassy began scrolling through her phone as she left the table.

'Would you like one?' Beatrice offered Jae a plate of shortbread.

Jae nibbled a piece.

Beatrice turned to me with the same offer. 'Cassandra has talked so much about you, Sandi.'

That seemed a strange thing to say, given Beatrice couldn't remember my name earlier.

'Cassandra said how helpful you've been with her work.'

I was about to answer, when she shifted her focus.

'I'm so pleased that you're here, Jae. It is so wonderful that I am able to be of assistance in these terrible circumstances.'

Jae smiled, though her brown eyes were wide and vacant.

'It's so lovely that Cassandra has this position.' Beatrice's eyes searched mine. 'She seems settled at last, don't you think?'

I murmured half-hearted agreement.

'At one stage, she wanted me to leave her father, you know.' She blinked rapidly, in the way Cassy did. 'All those anti-Christian ideas being flung at her at university, I suppose.'

I considered saying it had more to do with Cassy's father's behaviour than any radicalising, but instead made an excuse to use the toilet.

Upstairs, I found Cassy tucking in a sheet, hospital style, on a double bed. A vase of pink roses spilled petals onto a hardwood dressing table.

The walls were covered with posters of singers like Amy Winehouse and Courtney Love. In contrast, floral curtains with lace trim were neatly gathered on each side of the window. Outside, through an arc of conifers, the view of the bay distracted me for a second.

'Hey, Cassy, you were going to ring your boss.'

Cassy flitted past me to the other side of the bed. 'Look, Sandi, thanks for your assistance; it's been really great, but we'll be able to manage from here.'

'You and your troop of Jedi knights?' I snapped. It felt like she'd slapped me. I thought we were on this mission together.

'Bani will be fine with the arrangements,' said Cassy. 'Meantime, Jae's exhausted and needs a rest.'

'I'm calling the cops. I'm done with this.'

'It's not up to you. You're just the—'

'What? Hired help? I can't believe I've risked my life for some wacky B-grade movie.'

Beatrice poked her powdered face into the bedroom. 'Everything all right, dear?'

'Sandi's just about to head off, aren't you? Would you like us to call a taxi so you can get to the station?'

I angled past her mother, thumped down the stairs and grabbed my backpack from the living room. Cassy and Beatrice's footsteps followed.

As we stampeded back into the living room, Jae sat stiffly on the straight-backed chair, silently noticing our interactions. No doubt she'd become an expert in subtle observation.

I pulled up a chair next to her. 'We need to call the police to find you somewhere really safe.'

Cassy barged in front of me. 'Don't worry Jae. We've got everything under control.'

I curved around Cassy to explain the situation to Jae. Not to be left out, Cassy's mother placed a protective hand on Jae's shoulder.

Jae insisted softly, 'I'm happy here.'

Now it made sense. Cassy had manipulated Jae into believing I was the enemy and Cassy was the heroine. Curbing my desire to tackle Cassy to the ground, I strode out the front door and slammed the heavy security door behind me. As I unbolted the gate, footsteps tapped on the pebbled concrete behind me.

'You sure you don't want us to call a taxi?' Cassy called.

'I'm fine.'

As I reached the next mansion, a loud click signalled the Joynson's gate being bolted. When I turned back, there was no-one to be seen.

Mount Eliza to the closest railway station was over an hour's hike according to Google maps. I could have organised an Uber, but resented coughing up the money and the idea of sitting on a train by myself all the way back home made me steam.

I rang Stewart and he answered on the second ring. All I said was I needed a lift. Amazing friend that he was, he agreed to come get me with no questions asked. He was used to my wacky requests. I'm not sure if he tolerated them or embraced them; either way, I appreciated how he was there for me.

With heat simmering across from the bitumen, I made myself run in 100 metre sprints along the road shoulder of Nepean Highway, though with a lack of running shoes and the scorching sun burning my cheeks, that idea got the boot. Instead, I kicked stones out of my way under the lanky gums lining the road, where the sun slanted through the trees.

After arriving at Oliver's Hill Lookout and focusing on the choppy sea below, I texted Stewart to tell him where to find me. I figured he wouldn't be far off. About ten minutes later a beep made me turn. His white Holden drove past on the other side of the road. There was no way to do a U-turn at that point, so I waited for the car to reappear. When my mate pulled up, I collapsed into the passenger seat with relief.

Stew was his typical perky self. 'Decided on a bush walk?'

I filled him in on the whole gnarly Cassy soap opera as he took the beach route back towards the city, where glimpses of the sea reflected the late afternoon light in between dense scrub.

'You should find a nice partner like Ben,' he said.

'I thought there was an issue about him two-timing.'

'Two-timing.' Stew's voice was theatrical. 'If only there were two!'

I chortled and Stew joined in; he could lift my mood within seconds.

By the time we were in St Kilda, I was famished and suggested we stop to grab a bite to eat. When we passed Cassy's apartment on the foreshore my throat constricted. How had I let myself be duped?

Fitzroy Street was its usual pulsating self, with restaurants flowing onto the streets and music booming from speakers.

We began with pizza. After that we mooched on to the packed Espy pub and it turned into another long night. Cassy slipped from my mind, though Jae was a spike in the corner. The more alcohol blanked my mind, the less she occupied my thoughts. My job was done; hopefully they'd pay me the balance. I resolved to call the Coalition the next morning and provide a comprehensive handover.

18

SWEAT POOLED IN MY STERNUM. HAD THE BANG BEEN IN MY NIGHTMARE? Snatches of a stalker flashed through my mind, and escape – scrambling out of a train window, like in an old movie. With my head raised off the pillow, I listened: my rapid breath and swallowing the only sounds.

Maybe I'd imagined it. I'd snuggled back under the sheet when pounding on the front door tore apart the stillness.

I sat bolt upright and snapped on the bedside light, my heart thumping. Flicker was poised on the end of the bed, ears pricked. My thoughts raced in a brain thickened with beer. Who could it be – I checked my mobile – at 1.24am? Skull? My ex, Diana? Nah, that was just wishful thinking.

From the pile on the floor, I whipped on a T-shirt and undies and grabbed my hardwood aikido staff from under the bed. Stick in hand and mobile tucked into my undies, I snuck out of my bedroom and edged across to the front door. Flicker flew with me but changed her mind and dived under the couch. I was on my own.

As I waited for the door to be smashed in, I raised the staff above my head, shivering despite the warmth of the night, and braved a glance through the peephole, fully expecting to be met with Skull's thick, dark beard and savage mouth.

Instead, cropped black hair and the glint of a nose ring appeared.

I propped the staff against the wall and opened the door. 'You didn't think of calling before coming all this way?'

'A phone call wouldn't solve things. Too important,' Cassy said. 'Anyway, thought you mightn't answer.'

'Why would I ignore you after being dumped in the wilds of the Peninsula?'

Cassy rocked from foot to foot. 'Oh, earlier. That was all a misunderstanding.'

'Like World War I.'

'It wasn't meant to end that way. We were all stressed, weren't we?' said Cassy.

'That's a bloody understatement and you know it.'

Cassy stared at the floor of the concrete entryway. Satisfaction, that she was embarrassed, gave me a moment's pleasure.

'Look, you had a good point. My manager agreed. Jae's been moved into a hotel, somewhere secure, for the night, then tomorrow we'll work out next steps.'

I was pleased she'd listened to me. Maybe I'd overreacted about Cassy turning Jae against me. After all, it was Jae herself who had made the decision to stay at Cassy's mum's, despite the obvious risk to all involved. Still, Cassy had treated me like scum and that stung.

Cassy peered past me, checking out the living room, or what she could see of it with me standing in the doorway. I hadn't cleaned up because, strangely, I wasn't expecting visitors in the middle of the night. I followed her gaze. A pile of papers, takeaway wrappers and dirty mugs decorated the coffee table.

Cassy took advantage of my distraction and slipped inside. She scanned the room and settled her gaze on the low ceiling adorned with white paint peelings.

'I don't get it, Cassy. How you could put your mum in that sort of danger?'

'Jae needed to be somewhere where she could get some TLC. It wasn't dangerous until that sadist from the brothel chased us.'

'Talking of which,' I said.

'I'm using Mum's car tonight, just in case.'

I was about to say that decision was hardly a comprehensive safety strategy when Cassy sidled further into the room.

She tried to draw the red throw-over across the back of the couch. Perhaps realising it needed more than a subtle tug, she abandoned the task. 'Jae's told me more than she did for months. Thought you might be interested.'

'And it couldn't wait till morning?'

Cassy padded over to the bookcase at the far end of the living room.

She stroked the spines of novels with her fingers and drew out the sandy coloured *A Game of Thrones*. After inspecting the cover, she slid it back then traced her fine fingers along the rest of the series. A soft thud accompanied the drop of each book as she neatly lined them up on the wooden shelf.

Cassy twisted around, hitching her shoulder. 'Well, now that we're here.'

What was she thinking? What was I thinking?

My brain was as muddy as the Yarra River. 'I'm going to put something warmer on.'

I thumped into my bedroom and pressed the door shut. God, a coffee would help, though that would mean offering Cassy one. I gave my cheeks a wake-up slap, my head throbbing in response. After dragging on black jeans and a long-sleeved T-shirt, I nipped into the bathroom, dissolved a Berocca and sank the fizzy drink along with a couple of Panadol before emerging to find Cassy in the kitchen.

'Hope you don't mind?' She indicated the boiling kettle.

'I guess you're here to apologise.'

Cassy grinned, transforming her intense face. 'Yes.'

I knew I had to settle for that. Cassy could never actually *say* sorry.

'Cups?' she asked.

As she stretched to the top cupboard, her shirt rode up, above pinstripe pants, revealing a crimson rose, about the size of a cat's paw, with four open petals and the rest forming a tight heart. I remembered how soft it was to touch. *That was in the past*, I scolded myself. As Cassy's heels made contact with the floor, the rose vanished.

While Cassy fetched the milk, I made coffee in a plunger, in the usually cramped but tonight cosy kitchen.

I grabbed the junk off the coffee table and deposited it in the kitchen, then rearranged the throw-over across the three-seater. Mug in hand, I lowered myself onto the other end of the couch from Cassy.

Flicker emerged from under us. After rubbing herself back and forth along Cassy's legs, she sprang onto her lap demanding a pat, acting like they were old friends. Just as Flicker was about to settle down for a snooze, I leaned over and picked her up by the scruff of the neck and dropped her lightly on to the floor.

'It's okay,' said Cassy.

Flicker extended her back leg and licked it.

'This afternoon was complicated, with Jae, Mum, you.' She was expecting a response.

I crossed my arms, not yet able to ditch my resentment.

'Mum knows about the Coalition and asked if there was anything she could do to help. You know how it is. It helped Jae feel comfortable. Mum and Jae were having a good old laugh together in the end. That made it easier to talk to Jae about moving.

'Christ, she's been through a lot. She told me that one night when she was waitressing – in a disco club in Seoul – a man approached her about a lucrative job in an Australian karaoke bar. He organised her passport and visa, though Jae never saw any of her documents.

'When she arrived here and was taken to Amsterdam Angels, she refused to get into her work clothes. Courageous, hey? The brothel owner said she owed him the equivalent of 750 customers and each one was worth $110. If she gave him the money, he'd give her passport back. If she tried to escape without repaying her debt, he'd kill her family. Bastard. Typical though.'

I pictured Jae as she tried to stand up to the thugs. She didn't stand a chance – no-one in her situation did.

Cassy sipped her milky coffee, her lips elegantly poised between each mouthful. 'She wants to get in touch with her family to warn them, but she's also ashamed; she doesn't know what to tell her mother.'

'She has nothing to be bloody ashamed about.'

'Yeah, you can know that intellectually,' agreed Cassy. 'Anyway, the brothel owners will be more concerned about finding Jae than her family at the moment.'

'That's exactly what I was worried about.'

'Yeah, me too. But she's safe now, Sandi.'

A weight began to dissipate from my chest.

Cassy flicked the handle of her mug. 'There's another woman to be worried about now.'

'What do you mean?'

'Jae made a friend at the brothel, another trafficked woman, Yun-seo Kim, also from South Korea. Yun-seo tried to escape. In fact, she did. Briefly. A couple of days later, they found her and dragged her back. Jae found her sprawled on a bed, beaten black and blue.'

'You're joking.'

'You wouldn't believe what the traffickers do.' Cassy squeezed her eyes shut as if trying to block out the image.

'Is she all right?'

'Jae fetched the madam, who ordered Jae to stay in her room. From behind her closed door, Jae could hear someone in the corridor and hoped it was a doctor. If only. After that, Yun-seo disappeared. A few days later a new sex worker arrived, as though nothing had happened.'

Cassy picked up a red cushion lying between us and hugged it – small comfort against the traffickers.

'Now Yun-seo's vanished we'll have to involve the cops,' I stated.

Cassy tossed the cushion aside. 'No way Sandi, they'd want to grill Jae and she's more terrified of them and being deported than going back to the brothel.'

'Come on. Seriously? Surely now Yun-seo's missing, perhaps even dead, Jae's willing to tell them what's happened.'

'Yun-seo's worth more to them alive than dead. They protect their assets.' Cassy slowly turned towards me, her eyes softening. 'Look, why don't you come with me tomorrow and talk to Jae. It'll be easier with the two of us, with your investigation skills. We'll find out what's going on, then make a decision about what to do about Yun-seo.'

As well as believing the best course of action was to call the cops, no way did I want to get hooked into another rescue operation. But if I tackled the issue head on, Cassy would wriggle her way out of it like she always did and if I rang the cops, all the information was hearsay unless Jae agreed to cooperate. It'd be better if I could convince Jae, though whether she'd be willing to even talk to me was another question. 'Yeah right, like Jae's going to trust me, after what happened at your mum's.'

'She realises you were worried about her.' Cassy half laughed, half sighed. 'Worried about all of us, weren't you?'

Cassy adjusted her luminescent green shirt with one hand. The shirt splayed, revealing a sliver of a black bra. 'Today, the stress got to me. But really, thanks for everything you did to get Jae out. It's been amazing, working with you. Don't know what we would have done, otherwise.'

A tinge of embarrassment at the praise heated my cheeks. Perhaps I'd been too hard on Cassy. Even though she could be a pain, she did have Jae's best interests in mind.

She edged next to me, eased her arm across my shoulders. Speckled with emerald green, her cat-like eyes sparkled. The old desires sparked in me again, and I was prepared to forgive all her stress-induced slights when she smiled and stared at me like that; the way she used to.

Cassy's lips were soft, her back smooth. I felt the strength of her legs as she wrapped them around me. Her lips parted, her tongue found mine. We fumbled together undoing buttons that were too tight, laughing. I flung her shirt on the floor, wrapped my hands around her back, and unclipped the black bra. Then I sank into her soft, delicious breasts and sucked her erect nipples.

For a moment, I chided myself for my decision, but as we made our way to my bed, there was no going back.

19

I WOKE FEELING EQUALLY RELAXED AND PRIMED, THE MEMORY OF SOFT curves and strong muscles pulsing through my body. I turned over to find the other side of the bed empty, though the sheet was still warm and the pillow indented. Quiet but distinct sounds of cutlery clinking on crockery emanated from the kitchen, the sound of the kettle a bass line underneath.

I must have drifted off, because the next thing I knew the bed had shifted weight and Cassy was beaming at me. She was swimming in a T-shirt of mine and it woke up my body like the night before. Reaching over to stroke her bare legs, I was disappointed when she drew them up to her chest and under the shirt, far from my keen hand.

'Coffee?' She handed me a steaming mug.

'Seriously?'

'I've been awake for ages.' The smell of Vegemite toast wafted from her side of the bed.

We perched side by side, as if we'd been long married.

'I'm starving,' said Cassy.

'Me too.' I kissed her lips.

She pecked me back then took a bite of toast. 'We need to eat up and head off.'

I leaned in a second time to kiss her neck but she angled away and patted my hand.

'Don't let a little passion interfere with your mission, Cassy,' I jibed. Her knockback reminded me how she used to have to be the one to initiate. Seemed she hadn't changed.

'We're investigating a disappearance now,' she said.

'Last night that didn't seem to be a problem.'

'Do you know what time it is?'

'Oh come on, a short intermission won't cause a catastrophe.'

She shook her head and giggled. 'Well, you were irresistible. Brought back memories.' She kissed me hard and poked me in the ribs.

I gave in, indulging in breakfast in bed, though it was short lived. Cassy scooted off for a shower and when she was done, I felt obliged to follow suit.

In the car, as Cassy drove across the West Gate Bridge, she explained she'd moved Jae to a secure boutique hotel in Mornington, owned by friends of her mother's. 'The Campbells are totally trustworthy. In fact, they go to the same church as Mum.'

'Wow. That makes me totally confident.' I stared through thick steel barriers at the city skyscrapers, keeping my concerns to myself. Before risking another confrontation with Cassy, I decided to check out the accommodation.

We emerged from the under-river tunnel onto a Monash freeway, swarming with Friday morning trucks. A wall, buffering the neighbourhood from traffic noise, prevented me seeing beyond. Straggly gums leaning over the concrete structure flashed past.

Cassy kept glancing my way. 'How about some music?' she suggested, as we swung onto Eastlink.

We listened to Lady Gaga's *Million Reasons* on Spotify, Cassy singing while I jived. Her sense of fun was contagious and my skin trumpeted with happiness in a way that had been missing for ages.

When we parked outside The Royal Hotel, I was gobsmacked. "Boutique" suggested small and quirky, not a palatial stuccoed mansion, smack on the Mornington foreshore. Jae had soared from squalor to splendour in a day.

We clacked over burgundy tiles and time warped into a chandeliered reception. A woman, whose hair was as bouncy as she was, hugged Cassy. Gloria Campbell was about to embrace me when I hopped backwards and stuck my hands in my pockets, not ready to be taken into the fold.

'Cassy is like the daughter I never had.' Gloria clucked over Cassy, who shuffled from foot to foot.

At last the owner entrusted Cassy with a key.

We climbed the crimson carpeted stairs to the guest rooms, making way for an old man with a cane and a narrow-rimmed trilby hat.

At the top, in a luxurious room, we found Jae huddled in a corner of an antique queen-sized bed. She wore an over-sized floral nightie, probably courtesy of Gloria. Without make-up she appeared like a teenager, her skin pulsating with pimples, no doubt as a result of wearing cheap make-up twenty-four seven.

The window to the door of the balcony framed the blue expanse of tranquil sea, so different from the turbulence yesterday. I would have loved to slip outside to inhale fresh salt air, but the potential danger of Jae being discovered made me cautious.

Jae slipped off the bed and bowed to us with her right hand placed on top of her left. I cringed as she thanked me endlessly for my part in her escape.

'Have you had breakfast?' I interrupted.

'Yes, the nice lady cooked me eggs.' Jae smiled wistfully, as if remembering her own mother's cooking.

She invited us to sit down and I chose an elegant hard-backed chair while Cassy settled herself next to Jae.

'Did you get in touch with your mum?' asked Cassy.

Jae clasped her hands together. 'I told my mother that those men made me do terrible things. I'm free, but they might try to hurt my family.'

'What did she say?' I asked.

'Maybe she'll move. She's a very clever lady.'

'That must be a relief,' I smiled. 'And great you're being so well looked after here. Cassy told me you're worried about your friend, Yun-seo.'

Jae stiffened.

'We won't tell the police unless you want us to,' said Cassy.

She drove me mad with her promises to Jae, especially now Yun-seo was missing. I glared at her, but her attention was on Jae. It was obviously what Jae wanted to hear, as she relaxed back on the white pillows piled up behind her.

Cassy dived in again. 'Whatever you feel comfortable saying, Jae.'

I would have loved to march Cassy out of the room right then, but reminded myself to keep it nice. 'Hey, Cassy,' I said, trying to keep my voice calm.

She side-glanced at me, all innocent. We'd agreed in the car that I would take the lead; following was a new concept for her and working in partnership was alien for me.

'I just need to ask you a few questions about Yun-seo,' I said to Jae.

Victorian scrolls jabbed into my back so I reversed the chair and straddled it. 'To find Yun-seo, we need to know what she looks like. I've got photos of you and the other women. Can you point her out?'

I moved onto the bed and twisted so Jae could see the laptop screen. As I scrolled, Jae named other women but not Yun-seo. It seemed she must have disappeared by that stage.

'Can you tell me what happened to Yun-seo?'

Jae shuffled down the bed closer to me, her forehead dotted with perspiration. 'One day, Yun-seo said to a customer he had to have a condom. She was pregnant before. When they found out, Thumper and Spike hit her. Later she said, "I have to run away." "Wait," I said, "The nice lady will help us soon." "I can't wait," said Yun-seo.'

Jae's mocha-coloured eyes were unfocused. The event was a film stored in her brain.

'And then, the next day, there was no Yun-seo. Madam said, "Where's Yun-seo?" I shook my head. She slapped me again and again. Next day Yun-seo came back with a big black eye. I heard her scream. I went to her late at night when the men stopped coming. She was on the bed, groaning. She was black all over.' Jae indicated her stomach and ribs. 'I was very sorry for her.'

'Do you know what happened to Yun-seo?'

Jae's eyes widened. 'I said to Madam, "Where is Yun-seo?" She said, "Who is Yun-seo?"'

'Do you think she died?' I made myself ask.

A silence pervaded the guest room. Jae squeezed a fold in her nightie.

'You don't need to answer any more questions,' Cassy intervened.

Jae's reaction surprised both of us. 'Miss Sandi helps me. I help Miss Sandi. Please find Yun-seo. I don't know what happened. I hope she's okay. Another girl said she went to Sydney.'

Now was the moment. 'Since we don't know where Yun-seo is and we don't even have a photo of her, it's going to be virtually impossible to find her. Now you're safe, we can help all the other trafficked women in the brothel, including Yun-seo, by going to the police and explaining what's happened.'

Cassy glared at me with disgust, her mouth twitching. 'Don't be ridiculous.'

'They'll kill my family if I talk to the police.' Jae's quiet voice wavered.

'That's just a threat Jae. How are they going to do that from so far away?'

'You have no idea about the reach and ruthlessness of these traffickers, Sandi,' said Cassy.

'Oh come on you two, it's the only way to help Yun-seo.'

Tears dribbled down Jae's gentle cheeks.

'This was a bad idea.' Cassy sprang up and gripped the door handle.

It was obvious where this was heading – with me being marched out of the hotel and having to make my own way home again. If only I could have talked to Jae by myself. Since that wasn't about to happen, I forced the angry bocce ball to dissolve from inside my chest.

I tried to make eye contact with Jae. 'I didn't mean to scare you. Perhaps we can find another way to help Yun-seo. Are you all right to go on for a bit longer?'

When she nodded, I asked, 'What about that man who drives you? Can you tell us about him?'

She wiped her eyes with a tissue Cassy supplied, as I showed her tons of perfect shots of Skull.

'Thumper.' Jae's hands shook, her fear of him no surprise.

'Is Thumper there all the time?' I asked.

'Not every day.'

'What are the names of the others?' I asked gently.

She held up a hand, tapping each finger as she reeled them off. 'Thumper, Spike, Tuffy, Shark.' She arrived at her pinky. 'Uh, Cliff?' Jae frowned.

'You're doing a great job,' I said.

She smiled shyly.

'Apart from Thumper, what do the others look like?'

Jae couldn't tell us much. They were all big men with black or brown hair. She described one with big hands, who seemed to be the head honcho.

'All those mongrels have attacked you, haven't they Jae,' said Cassy.

'Before I talked to Miss Cassy, I knew no-one in here in Australia. I didn't even know where I was living. If they killed me, no-one would know,' whispered Jae.

Cassy and I exchanged gazes, the reality of Jae's situation hitting me like a giant wave.

Jae's breath became shallow and soon she was wheezing, her face as pale as the crisp white pillows. As Jae's breathing became more distressed, I scrounged in my backpack for my asthma puffer.

When I turned back, Cassy was kneeling in front of her. 'Breathe in. Breathe out.'

Jae followed Cassy's instructions, as they breathed slowly together. Jae's sense of panic resonated with me, no doubt she was suffering from the same condition as me – flashbacks. I offered the puffer but Jae shook her head.

Over the next few minutes, Jae's breathing became easier. She wriggled past Cassy and retreated into the ensuite.

Cassy paced as I stood at the bay window, looking out. White waves rhythmically formed and broke and grey-blue sea met sky-blue horizon. Seagulls called.

Cassy arrived next to me. 'Truce?'

I stretched my arm around her shoulder. We nestled in silence.

When Jae emerged, Cassy slunk away from me.

Jae's eyes were red, but glistening. 'Thank you.' She bowed to both of us. 'All the time in here – in this country, I'm too scared to cry. Now I can cry.' Her whole body was shivering.

'Are you cold?'

Jae crawled onto the bed and under the doona. 'I'm very sleepy.' She slid the pillows flat, her eyes drooping.

As we closed the door, Cassy wrapped her hand around my arm. She pressed her lips on mine, while I leaned on the banister, hoping the old structure would hold my weight. Holding hands we descended the stairs, Cassy letting go when Gloria came into view.

'We've got to head off, but will you check on Jae in an hour or so?' asked Cassy.

'Of course, darling. Poor dear,' Gloria said.

'How much did you tell her?' I asked, as we hopped into the car.

'Enough.'

I suggested a trip to the beach before we drove back to town and surprisingly, Cassy agreed.

'I know exactly where to go,' she said.

We parked under the shade of tea-trees. As we meandered down wide stairs built into the cliff, I caught glimpses of the bay and breathed in the scent of eucalyptus.

Multicoloured beach huts curved around the foreshore and left a narrow strip of sand. The beach was all ours.

The sun was searing and I whisked off my jacket and runners. As we strolled along the sand barefoot, Cassy caught my hand. She drew me closer to the sea and we let waves caress our feet. The freezing water soon felt refreshing against the warmth of the day.

When we'd had enough, we wandered along the sand to a wider spot in front of the beach huts. I lay on my back, my elbows supporting me, with Cassy alongside.

'What do you think we should do?' she asked.

When I gave her a wink, she added, 'About Yun-seo.'

I wrestled my thoughts into focus. Surreptitiously risking a hand on Cassy's thigh, I brainstormed options about Yun-seo that didn't involve the cops, but my mind was on the woman next to me. When I leaned towards Cassy and kissed her soft lips, she responded. I was completely absorbed when she withdrew and sat up.

'Not here. This is my old stamping ground.' She glanced up the beach. 'So many people know me around here.'

Following her gaze, I spotted a man and his kelpie descending the steps to the beach.

'Come on Cassy.' I tugged her back towards me, but she resisted.

As the moment fizzled, my frustration turned to anger. 'Oh yeah, you have to protect your reputation, I totally get that.'

I retrieved my sunglasses which had leaped a metre away and masked my eyes with them.

'Well anyway, things to do, Cassy, crimes to solve; better hit the road.' A flash of dizziness hit me as I rocketed upwards too fast.

The sand was thick and hard to walk across. I tried to stride, but the slippery terrain made it impossible.

Cassy lingered behind. I seethed as I waited in the car park for her to catch up.

When she finally joined me, she said, 'How about going out, properly, you know. Maybe next Friday night?'

I buckled my seat belt. 'I'll check my diary. See if I can squeeze you in.'

On the excruciating trip back to town, Cassy made small talk and patted my knee.

I didn't respond to any of it; I'd had enough of this cat and mouse game.

20

THE PROMISE OF A SUMMER JAM-PACKED WITH HOT SEX FIZZLED. MY ANGER spiralled with Cassy, but mostly with myself. My planned return to Bob's Motors to grill his offsiders about Ricardo seemed the perfect antidote.

After tussling with Friday afternoon congestion and pre-Christmas mania, I finally pulled up at the mechanics.

I marched into the workshop determined to shove boss Bob aside and interrogate his employees. The puff went out of my resolve when Bob was nowhere to be seen. Inside was a guy with surfie-blond hair yanking off a grill from a Camry and an olive-skinned mechanic whose hand converted to a stop sign when he spied me.

'Bob here?' I demanded.

The olive-skinned mechanic, his face chiselled with Greek angles, fast-tracked towards me. 'Stepped out.'

'I'm working for a solicitor representing Ricardo Lopez – Rick.'

The mechanic retrieved a metal nut from the floor and spun it between his fingers.

'Bob's aware we need to speak to Rick's workmates. I have to tie things up with his solicitor this arvo. Just need to speak to you guys and we're ready for court.' I stuck out my hand. 'Sandi Kent.'

He wiped his right hand on his trousers and reluctantly shook mine. 'Chris. We're flat chat. I'll get Bob to give you a buzz. Leave your number.' Chris guided me into the reception area.

'I'll take two minutes max.' I said. 'My job's to find out if there was anything else going on for Rick before he left his employment here. Do you know who he was always talking to on the phone?'

'Dunno.' Chris blew on the nut and pocketed it. 'Bob and I go way back. He needed to do what he did.'

'Sure, I get that. You ever heard Rick talk about his cousins?'

'Nah, Rick kept to himself. Didn't mix.'

'Were you here when his cousins dropped by?'

'Don't remember.'

I could tell this guy wasn't going to give me a smackerel.

'Maybe your workmate out back might be better able to assist.'

When he hesitated, I shrugged. 'If you'd prefer, the solicitor can issue a subpoena and you can appear as witnesses at the trial. Days off work.'

Chris was giving the metal object in his pocket a workover. 'Won't hurt for a minute, I guess.' He stepped into the entranceway and called out, 'Hey Todd.'

Lanky Todd appeared in the reception doorway. Although he was young, his shoulders were hunched, presumably from leaning over cars.

After introducing us, Chris said, 'I know you and Rick worked together a bit. Guess he might have said something to you even though he could hardly speak a word of English.' Chris guffawed.

Todd shuffled from foot to foot, clearly uncomfortable with the taunt. 'What'd you tell her?' Todd tipped his chin at me.

Chris gave a sharp laugh. 'Don't know nothing, mate, except Rick was a complete pain in the arse. Bob was a bloody saint putting up with him for so long. Giving him a go in the first place.'

Chris's dark chocolate coloured eyes held my gaze. He would have been late thirties or early forties, so I imagined he might have been working with Bob most of his adult life. Had Bob given him a go when he started work?

'I'd bloody order Rick back to work when he was slacking off, just to give Bob a break from telling him off,' Chris said. 'Rick cracked it with me one time. Got a temper, all right.'

'Bob said Rick was always on the phone,' I said to Todd.

'Yeah.' Todd flicked his ponytail from one shoulder to the other.

'Do you know who to?' I prompted.

Todd scratched his eyebrow.

'Did you ever overhear what he was saying?'

'Overhear anything?' he repeated.

My interview with these guys was going nowhere fast. I wasn't sure if Todd was worried about Chris' reaction or had something to hide. I decided to warm him up, find out who was under that laid-back persona. 'You into surfing?'

Todd looked surprised. Surely I wasn't the first person to come to that conclusion. *Never assume,* I reminded myself.

'What you up to this weekend then? Looking forward to finishing up?'

Todd looked sideways at his colleague. 'Yeah. Going shopping with me girlfriend.'

'What's this got to do with Rick?' demanded Chris.

'Want to step outside for a sec?' I suggested to Todd.

'You said you'd be two minutes; we've still got a dozen cars to finish off.' Chris made a sweeping movement with his hand that ended up as a wave.

A man was silhouetted in the doorway to the garage. At first, I thought it was Bob, but then realised the man was wearing a suit.

As Chris attended to the customer, I snatched the moment.

'Todd, what you say won't get back to your boss. Rick's pretty much up shit creek unless I can get a few leads, so it'd be great if you could give me any info.'

Todd leaned against the counter. 'Guess it'll be okay. Hm, you know we worked hard and all, but sometimes we had downtime, a beer after work. Not that Rick drank much; he was pretty clean, you know. Didn't go out with the others. He knew they had the shits with him. His English was crap, but he got his meaning across, you know. He was having a hard time.'

I tried hard to match his languid pace of speech, even though I had the urge to pinch the information out of him before Chris came back. 'Was he in trouble?'

Todd screwed up his long face, resembling a caricature of himself. 'Sure.'

'With his cousins?' I asked.

'I reckon. But the phone calls – that was all chick problems. I used to hear him on the phone. "Don't worry," he'd say, 'I'll fix it up, you can come live with me."

'She'd be ringing him all the bloody time. He used to try and hide it, 'specially from Bob. She didn't give him a moment's peace. You know how demanding some chicks are.'

Maria would have been proud how I kept my eyebrows in line and resisted carving his attitude apart.

'I don't know why she was so upset. "Don't cry," he'd say, "it'll be okay." Seemed like he'd do anything for her. I told him he should get a girlfriend who was easy-going.'

'You know her name?'

'He never said.' After a moment's thought, Todd said. 'He did say he was trying to work out whether he could rent a pad for them both. He seemed worried. Yeah, real worried.'

'How?'

'I don't know, kind of found it hard to do his work.'

'The whole time he was here?'

Todd tapped the counter, considering the question. 'At first he seemed fine, but in the end he'd spend half his time on the mobile. When the boss gave Rick the flick he was mucking things up, not tightening bolts back on proper. You know, risky stuff. I helped out where I could, but he was getting worse.'

From inside the garage, I heard the revving of an engine.

'What about his cousins?' I asked Todd.

'Oh yeah, they were bad news, all right. Even Bob shat himself when they barricaded the doorway.'

'Barricaded?'

'Well, felt like it; didn't think we were going to see the light of day again.'

I noticed Chris returning.

'You know the truth? I reckon–' Before Todd could finish, Chris barged past us and headed to the cash register, his suited customer following.

Once the customer had been dealt with, Chris glowered at his colleague. 'What you been crapping on about?'

'Just stuff about Rick's cousins.' Todd jammed his fists into his pockets. Whatever he was going to tell me would remain locked under a bonnet.

'What the heck?' From the entrance, Bob's raspy voice reverberated off concrete. He strode into reception, his limp not slowing down his pace.

'What the hell are you doing back here?' His spit fired onto my lip.

I wiped his saliva away. 'As I explained to your colleagues, better to talk now. A quick, painless five-minute chat is way less drama than a subpoena for a month-long trial.'

Todd dodged past his boss and disappeared into the workshop.

'You have no bloody right coming in here.' Bob's face was fierce, his voice an explosion on each word. He spun towards Chris. 'What the hell were you thinking?'

'She threatened taking us to court.'

'Threatened, did she? This is private property, you con artist.' Bob strode behind the reception desk, and as he and Chris stood shoulder to shoulder, picked up the phone. 'I'm calling the cops.'

With a greasy finger pointing at my face, Chris hissed, 'I knew you were trouble.'

I was tempted to yell back at them, but knew it would escalate the situation. 'Just going anyway, Bob.'

After striding out of the workshop and diving into my car, I spied Bob scowling at me in my rear-vision mirror as a mountain of trucks prevented a quick exit. Finally, I hit the accelerator and made my escape.

21

MY VISIT TO THE MECHANICS HAD ADDED TO MY INTEL ON RICARDO: HE had "chick trouble". We had something in common.

As soon as I was inside my flat, I planted my mobile on the iPod dock. Beyoncé's voice couldn't cover Flicker's insistent demands. Her appetite was ferocious and like me, she had a fast metabolism. While she tucked into her tinned dinner, I strutted around the loungeroom to an old favourite, *Run the World*.

My mobile buzzed with an incoming call from my sister, which never happened, so I guess I should have been rapt. Iris, on speaker, filled my flat with her whiney voice. Unlike friends who were close to their sisters, Iris and I had never clicked and our father had ensured it stayed that way. Nowadays, Iris lived in an alien religious solar system that I had no desire to fathom.

After I asked how she was, our conversation plummeted.

'I'm sick of having Christmas at my place,' she said. 'It's so much work. You have no idea what it's like with children.'

My niece's sweet voice chimed in the background.

'Wait, Amber,' said Iris, 'Mummy's talking now.'

I glanced at the black and white framed photo I'd taken of earnest Amber and her wistful sister Chloe as we'd played Go Fish. 'Hey, I'd be happy to play hide-and-seek in a park after sharing a few sangers.'

Iris clicked her tongue and I could visualise her impatient study of newly painted fingernails. 'We can't have the girls at risk of bee stings and salmonella poisoning.'

If Iris had inhabited my world, she'd have developed a reality check about what risk involved. I gritted my teeth to stop myself reacting: the longer the gap, the less likely something bitter would come out of my mouth.

146

Luckily, Iris took up the slack. 'For goodness sake, Sandi, can't you just grow up and get a decent place to live?'

She couldn't get away with that one.

'Yeah, I'll find a sugar mumma to buy me a mansion in the 'burbs like you.' I waited for the phone to go dead.

'Good idea,' she said.

My sizzling sarcasm skills had clearly taken a dive.

'Look, how about I make dessert and clean up the dishes after?' Her kids loved my trifle.

After a pause, she said, 'As long as you promise to keep it in the fridge until the second before you leave, then keep it in an esky surrounded by ice packs.'

'For God's sake.'

'And please don't blaspheme.'

Hanging up was the best option. 'Say "hi" to the kids and see you in a couple of weeks.'

'It's only 11 days,' said Iris.

After jabbing "end", I let out a series of curses. If it hadn't been for my nieces needing a sane adult in their restricted lives, I would have ditched Iris.

I scooped Flicker up for a cuddle. She succumbed to a couple of pats then wriggled out of my hold and started darting around the flat. I tossed her a golf ball made of alfoil, chuckling as she batted it across the living room carpet. Her playfulness was an antidote to the rest of the crap in my life.

After a dinner of left-over pasta, I rang Mum to let off steam.

'We'll work out something different for next year,' she slurred.

'Totally, I'll be in New York, catching a show.'

'Save your pennies,' chortled Mum, her laughter spiralling.

Given I couldn't match her drunken jolliness, I made an excuse to finish the call.

My laptop hummed as I logged on. There was email from Maribyrnong Aquatic Centre hassling me about January work rosters and another reminding me my mobile phone bill was overdue. They could wait. One email's subject line jumped out.

Further evidence received

I signed into the encrypted message sent by Maria's secretary, curious about what it would reveal. The Office of Public Prosecutions had responded to my request for further information.

The first attachment provided a transcript of Ricardo's phone communication with Lee. His texts to Lee, or Petal as he called her, were all minimalist.

Soon Petal or *Tomorrow Petal.*

Lee's texts were all one-liners in English. I wrote them out in my notebook and read them aloud.

Come visit sweet man.

I need your soft eyes.

My heart is heavy.

My soul is in pieces.

I can't breathe.

My heart sinks, with my body.

I retrieved the toilet paper from Lee's file and compared her text messages to the poem hidden in the garage. I re-read the first line.

I'm saddened by the thought that my mother's cheeks are lost.

Any doubts about who had written that poem evaporated.

Only two voice messages were provided, both from Lee to Ricardo, and both the night before she was murdered. I played the audio.

'Please ring me.'

'Ricardo ring me.'

It was haunting listening to her soft, shaky voice. She sounded terrified. It fitted with the mechanic saying a woman had rung Ricardo crying. Tears even welled up in my eyes, listening to the voice mails a second time.

I checked the next attachment – Ricardo's mobile phone records – and double checked who he'd been ringing. Apart from calling Lee, the numbers matched his work at Bob's Motors and his sister. When I rang the only other number he'd called, a recorded message to Autobarn played. Lee must have been the woman that the surfy-looking Todd had overheard.

As I closed down the laptop, my brain pounded with information, trying to make sense of what had happened to Lee and whether she'd really fallen for Ricardo.

With Flicker ensconced on my lap, I watched a humourless comedy on TV until restlessness made my legs twitch. How tragic, spending a

Friday night in front of the box, but Stewart was at work and it was probably too late to organise a catch up with other friends.

My thoughts drifted to Jae and her friend. I wondered if Yun-seo had been moved interstate or was lying dead somewhere. The inane chatter on TV jarred. As I snatched up my keys, Flicker scowled.

'Not my fault you're agoraphobic,' I said.

I drove on automatic to Amsterdam Angels in Richmond. Red lights doused the top storey and its cast-iron balcony, while next door black graffiti on the red brick wall seemed to throb. Sordidness and dismay crept along my skin; Jae's account of Yun-seo being beaten after she'd escaped made it all too real.

As I prodded the central locking button, the car doors clicked. I left my window down a fraction for some fresh air and once again settled in for the long haul.

After surveilling an endless stream of punters, the van pulled up. Strangely, it wasn't their usual minder who jumped out of the driver's seat and swaggered into the brothel. The new escort slid out lightly, unexpected for a big fellow, and glided through the front door.

A troop of men exited soon after 11pm. A new one entered, but scuttled out almost immediately. I checked online under Melbourne brothel hours, which stated Amsterdam Angels was closed. Why so early on a Friday night? Not enough demand?

Soon after, the lights were extinguished and the women dribbled out with their escort. Another woman had replaced Jae; supply was obviously no issue in this business.

The escort pinched his spiky black hair as he waited for his prisoners to pile in. My camera copped a work out, capturing his image. I thought he might be Tuffy, as he matched Jae's description of "a big man with black hair and big hands". He looked familiar. He sprang into the driver's seat and navigated towards the city with me close behind.

In the city centre, the van sank into the underground carpark in Lonsdale Street. There was no point pursuing that dead end again, so I pulled over at an empty bus stop and picked up the hard casing of my camera. As I scrolled through, my arms jolted: close-ups of the escort revealed a round face, jet-black eyebrows and thin dark eyes. I'd definitely eye-balled him before, his sumo wrestler build, his massive chest and wide shoulders. My skin had prickled from his paws.

As I considered options, the car-park gate crept upwards and the van loomed from under it. I stashed the camera, my next step clear.

He sped towards the northern suburbs and I had to dodge traffic to keep up as we flew past my old neighbourhood of Thornbury and into Preston. When the escort turned into a road with a playground, it was obvious where he was destined: back to where I'd first inhaled his overpowering aftershave.

He parked in the driveway of the fibro-built Club 96, behind Qiao's Mitsubishi. I pulled over outside the park and drummed the steering wheel with morbid satisfaction. This was confirmation that Tuffy, head honcho of Amsterdam Angels – prison for trafficked sex workers – and Ju-Long Wang – witness to Lee's murder – were one and the same.

My neurons sparked, connecting disparate sources of information. Cassy's question about whether Lee was really a student from China bounced back to me. Despite her faults, Cassy did have expertise on the subject of sex trafficking.

I snapped more photos as another load of women piled into the van. Then we were off, back to the city and into the underground car park in the Greek precinct. How many women could they fit into one apartment?

Even though it seemed certain Ju-Long would now be snuggled up in one of the apartment's beds for the night, I decided to hang around for 15 minutes to make sure. While waiting, I studied the hundreds of photos in my camera, still shocked by the connections. A flash of a headlight caught my eye. I'd almost missed the van surface, with Ju-Long at the wheel.

He cruised through the city, down Russell Street and right into Flinders, where footpaths were packed with straggly revellers desperate for taxis. Women had abandoned high heels and tiptoed barefoot, their shoes hooked over fingers.

We traversed south of the city and along arterial roads to Bay Street, the main thoroughfare running through Port Melbourne to the beach. Without indicating, Ju-long spun left, entering a narrow side street. Single-fronted houses lined one side of the street, graffitied roller doors on the back of businesses graced the other, guarded by stinky industrial rubbish bins, their contents bulging.

Ju-Long screeched to a stop outside an old red-brick house, fierce red globes strung across its frontage.

Once he strode inside, I eased past the sign: Sweet Dreams. I parked hidden in an alleyway, the nose of my VW poking towards the street.

Within five minutes, Ju-Long appeared with a stream of eight hunched women. The last in line, an emaciated woman, limped towards the van. Ju-Long shoved her inside.

The loaded van took off. Surprisingly, instead of heading back to the city, Ju-Long turned down Bay Street towards the beach. Trees loomed overhead and drab businesses, now closed for the night, lined both sides of the avenue. The closer we got to the bay the more the median strip was dominated by palm trees.

Close to the beach, Ju-Long turned into a side street. As I followed, the van halted in the middle of the road. I killed my headlights as his white reverse lights flicked on. I checked the rear-vision mirror and gripped the steering wheel ready to bolt if he'd caught me. He backed into an angle park and leaped out.

My nerves jangled as he glared in my direction and strode towards me. *Fuck.* I shoved my VW into reverse, my toes poised over the accelerator.

Ignoring me, Ju-Long ripped open the van door and yelled into its interior. As the women scurried out, he corralled them across the road and into an upmarket apartment block opposite.

I moved to a less conspicuous spot and stared at a blue stone church on the corner seeking inspiration. When that failed, I noted the address of the apartment in my mobile and stared up to see if a window would light up under the sail-like eaves. No clues there.

Within a couple of minutes, Ju-Long's figure appeared through glass doors. How many brothels were part of this ring? And where were we headed now? My eyes drooped with fatigue, but there was no way I was going to bow out at this stage.

Instead of hopping into the van, Ju-Long eased into a silver Mercedes parked alongside. The ringing of a hands-free phone burst through the silent night, as he reversed out of the car park.

Still nervy, I drove behind him with a good margin between us. Concentrating on the route was beyond me; keeping safe was as much as my weary mind could manage.

Ju-Long entered an elegant tree-lined street in what I was pretty sure was now South Melbourne, parked on the road, and slipped inside a three-storey townhouse.

Desperate to call it a night, my legs aching from tiredness, I turned my car for home just as a Toyota pulled up outside the house. Ju-Long promptly emerged from the front door, a purple jacket looped over his arm, and slid into the back seat. An Uber or associate?

We were off again, back towards the city via Clarendon Street. As the garish Crown Casino and Entertainment Complex sign came into view – the image of the crown made up of giant 3-D silver buttons pinned to a background of peach and imperial blue – the Toyota suddenly turned into the complex drop-off point.

Ju-Long left the car, skated through rotating glass doors and vanished.

I wondered what facilities would be open at Crown at that time of night – gambling for sure, movies maybe, dining doubtful. The idea of following him flitted across my mind, though I would have had to find a car park and pay a bomb. More critically, my intrigue had been overtaken by exhaustion.

Uncovering Ju-Long's nocturnal tastes would have to wait.

22

Northland Shopping Centre, grotto of artificial light and credit-card mania, was where Erica García, the friend of Ricardo's fiancée, wanted to meet.

The car park resembled a piranha attack, everyone fighting over one vacated space. Having slept in after my late-night brothel tour, I was already 15 minutes late and frazzled. After finally nabbing a park, I jogged across the bitumen around frustrated driver's cars, pushing through the thick heat.

As the electronic glass doors slid open, a wave of cool air enveloped me. It was a quick walk to our meeting point, through the Myer perfume section, the scents of multiple subtle aromas an antidote to the clammy petrol stench outside.

A woman whose turquoise coloured dress rippled as she zigzagged towards me, seemed in a dilemma as to whether to introduce herself. Her fingers were loaded with thick plastic bags. As she voiced my name, her cheek muscles lifted in an attempt to smile.

Erica had recognised me from my description: tall, solid; bleached hair, spiky at the front, shaved at the back; not to mention my paisley-patterned shirt, courtesy of the op shop. I'd wanted her to notice me.

In a soulless café stuck in the middle of a shopping corridor, with no walls and no atmosphere, I ordered coffees at the counter while Erica decided on a table. For a second, she looked like she might scurry away into the crowd, her eyes flitting from me to the exit. The queue progressed at a seahorse's pace, and I kept a close eye on Erica in case she vamoosed.

Order number finally in hand, I joined her at a table on the edge of low black barricades that divided us from the shoppers. As I attempted to squeeze into an aluminium chair opposite Erica, it knocked into the back of an elderly woman's seat behind me.

'Sorry,' I mouthed.

It seemed that our conversation would be public, whether we liked it or not.

Erica massaged her belly. Although she was on the chubby side, it was clear she was heavily pregnant.

'Kicking?' I asked.

'Constantly,' she answered quietly.

'Have you got other kids?'

'He'll be the first grandchild in my family. Everyone is very happy. I have family back in Colombia, so when he's a bit older, we'll take him to visit.'

'That's exciting.'

Erica smiled half-heartedly. Given we were here to talk about Valentina disappearing, I guess it was impossible for her to be fully joyful. Now seemed the moment to jump into the reason we were meeting.

'Luz told me that you and Valentina Rojas were good friends.'

'She was my best friend,' said Erica.

'You must miss her.'

'Too much.' Erica rubbed her collarbone as if grief had lodged there.

I waited until she'd regrouped. When she made eye contact, I asked, 'Did you know Ricardo well?'

'He was a private person. Valentina was the lively one, always joking and laughing.'

'What did you think of him?'

'Valentina and I were going to be married within a week of each other,' she answered. 'She liked how much Ricardo loved his sister Luz; how he played with his nephew and niece. He went to church and he was good looking too, of course.'

'Did Valentina need to get married to stay in Australia?' I asked.

'She loved Ricardo.' Erica's tone was strident.

The arrival of a waitress with our coffees interrupted our conversation. Erica sipped her short black, as I sank my latte, considering her responses.

'There was another problem,' I guessed.

Erica's cheeks flushed, perhaps as a symptom of pregnancy or the strain of dredging up painful memories. 'Valentina was a strong person. I admired how she'd speak her mind. In the end though, that didn't help her.' Sadness clouded Erica's face.

'Couples always argue about something, hey. What did Valentina and Ricardo disagree about?'

Erica hesitated.

'Valentina was your best friend and best friends share confidences, don't they?' I said.

'She didn't like how Ricardo spent too much time with his cousins,' she blurted.

'How come?' I played naïve.

Erica's tight-lipped lack of response told me she wasn't about to offer up the answer.

'I know they're drug dealers,' I said.

Erica scrutinised the shoppers around us as though Ricardo's cousins had spies everywhere. My eyes darted around, but I only spotted families with pushers and parcels.

We turned back to each other and I asked, 'How did Valentina know?'

Erica leaned her elbows on the table and circled her mouth with her hands trying to ensure the secret stayed between us. 'Valentina and Ricardo used to go out with them to gourmet restaurants. The cousins paid for everything. Ricardo never answered her questions about how they earned their money. She hated that he was involved with them.'

'By *involved* you mean he worked for them?'

Erica lowered her eyes, shielding her belly with a bulging plastic bag. I assumed I was right.

'Did Ricardo stop?'

'Valentina pleaded with him not to see them anymore. He said it was impossible to walk out on them. We talked for hours about what she was going to do.'

The echoing noise of chairs scraping and children squealing made it hard to hear Erica, whose voice had turned into a whisper.

I leaned towards her, thinking about how Luz's husband had heard Ricardo and Valentina argue, according to the police file, three days before Valentina disappeared. 'What did you tell the police when Valentina went missing?'

'Only that she was thinking of calling off the engagement. I didn't say why. There was no way I was going to tell the police more, though I wanted to. Ricardo's cousins are dangerous. I had to keep my family safe.'

'When you say "dangerous", what do you mean? What have they done?'

Erica shuddered and shook her head. 'I don't know.'

Everyone who spoke about the cousins put a new scary spin on them. The descriptions were escalating and Ricardo was firmly in their pocket.

'What do you think happened to Valentina?' I asked.

'I don't want to think about it.'

'The cousins?'

She shrugged, avoiding eye contact.

'Any chance she just up and left?'

'No. Where would she have gone?'

'Back home to Colombia?' I asked.

'No. She would have told me, or someone from home would have let us know.'

'Was there anyone else who might have hurt her?'

'No-one would want to hurt Valentina. Everybody loved her and apart from work, she only saw friends and Ricardo.'

'Do you think Ricardo could have hurt Valentina?'

'I never saw him say a nasty word to her, but you don't know what happens when a couple are alone together. If he was working for his cousins, who knows what he was capable of.' Erica clasped my hands. 'Please don't tell anyone about Ricardo working with his cousins. We could all be in danger.'

'What danger?' I asked.

She shook her head.

'What was Valentina so scared of?'

'All I know is she saw something terrible and had to keep it secret. She didn't say what, but she was scared for her life.' Erica's hands trembled. 'Then she disappeared.'

Suddenly Erica struggled to her feet. She waddled away as fast as she could through a wall of consumers.

23

I PULLED INTO THE DRIVEWAY OF MY CHILDHOOD BENTLEIGH HOUSE. 'HEY Mum, maybe you should move somewhere smaller, easier to maintain.'

'Nice to see you too.' Mum wiped her face with the sleeve of her beige button-up shirt.

Preoccupied with what Ricardo's fiancée might have witnessed and how to expose Ju-Long's crimes, I'd been tempted to cancel this catch-up, but I knew the consequences.

My DIY mother was weeding her front-garden-cum-veggie-patch, now overshadowed by an ugly grey apartment block next door. The neighbourhood's large suburban blocks were a developer's dream.

Mum knelt on a foam cushion that I'd gifted her last Christmas, replacing a threadbare towel she'd always used. A khaki floppy hat was firmly attached by a cord under her chin – the epitome of fashion. She'd become obsessed with making the weatherboard environmentally sustainable and had installed water tanks and solar power. She also seemed to have aspirations of self-subsistence, with front and back yards converted to a vegetable garden and fruit orchard.

She edged into an "on your marks" position, her hands in a high bridge, and pushed herself up. 'Lunch is ready.'

That was code for "you're late".

'Yeah, sorry about that. Work's been hectic.'

The way she blinked indicated she was unconvinced.

'Truly, I haven't even gone out all week.' I hated how I regressed into an adolescent the moment I returned "home".

'How restrained.' She ripped off gardening gloves.

Our old yellow Lab waddled over to me.

'Hey, Sparky.' As I scratched under his chin, a waft of stinky dog flew up my nose.

Mum flicked long brown hair from her perspiration-spotted face and closed in to kiss me on the cheek.

'You're all sweaty,' I ducked to one side, 'and Sparky needs a bath.'

Despite my follow up smile, Mum frowned.

'I can wash him if you want,' I offered as a truce.

'It's all right, that's my job for this afternoon.'

'You sure?'

'Yes, it's fine, Sandi. I want to talk to you while you're here, not have you do chores.'

I linked my arm through hers as we meandered inside.

While she disappeared to get changed, I headed into the ranch-style kitchen. Fresh herbs lay in piles on the laminated bench. I crushed mint between my fingers and breathed in the scent.

Mum reappeared and took out a green salad from the fridge. 'Courtesy of the garden beds.'

'Wow,' I said, with more enthusiasm than I felt.

Mum extracted a spitting chicken and potatoes from the oven, the oily aroma reminding me of Sunday night roasts when I was a kid.

'No visitation from Iris?' A grass seed of hope burrowed into my side that I might get to see my nieces.

Mum grimaced, shook her head. 'Christmas is soon.' Her voice feigned jolliness.

'We'll be lucky if Iris lets us play Snap with the kids.'

'She's a good mother who's protective of her children,' Mum said.

'Oh come on, don't defend Iris. She's an over-involved born-again, who should go back to work and let her kids breathe.'

'It's hard to know what it's like until you've been a mother.'

My fury multiplied. She must have felt the laser beam firing into her back.

'We have to be patient until Iris feels more confident,' she said.

'It's been seven years. What's going to change? Some message from God that she should include her sinning family? That maybe we won't turn her kids into salt just by playing with them.'

'Don't be ridiculous. If only you–' she said.

'If only I what?'

I fetched knives and forks and banged them onto the dining table.

'It would be difficult to have a child in your situation, wouldn't it,' she said.

'Where do you get your information from? *Women's Weekly*?'

It was an unfair gibe. I was the one who read *Women's Weekly*, though only in waiting rooms of course.

'You wouldn't have one on your own, though, would you?'

'You brought us up by yourself, without any help.'

'Mmm,' she said.

According to my mother we'd been deprived by not having a father around and that was why Iris was mad and I was gay. Not that she'd said it so clearly, but it was obvious. When I was 19, I told Mum that Maria was my girlfriend. She was shocked, even though my lack of boyfriends should have been a flashing neon sign. Mum was still stuck in the hope that this was a phase. Although, compared to other friends, I was lucky. Stewart's father banned the words "gay" and "queer" in his family and Stew could never bring a boyfriend home. At least Mum had always welcomed Maria and other girlfriends who'd hung around long enough to meet her.

Mum swept newspapers, books and letters up one end of the pine dining table as though they were leaves. Tidiness had never been her strong point, an asset I'd inherited. She sat in her favourite position with a view of the garden.

Mum fanned herself with an electricity bill. 'How are your swimming classes going?'

My mother thought my PI business was a waste of time at best, and a suicide mission at worst, making it another topic that was off limits. She'd made it clear I'd let her down by abandoning my law degree, when she'd put so much effort into our education. I guess my job as a swimming teacher at least followed her career direction.

Before I had a chance to answer her, my phone screeched. She-Who-Must-Not-Be-Named, my latest name for Cassy, flashed up. I jabbed "end" and turned my phone face down.

The day before, after my meeting with Erica García, I'd rung the Mornington hotel to check if Jae Shin was alone so I could pop down and show her the photos of Ju-Long. I'd thought the phone was going to ring out, but finally the owner, Gloria Campbell, answered breathlessly. When I'd asked to speak to Jae, there was silence.

'I am so sorry.' Her voice sounded shaky. 'Jae's gone.'

My stomach plummeted. Visions of Ju-Long wrenching Jae by her hair into the van projected onto my retina.

'Didn't Cassy tell you?' Gloria queried. 'She found Jae somewhere more secure, which is wonderful, isn't it? We loved being able to help out, but I'm sure Jae will be better off where she is, though she did enjoy the home cooking.'

I should've been pleased that Jae was safe and Cassy had moved her. After stewing for an hour, I'd texted Cassy. She hadn't replied until now.

'Not answering?' said Mum.

'Nah, it can wait. We're in the middle of eating.' My tone was stroppy.

'Never stopped you before.'

In the middle of a mouthful, my mobile rang again.

'Someone's obviously desperate to talk to you.'

If only Mum had known the whole story.

I leaped out the back door under the passionfruit and in amongst the raised vegetable beds, Sparky panting behind me. 'Cassy, for Christ's sake, days without replying.'

'Listen,' her voice sounded tight, 'Jae's begging you to come see her. She's been up all night. She's terrified that Yun-seo might have been killed, and if that's the case what does it mean for her? She's been talking about going back because she's so scared they'll find her and kill her or her family.'

Above, a dark cloud dominated the sky.

Mum studied me through the window, while Sparky was poised at my feet with his ears pricked. I roamed further down the garden where the fig was, the only tree that remained from my childhood. The rope swing had disappeared years ago.

'Not sure what to do,' said Cassy.

'You're the bloody wannabe social worker.' I kicked the gnarled trunk of the fig tree. 'Your feminist collective at the Coalition should be able to band together and work something out.'

'Unfortunately, it's Sunday and no-one's working.'

'Unlike the rest of your dedicated crew, you expect me to obey whenever you decree. Sorry to inconvenience you, but I'm visiting my mother.'

'It's fine, we'll deal with it. Sorry to bother you.' Her voice was flat.

I considered telling her that I wanted Jae to have a look at the photos, when she hung up.

I kicked the tree again – bad mistake. A sharp pain fired up my big toe and into my ankle. Whipping off my runner, I massaged my foot until the pain eased, then reached up and hung from the branch where the swing used to be.

The ground below me was littered with squashed figs. If they'd been any other fruit, they would have become jam. My bet was that the only reason Mum had kept this tree was because she knew how much it meant to me.

As I plucked figs from the heavy branches, a cold touch on my arm made me look up. The cloud hanging above was letting loose. I retreated inside.

Mum's eyes were on me. 'Rain. Wonderful. Everything all right?'

'Yeah, fine, just a case I'm working on. Bit complicated to explain.' I took a bite of chicken breast, the thickness making it hard to swallow. 'How's your job going?'

The lines on Mum's cheeks became accentuated as she smiled. 'How I lasted 25 years teaching rowdy kids, I'll never know. It's a dream working with students one-on-one. I get to talk to them about my favourite topic and I can take my time to catalogue the books and order new ones. It's fabulous.'

Mum had worked full-time as a teacher since I could remember. She deserved some peace in her fifties.

'I love the Year 9/10 reading list. I've been reading Amie Kaufman's, *Illuminae Files*. You read them?' she asked.

I shook my head.

She swooped towards one of her bookcases. Mum had collected every piece of literature since *The Odyssey*. Having resisted all her encouragement and pressure as a teenager, I'd only read a fraction of the books. Eventually she'd worked out if she gave me a fantasy or science fiction novel, I'd devour it, especially if there was a heroine.

'Not sure I've got time at the moment.'

Her bottom lip pouted.

'I'll take them anyway.' I forced a smile. 'Hopefully, I'll have some downtime over Christmas.'

I took my plate to the sink and put the kettle on. 'Want a coffee?'

'All right.'

'I won't be able to stay long though.'

'Oh,' she said.

'I've got to wind up a job.'

She tried to smile, but her eyes were glum.

A shard of guilt wedged in my gut. I should have stayed longer, visited more often, kept her company.

Before I could censor myself, I said, 'Maybe we could go away somewhere over summer.' My chest constricted as soon as the words left my mouth. I loved her, but with so many topics off limits it made spending time together a strain. 'For a weekend.'

Mum looked surprised. 'That'd be lovely, pet.'

'I'll check my calendar,' I said.

With our coffees in hand, Mum gave me a tour of her corrugated-iron garden beds, innocent fluffy clouds now dotting the sky.

'So Christmas is settled?' asked Mum.

'Despite Iris complaining that having it at her house will be the greatest imposition since childbirth. Well, the alternative of a dinosaur-occupied park was the clincher.'

As I was leaving, with sci-fi books and figs in hand, I hugged Mum and drew in her familiar scent of coconut. She'd started using coconut milk products to treat her thinning hair, one of the few luxuries she allowed herself. I made a mental note to check out dates for our weekend away. We both needed it.

Pointing my car towards home, my focus zoomed back to my phone call with Cassy. I grabbed my mobile to ring her but decided against it and shoved it in my backpack.

'Shit, Cassy!'

A hundred metres down the road, I pulled over and retrieved my phone to text, *Where are you?*

Within 10 seconds she replied with an address nearby.

24

SET BACK IN THE SERVICE LANE OF NEPEAN HIGHWAY, THE CREAM
weatherboard blended in with its neighbours. A row of dwellings with
high fences shielded residents from prying eyes and the racket of trucks.
I wondered if Jae had adapted to the change from Mornington's seaside
views to a massive business district visible through six lanes of traffic.
The highway was a means to get places, not a place to live. The Refuge
was safer than Cassy's mum's, though, I reminded myself, and way safer
than Amsterdam Angels.

After texting Cassy, she and Jae met me on the porch.

Following a perfunctory 'Hi', I entered the hallway after them, the
black security door banging behind me.

'Thank you, Miss Sandi.' Jae reached out and clasped my hand and I
squeezed reassuringly.

As Cassy tried to lay thin fingers on my forearm, I dodged her.

She ignored my snub. 'Have you got any leads on Yun-seo?' Her
voice was steeped with desperation.

My contract with the Coalition – to plan Jae's rescue – had blown
out of all proportions. As knotted muscles gripped my shoulders with
worry for these women, it struck me that Cassy had transferred the
Coalition's job onto me. And I'd fallen for it. A bad habit of mine and
this time I'd had a gutful.

'What have you and the Coalition achieved?' I threw back.

Apart from blinking rapidly, Cassy offered no response.

On the brown flecked carpet, I knelt near Jae and extracted the
camera from my backpack. 'I think I know who Tuffy is.'

Jae flattened herself against the tan-coloured wall.

'Hold on, we need to speak somewhere *private*,' Cassy pointed down
the corridor. 'We can use the office. The staff are only here on weekdays.'

I hurtled to my feet. 'Like it was totally cool with your boss when we met in her office? How come it's even fine for me to be here? Don't refuges keep their locations secret?'

Cassy spun away and slunk down the hall. Jae and I followed into the kitchen awash with voices and aromas. On the four-burner gas stove, saucepans boiled and frypans hissed. I breathed in the sharpness of garlic and subtler aromas of tangy coriander and sweet cinnamon.

One woman, her purple extensions macraméd through thick black curls, stirred a large pot as she talked in an African language to a boy who grinned and chatted back. A skinny Anglo woman, slumped at the kitchen table, gazed blankly at her mobile. At her feet, a toddler lay like a beetle and screamed.

'Shut up, Adam,' the skinny woman pleaded.

As Cassy introduced me to the women, the thought hit me that this could have happened to my family. Mum, my sister and I could have been hiding here, torn away from friends. We'd been lucky my grandparents had welcomed us into their home for as long as we needed.

As we made our way out the back, Jae carrying a chipped teapot and old cups, we dodged a group of kids playing Mr Wolf.

The bungalow-cum-office had a small meeting table up one end. Posters and flyers about different events, mostly protests, littered lime-green walls. Folders, notepads and unwashed cups clogged desks.

Jae carefully positioned the teapot in the centre of the table as I plonked down next to her, cradling my camera on my lap. Opposite me, Cassy tried unsuccessfully to make eye contact.

Jae poured the pale green tea. 'Please.'

We all sipped in unison. It was strong, but not bitter like I've sometimes tasted in restaurants in Footscray. Jae smiled shyly when I commented on how tasty it was.

Jae reached out and moulded her fingers over mine. 'Please help me. I'm scared.'

'I think we're close to getting enough evidence to have these thugs charged.'

Jae tipped her head to one side, clearly trying to understand.

'These photos show that Tuffy is keeping women prisoners.'

When I raised the camera onto the table, Jae tensed but bowed her head in agreement. It didn't take long for me to arrive at the shots of Ju-Long as he left Amsterdam Angels. I angled the LCD screen towards Jae.

'That's Tuffy, that's Tuffy for sure,' gasped Jae.

My hands couldn't stop scrolling through the photos. Jae's identification was another confirmation that Tuffy and Ju-Long were one and the same. I pumped my fist under the table. Pieces of the nightmare puzzle were slotting in.

'Have you heard him called Ju-Long Wang?'

'No.'

'Who?' Cassy's voice was impatient.

I raised my hand to Cassy. 'Did he stay with you in the city, like Thumper did?'

'Sometimes. Thumper stayed most nights.'

'Did you have women from different brothels in the city apartment?'

'Yes, some worked at other brothels,' Jae said.

'What's going on, how come you're calling him Ju-Long?' Cassy jumped up and tried to snatch my camera, but I shielded it with my elbows.

'Show me.' Cassy fabricated a smile.

Despite my desire to exclude Cassy, I flourished the camera in front of her.

I faced Jae. 'I think he's the boss of a string of illegal brothels. I'm going to find out more about Ju-Long – Tuffy. That way we can work out what happened to Yun-seo and help the other women. I want to show you photos of other brothels, where I've seen Tuffy. See if you know anyone else.'

Jae cupped the rough side of the camera with one hand as we both gazed at the screen. Although she was too polite to ask, it was clear she was itching to search through the images herself. My camera never left my possession, but I guided it into her grasp.

'She's a lovely girl,' said Jae about one woman at Club 96. 'I went to that brothel a few times.'

She arrived at photos outside Sweet Dreams, the new brothel Ju-Long had led me to a couple of days ago.

Jae breathed choppily. 'Yun-seo.'

I expanded the photo, recognising Yun-seo as the emaciated woman with the limp.

'She's alive.' Cassy was ecstatic.

Our heads converged as we focused. Cassy's mint-tinted breath floated my way as she wrapped a hand around my neck. A warm relaxed sensation enveloped my spine. I caught myself and wriggled away from her touch.

'Where's the brothel?' asked Cassy.

'In Port Melbourne. No clear way to get her out of there.'

'You got Jae out. You can get Yun-seo out too.'

Jae nodded slowly at me, clutching my fingers. 'Thank you.'

As I started to extract my hand, Jae released her hold on me instantly, as if fearing punishment for expressing her needs.

'I'm already running the gauntlet pursuing Ju-Long. There's no way. It's too dangerous, not just for me, but for Yun-seo as well.'

So many young women needed rescuing. Doing it once was risky enough. They were all linked. Ju-Long and Thumper would do everything in their power to prevent another escape.

Jae's soft eyes pleaded.

'No way. This is huge. There are at least three brothels involved and 30 women. I can't take that on single-handedly. I promise to find out more about Ju-Long.'

I eyeballed Cassy. 'I have to go. Sorry, but I'm not some sort of paramilitary operation, just a sole private eye, without a weapon.'

I waited for Cassy to see me out so I could have a private fierce word, but she'd anchored herself next to Jae.

As I made my way across the backyard, two boys growled at each other. Mr Wolf must have ended in an argument.

25

I'D ENTICED MY OFFSIDER WITH THE PROMISE OF A MASSIVE HAWAIIAN PIZZA.

The moon sat high in the sky and the aroma of ham filled Stewart's Holden as he reversed into a parking spot facing what appeared to be Ju-Long's residence in South Melbourne – a concrete townhouse, one of four squashed between stately old buildings. Ju Long's was the only house with lights still on in the vicinity, standing out like bling. Parked out front, his Mercedes was less conspicuous in this well-to-do suburb. Behind us loomed the Railway Hotel, now closed for the night, its windows like eyes, dark and impenetrable.

In Stewart's company and with the camouflage of an alternative vehicle, my tension eased. I updated Stewart on the complexities of the cases and the tragic Cassy story.

'Cassy ditched?' he queried.

'No going back.'

He raised both eyebrows, an expression of scepticism.

'I was turned on and still kept my cool,' I insisted.

'Turned it off like a light switch,' he joked.

'You bet.' I laughed. 'Still employed?' I asked, preferring to shove my crap aside.

'I've forced myself to get there on time.'

'Yay buddy, I'm proud of you. So, how're things going with Ben after the photo issue?'

'Oh that.' He looked sheepish, staring down at the grimy carpet of his car.

'Instagram's the guilty party then.'

'Ben hasn't gone to Zanzibar recently, and we'll catch up later this week, so can't ask for more. Anyway, what's the plan here?'

'Let's hope the creep heads straight to Crown, like he did the other night. If you can drop me off there, that'd be fab.'

'How many nights you been staking out this joint, Sandi? Maybe you need a night off? Girls just gotta have fun you know.'

I stared at him. Clearly, he thought my life was as tragic as I did.

'My New Year's resolution exactly.' I couldn't keep the knife out of my voice.

'Whatever, girl.' He flicked shining blond hair out of his eyes.

'Who would have thought work would take over my life?' I sulked.

'The trick,' he tapped my wrist, as a piece of ham slid off the slice of pizza in his other hand, 'is to have a job that's totally superficial.'

'Another New Year's resolution. Speaking of which, there's no way I'm missing that.'

'Oh, thank God. Can't do New Year's without you. It's *tradition.*' Stew started singing the old musical number from *Fiddler on the Roof.*

Not daring to add my dodgy notes to his tuneful deep tones, my lips remained closed. Despite this, I knew heaps of scores by heart, care of my mum being a devotee and subjecting her daughters to endless musical classics, especially *The Sound of Music.* I didn't know what my bestie's excuse was, though being a dancer could account for it.

I glanced up at Ju-Long's house, lights still glowing. Maybe he was having a quiet night in watching snuff porn.

Clearing my throat, I said. 'Hey, I might need your help again in the next couple of days. Any chance?'

Stew pulled out his phone, as the upstairs of the townhouse darkened.

'Well, as long as it doesn't clash with work. A boy has to pay the rent, sweetie, though looks like you're in luck. I'm free tomorrow.'

Wearing a lime-green shirt and carrying a dark jacket, Ju-Long's frame squeezed through the front door, at the same time as a white car pulled up outside.

'We're on,' I announced.

Stewart started the engine.

As the white car did a U-turn and drove straight past us, I tugged on the brim of my baseball cap, shading my face. 'Go,' I ordered.

Stewart lurched onto the street and when I peeked from under my hat, we were up the Uber's backside.

'Shit, slow down, keep back for fuck's sake.' I slid down in the car seat.

'It's fine.' Stewart's lip pouted as he took his foot off the accelerator.

I softened my tone. 'You've got to spend more time on the foreplay, buddy.'

He sucked in his lips. 'Like you need to teach me, girl.'

Now at a safer distance behind, we followed Ju-Long's lift towards the city. Within minutes the gold letters of the "CROWN" sign appeared emblazoned on the entrance. The Uber turned into the parking area, under the dazzling archway.

'Stop here.' I ditched the baseball cap; it didn't match my high-waisted black pants and sleeveless pomegranate blouse.

'But there's no parking.'

'I'll be quick.'

The door to the Uber swung open and Ju-Long climbed out.

As I sprang out of Stew's car, I uttered, 'Thanks Stew, I'll be in touch tomorrow.'

'Let me know you're–' Stew's voice faded.

I dashed across the near empty road, skirting the low steel fence and bushy garden that bordered the footpath. Ju-Long strode into the Crown complex through revolving glass doors and entered the casino, with me on his tail.

Inside, my senses were assaulted. The carpet was a swirl of clashing colours: cacky orange collided with psychedelic purple. Hundreds of pokie machines emitted flashing images, entranced punters glued to them. Mechanical sound bites, pings and clicks competed with sixties music blasting from above.

I scanned ahead but could no longer see Ju-Long. Shit, how could I have lost my quarry? Speed walking between the rows of gaming machines, I narrowly avoided collecting an elderly woman steadying herself on her walker. Still no sight of Ju-Long. I'd had this operation totally under control and now it was blown in a moment of distraction.

Hurrying past five-dollar roulette tables to the sound of rubbers flapping, I glimpsed a lime-green shirt as its owner veered off into a separate room to the side. I reached the entranceway in time to see Ju-Long scanning the clientele. As his gaze fired my way, I slipped behind the wall, my heart pumping. I waited a few seconds, and, with no hulk appearing to pummel me, poked my nose around the corner.

Crammed with patrons, a quiet intensity charged the room. Closest to me, eight gamblers perched on cream chairs, with a row of eager onlookers hovering behind them. A new betting round began, and I was gobsmacked when the woman nearest me, her jasmine scented perfume wafting my way, extracted a wad of hundred-dollar bills from her gold crystal purse, exchanging the cash for orange-and-black tokens.

Ju-Long had joined a table on the far side of the room, blue chips stacked in front of him. When the dealer swept everyone's bets away, Ju-Long scanned the room and I positioned myself behind the onlookers nearby until he refocused on the dealer's cards.

A grey-haired man appeared behind Ju-Long, his turkey neck wobbling as he moved his lips. Ju-Long leaped to his feet, indicating for the older man to take his seat and stood behind him, leaning over to talk. After edging a bit closer, I discretely produced my mobile and with my phone at waist height, snapped photos of them.

An attendant, whose boy-like face, baby blue eyes and chubby cheeks made it hard to tell his age approached Ju-Long, spoke to him and pointed towards the ceiling. He nodded at Ju-Long's reply.

As the attendant strolled away, I intercepted. 'Excuse me, can you tell me what this game is?'

'Baccarat.' He smiled, exposing large glossy teeth.

He explained the rules and I let his cheery voice float over me, while studying Ju-Long and his companion.

'Wow, thanks for your clear explanation. How much are the blue chips worth?

'$500.'

'Does it go higher?'

'Up to $10,000, down here.'

'This looks more like my scene rather than the budget blackjack tables out in the corridor. I just received a massive bonus so I'm ready to splash.'

'Would you like to join a table?'

'I actually had my heart set on the Mahogany room. I've heard it's like a six-star resort and you can bet as much as you want.'

'Up to $300,000. Are you a Crown rewards member?'

I shook my head.

'Well, it might take a little while to build up enough points to achieve the platinum membership needed, unless of course you accompany someone.'

'Happen to know anyone who might be heading in that direction tonight?'

'Well I'm afraid I can't really help you there.' His mock serious expression matched my tone.

'Outside the PD? I'd be betting those guys over there are members.' I nodded discretely towards Ju-Long's table. 'They've been betting a packet. Regulars?' .

He glanced in the opposite direction.

'I'll assume that's a yes,' I said.

'I haven't said a word, but would you like to join that table?' he asked.

'Might just watch a little longer before making my move. Thanks for all your help.'

The attendant moved on to help an elderly man carrying a tray of drinks as my attention returned to Ju-Long. He'd taken up a vacated seat next to his associate and the dealer was sweeping up another pile of his blue chips. The older man raised his over-sized phone to his ear and abandoned the table. Ju-Long calmly finished his hand and collected his remaining chips before joining him. I stepped back to my spot at the entrance to the room, where I had an accessible escape route.

They headed my way and I fast tracked out of the Baccarat room towards a game of blackjack, slipping behind the suited card dealer, his gold tie glinting under the lights.

I half expected Ju-Long to head back towards the casino entrance where Stewart had dropped me off, but instead, he and his companion headed in the opposite direction.

They exited the casino into an adjoining foyer featuring a palatial staircase and cascading waterfall. Spurts of water accompanied dramatic piped music. The two men entered the Crown Towers hotel on the other side of the foyer, with me following at a distance.

Suddenly Ju-Long spun around and stormed towards me. His dark narrow eyes were fixed on mine. I was caught in the middle of the foyer with no cover. Trying to seem unfazed, I fled behind the nearest black marble column. Of course, he'd recognised me from Club 96, idiot that I was, risking it again. His massive build was intimidating despite my five years of aikido.

I slid around the column away from his trajectory, my palms cold against the rock, my heart pounding. *Calm down*, I yelled silently. What would he do to me in public?

Straightening, I readied myself.

Ju-Long strode straight past my hiding place, back towards the casino. Perhaps he hadn't noticed me at all. A long sigh released the tightness in my chest.

It felt too risky to follow him. As Ju-Long was lost from view, I rounded the column to observe his grey-haired companion shaking hands with two other men.

Not being one to call it quits while I still had my body in one piece, I took out my phone, with still jittery fingers and zoomed in. One of the new men had his back to me, which was annoying, but I took the photo anyway.

Slipping the phone away, I spotted Ju-Long's spiky black hair, his jacket draped over his arm. I flattened myself against the dark marble.

Ju-Long joined the others and they edged deeper into the hotel lobby. The busy reception area provided cover as I darted around suitcases in pursuit. Spotting a sign to the VIP gaming room, I was surprised when they didn't head up in the lift. Instead they meandered outside and piled into a waiting taxi. I rushed outside, deciding to follow, but was thwarted by an empty taxi rank.

Frustrated, I retraced my steps out through the casino and with the promise of Stewart's help, plotted my next move.

26

INVADING SOMEONE'S LIFE IS SIMPLE. GPS TRACKERS, LISTENING DEVICES and hidden cameras are all purchasable online or in spyware shops, all legal to buy and easy to use.

The main customers for this gear are men. I know because I'd researched it earlier in the year, to assist a client with gathering evidence about her ex-husband breaching his Intervention Order. He'd used any means possible to track her down, including installing tracking software on his daughter's mobile. An IT degree was needed to escape family violence these days.

Usually I bought spy gear online, but this time it couldn't wait. Over breakfast, I checked out spy-shop websites, before driving to Brunswick.

To avoid the congested Sydney Road, I parked around the corner next to the library and strode along the footpath, spotting a freshly taped bunch of flowers on a pole outside Brunswick Baths: a tribute to someone who'd recently become part of the road tally. Cyclists dashed past, risking their lives in the jungle of trucks and speeding cars. As I crossed the road, a combination of young mums out for brunch and older folk lugging ALDI's shopping bags accompanied me. Greek music blasted from an old Valiant, stationary at the traffic lights.

Smart Spy's bright blue and green signs stood out from across the street. The shop was bang up against a bluestone church whose banner across the entrance welcomed asylum seekers and refugees. Even the churches in alternative Brunswick fought for the under-dog.

Inside the spy shop, the set-up was sparse, with locked glass cabinets lining the outside of the room. Behind the glass, small laminated signs explaining their purpose were sticky-taped to intriguing devices like telescopes sporting smartphone viewing attachments and hidden bug detectors.

The assistant behind the counter, a clean-shaven redhead, didn't let me browse for long, with a 'Know what you're looking for?' gruff demand accompanied by a massive sniffing episode.

'I'll let you know if I have questions,' I told him.

After a quick browse I requested a GPS tracker. The silent shop assistant extracted a small silver key from below the counter, unlocked the cabinet, retrieved the item, and placed it on the counter. With each new purchase, he repeated the same process.

I pointed to a listening device. 'I'm presuming this can be dialled into remotely?'

'All the information's on the packet,' he grunted.

Luckily an internet search provided the answer. The assistant ground his teeth as he waited for me to confirm my choice.

The pile of gear on the counter grew. It was expensive, but the Fair Sex Coalition's final payment had come through, enabling me to fund it up front.

As I tapped my credit card, I asked, 'Is your lack of assistance company policy or do you gift all your female customers the special silent treatment?'

My remark was met with a scowl.

I returned to my car, stowed the gear in the boot and called Maria. When I explained that Ricardo's case had led to some intriguing connections, she gushed, 'Fantastic work, *bella*. Got time to go to Flagstaff Gardens to fill me in? I need some fresh air.'

Fresh air was overstating it, but the gardens were green and tranquil. We agreed to meet outside her office block.

I drove down the wide and leafy Royal Parade and parked in my usual city spot – the Queen Vic Market. It was open, so finding a car spot was trickier than the last time.

When I finally arrived outside her office block, I texted Maria. She soon joined me, linking her arm through mine. With Maria squeezing my forearm and me shortening my stride to accommodate hers, we strolled to the nearby gardens.

When we entered the park, the noise of the traffic faded, pigeons purred and majestic Moreton Bay fig trees replaced skyscrapers.

Maria chose a shady bench under a giant elm, the tree's trunk dressed in a grey skirt to deter possums.

My friend's eyes looked haggard. She dropped onto the bench, collapsing against its curved wooden back and flipped off her high heels. 'Phew, I needed a breather. I've been on the phone all morning. My head is a sack of straw.'

As she drew breath, Maria's breasts rose and fell beneath her V-necked teal dress.

'That job is a parasite,' I said. 'The creepy sort that you only notice once it's taken over your body.'

Maria chuckled and stared skywards, where jagged green leaves created a canopy. I waited for her to initiate the conversation. She needed a moment of peace.

A few minutes later, she sat up straight. 'Intriguing connections?'

'I've discovered that as well as his job at Club 96, Ju-Long Wang is the driver for other brothels, including Amsterdam Angels. That's where Jae Shin, the South Korean woman, was trapped as a sex slave. And it seems the woman Ricardo's accused of murdering, Lee Wu, was also trafficked.'

'Whoa. Hold on. How do you know?' asked Maria.

'Did you read the texts from Lee?'

'No time,' she replied. 'I'll be lucky to have Christmas lunch with my family at the rate work's going. I know I suggested we catch up soon, but that might have to wait until the new year. Sorry *bella*.'

It was nothing new, but I'd been looking forward to it. Shrugging away disappointment, I filled her in on the OPP's information and showed her Lee's texts and the translated poem on my iPhone.

'Wow, that poem's a find,' said Maria. 'The police missed it?'

'Apparently. What do you make of it?' Worried that my reaction to Ricardo had clouded my judgement, I wanted an unbiased opinion.

'It seems Lee knew she was going to die.'

'It sounds like someone who's been subjected to torture.'

Maria nodded her agreement.

'I guess it's possible Lee could have suicided,' I hypothesised, 'or Ju-Long could have knocked her off, though I imagine he'd want to protect his assets. From what Jae says, Ju-Long's the head honcho of the whole operation. He's making a packet. Last night I reckon he gambled away $50,000.'

'Money laundering?' queried Maria.

'At Crown?'

Maria performed a juggling action with her hands, as she weighed up the possibility.

'On another note,' I added, 'Ricardo was definitely caught up with his drug-dealing cousins and that seems to be connected to his fiancée's disappearance.'

'We can't muddy the pond by focusing on Valentina.'

I smiled at her turn of phrase. 'I get that, except it's linked I'm sure.'

'What does Ricardo say?'

'He won't share.'

'Do you need to go back to remand?'

The thought of returning was like an anchor attached to my waist. 'Yeah, I should. Each time I get a step further, he retreats into his burrow.'

'You're making progress. We have the ingredients for a defence case now,' said Maria. 'Although the implication that Lee was a sex slave is only speculation at the moment, the texts and voice mail add to the weight of evidence that she viewed Ricardo as someone she trusted, not someone she feared.'

'True,' I replied. 'But it's not enough is it? I'm going to see what else I can find out about Ju-Long.'

'How?' asked Maria.

I was caught in a bind about how to answer. 'Well.' I brushed away leaves from the bench.

'Don't you dare.' Maria's voice was sharp. 'If you go interfering with a witness, that would compromise the whole case.'

Shit. The tone of my voice must have given it away. I should have been guarded; I'd become too caught up in the chase. 'I've done nothing Maria, I swear. Don't worry, I won't do anything to compromise the case.'

There had been another job I'd worked on for Maria, investigating a guy suspected of insurance fraud, only I didn't cover my tracks well enough after breaking into his house. That was early on in my career. There was no way I'd stuff up like that again.

'Seriously.' Her upper lip raised like a dog's snarl.

I lifted my hands in a "surrender" movement.

'Promise.'

I crossed my heart.

Maria squeezed her lips together and I could tell she reluctantly accepted my assurance.

A woman with a walking stick and a cloth bag shuffled along the path. She took out half a loaf of sliced white bread from a paper bag and scattered it onto the grass. Within seconds a flock of seagulls congregated, squawking and flapping their wings in a noisy squabble. Our peaceful break evaporated.

Maria checked her watch and pulled on her high heels. 'Better head back.'

As we fast-tracked back to her office, I asked, 'How's Kristin?'

Maria blushed and flourished her arms like she had an announcement. 'It's not just about my family. Kristin and I have thought long and hard. Now there's the option.' Her voice sounded more strained than usual.

A group of rowdy business men headed towards us, their laughter like a dawn alarm. Maria and I were forced to walk single file as they dominated the pavement, ignoring our presence. I considered having a go at them but was focused on what Maria was about to disclose.

Once they'd passed, Maria spluttered, 'We're going to get married. We want to cement our relationship and if we become wife and wife, our parents will be more accepting.'

A cyclone of emotions twisted my gut. 'Well, congratulations, Maria.' My voice sounded unsteady.

Maria beamed. 'Will you be my bridesmaid, *bella*? It would mean so much to me.'

This news was the clincher. Maria had found her life partner. Her whole adult life had been such a clear trajectory: finish a degree, land a lucrative job, get married. The cost of the bridesmaid's dress was a minor issue.

'Sure,' I reluctantly agreed.

She kissed me on both cheeks and trotted inside her office block.

The idea of returning to my flat grated. I was desperate to swim long and hard and decided to head to the beach. Swinging past home, I changed into my bathers. My car chugged, almost on automatic, under the West Gate Bridge towards Williamstown and after parking on the near empty esplanade, I hurdled over the bluestone wall and sprinted across yellow sand, dropping my beach towel and T-shirt on a dry patch.

The water was cold as usual. After a few minutes my body adjusted. The sea was calm and as I backstroked away from shore, white clouds eased along baby blue sky.

With the arm technique I taught the kids – reach, roll and relax – I spun over and freestyled out deeper. Stupidly, tears welled up as I propelled through the water back to shore.

'Hey, get a grip,' I ordered myself.

I knew just the antidote.

27

I HEADED TO BUSHY BULLEEN, A HOP, SKIP AND JUMP FROM WHERE I USED to live in Thornbury. Driving through the congested city and along the Eastern Freeway was uninspiring, until I turned off at Bulleen Road where parks replaced concrete. Staring at a gumtree forest lining the road, I passed Yarra parklands where the Heide gallery lay hidden.

I turned into Sheahans Road Reserve and took a spot in the near-empty car park. As soon as I entered the red-brick stadium, my feet lightened.

The squeak of rubber and the pound of the ball were like a familiar song, the odour of hard-yakka sweat almost sweet. Red lights announced the Space Jammers were trailing by four points. If I'd had my basketball uniform with me, I'd have slipped it on and lined up on the bench, hoping the coach, herself a former Space Jammer with a knack for darting between opponents' legs to score goals, would have forgotten my two-year absence.

I edged around the outside of the court to join a handful of onlookers, positioning myself on a hard-wooden bench, in front of the twenty-metre poster of Michele Timms, Bulleen's pin-up girl.

The ball was lobbed to my cop mate Alice, her pink number fifteen bold against the black uniform. She nimbly caught it, and in the same movement dribbled the ball towards the goal, where two defenders blocked her progress. Alice tried barging through, but was bumped hard and tumbled, rolling lightly on the floor, before bouncing back upright. The pre-pubescent looking referee signalled the foul. Alice positioned herself at the penalty shoot-out line. She scored and I whistled. She landed the second penalty with ease.

After the game, Alice settled next to me and dabbed her pink cheeks with a towel. She'd hardly broken into a sweat, fit beast that she was.

'Good game,' I said, 'Except you lost.'

She dragged out a hair tie and shook free her shoulder length blonde hair. 'Get back on the team, or tuck your head in,' she laughed. 'Seriously, when are you coming back to basketball Sandi? We miss your height.'

Alice was a centimetre shorter than me and a better goalie.

'As soon as I get my life under control.'

She folded her towel neatly and packed it into her unbranded sports bag. 'I'm starving. Time for some junk food?'

We bought a meat pie from the kiosk and sat on metal chairs at a table in the foyer, furthest away from the attendant. The scent of warm pastry made me salivate even before I tore the plastic off.

'How was Sydney?' I asked.

'All play and no responsibility. Perfect weather for swimming. Back into the thick of it now. What mischief you into?'

Once I'd licked tomato sauce from my fingers, I filled her in on recent events: staking out brothels, rescuing Jae, reconnecting with Cassy. Well, I didn't say too much about my ex-girlfriend. Alice shook her head in disbelief, or maybe it was the predictability of my life she was commenting on.

I showed her the photos of Qiao, Ju-Long/Tuffy, and his mates at the casino.

'Sounds like this is more of a syndicate than most of the illegal brothel arrangements. Not that I know huge amounts, just what you overhear in the mess room. Not all traffickers are physically violent either, but when they are, women are more likely to run – like yours.'

She stood and stretched her calves against the wall.

'If you're onto something, well, the Feds may already be investigating, and not have any proof. Be interested to hear what you find out.'

'Hey, I thought you were getting info for me.'

She flicked her legs one at a time, before dropping back next to me. 'Bit of give and take won't go astray,' she laughed.

'I got some goss on the guy you're investigating,' she lowered her voice. 'Sounds like Ricardo Lopez is strongly suspected of drug dealing and murdering his fiancée, but there isn't enough direct evidence to charge him. The investigating officers have been looking for other ways to convict him, so the murder of the sex worker was perfect. They haven't been able to find anything else even though they've kept a close eye on him for the past eighteen months. He hasn't even copped a speeding fine or a drink driving offence. Made the officers involved mighty frustrated. Not now though. They're rapt he's been arrested for murder. That would trump drug trafficking, as long as he gets convicted. A conviction does sound pretty likely given all the evidence.'

'What about his cousins? Heard anything about them?'

'Seems his cousin Santo Perez is the brains behind the operation. He's had no convictions against him. But he's been connected to drug importation, not just dealing.'

She nudged me with her elbow. 'As usual, not a whisper outside this hallowed turf.'

I saluted her and when she frowned, reassured her, 'Don't worry Alice, my lips are eternally sealed. Hey, one more thing, a friend of Ricardo's fiancée said Valentina witnessed something that made her scared about her own safety.'

Alice shrugged. 'Wouldn't surprise me. You don't get involved in that sort of business without violence being part of the deal. I haven't heard anything that links that intel though.'

With her grey bag slung over her shoulder, Alice spun me around to face her. Her blue eyes were fierce and her usually bubbly voice terse. 'Hey, stay out of trouble girl. You're dealing with some nasty pieces of work here. You should think about becoming a police member. Regular work, decent pay, and protection.'

I rolled my eyes. 'Can you see me bowing down to the hierarchy?'

Alice guffawed. 'That's true, no hope for you. But if you're going to shut these guys down, you need more than a Jessica Jones routine.'

Problem was, that was exactly my plan, without the superpowers.

28

THE GUM TREE ABOVE ME SHUDDERED AS THE NORTHERLY WIND WHIPPED through its branches. After turning on the tracking device, I dropped to the bitumen behind the back-bumper bar of Ju-Long's Mercedes. Torchlight showed the best position to attach the device, away from the exhaust pipe. The magnet on the underside of the tracker gripped the metal with a click.

I sprang to my feet and entered the small front yard of the townhouse. The streetlight provided sufficient light and a bottlebrush kept me relatively hidden. Outside the grey front door, I crouched at eye level with the door handle.

Lock picking is usually quick – the handful of times I've done it for real – but the pins in this keyhole were obstinate. I changed to a curved pick and reset the wrench. My right hand began to cramp. My fingers weren't designed for such fine work.

When I eyeballed Stewart across the road in his car, he waved. Apart from my accomplice, the suburban street was empty, the hotel opposite once again closed for the night. I took a deep breath, flicked my hands to relax them and tried again.

A series of faint clicks signalled success. I twisted the wrench and the door popped open. To ensure the break-in was undetectable, I returned the lock to its normal position.

Flicking on my torch, I checked for an alarm in the hallway. Surprisingly, nothing. Was Ju-Long so blasé? The room to my left was full of gym equipment: a bench press, treadmill and dumbbells. Further down the corridor lay a laundry.

After slipping on gloves and closing the front door, I stole up the stairs. My torch highlighted sections of an open-plan living area. I scanned for a security system, but there was still nothing obvious. A flat screen covered a third of one wall and three white leather couches created a TV-room divider.

As I ran my hand along the island bench in the kitchen area, the stone's coolness seeped through my kid gloves. The bench and stainless-steel cooktop were shiny and spotless. Either Ju-Long Wang had a house cleaner or he didn't cook much. I doubted he spent his free time sponging and polishing.

Opening the stainless-steel fridge out of curiosity, a putrid stench emanated. Plastic takeaway containers with rice and meat occupied the bottom shelves, some definitely outstaying their welcome. The top shelf was packed with tins of Red Bull and Coke. I eased the fridge door shut.

In one corner of the living room, snug up against the balcony window, a desktop computer reflected my torchlight. After unplugging the computer cords, I stowed Ju-Long's white power board in my backpack and replaced it with another, the same colour but a different design. Hopefully, Ju-Long wasn't a fine detail sort of a bloke.

My mobile indicated I'd been there five minutes. It felt like hours. As there was no word from Stewart, I headed up the stairs to the third storey comprising a bedroom and ensuite. After a quick look around, I slid open the doors to the half-empty built-in robes. Suits of different shades of black and grey hung neatly alongside plain shirts, covering off on primary and secondary colours. Two black suitcases were stacked up the top of the wardrobe. Standing on my toes, I slid them out one a time. Both were light. I dropped them quietly onto the carpet and swept the torchlight under their covers – both were empty. I sprang up and positioned them back exactly as they had been. Surprisingly, the room lacked any other personal items.

My next step was to check power points. One was perfectly situated beneath the unmade king-sized bed. I crawled under it and replaced the existing double adaptor.

Off to the side of the bedroom, a glary white ensuite contained the basics for washing and shaving. The lid to a bottle of Barbasol unscrewed easily. The smell was a match for the sickly-sweet aftershave that had revolted me at the fibro brothel. The only item in the cabinet drawers was a packet of Valium. Was that for him or his prisoners?

Downstairs in the living room, I took a seat in Ju-Long's executive office chair in front of the monitor. Floor-to-ceiling windows provided a mesmerising view, past the balcony, of city skyscrapers.

Dragging my attention back to my task, I unzipped my jacket pocket and extracted a USB. This could provide the answers to the questions sizzling in my mind. I pressed the computer start-up button and simultaneously inserted the USB. Even though it was expected, the start-up tune made me jump. So many outcomes were riding on the success of this operation, not least the safety of Stewart and my butts.

In a few moments, thanks to the boot-up program, I invaded Ju-Long's life in a parallel profile. All his document folders appeared on the screen.

First, I conducted a jpeg search. Thousands of them showed that Ju-Long was either a prolific photographer, or a photo librarian. I reduced them to thumbnail images and had a quick squiz. Madam Qiao Zeng and other women at the brothel appeared in endless erotic positions. I recognised Lee Wu, now deceased, in a particularly compromising pose. It wasn't an image her mother would treasure.

Other photos featured Alistair Payne, who Qiao had been chummy with at the mansion in Ivanhoe. I was surprised to find wedding photos of Qiao in a lavish white dress with a suave looking Alistair. Somehow, I'd pictured her as a courtesan, rather than Alistair's "lawfully wedded wife".

In another series of shots, all the motley crew, including Skull aka Thumper, were captured dining at a Chinese restaurant cheerily eating Peking Duck.

Other photos of Ju-Long and Qiao were dated two years ago, one taken outside a business. I zoomed in and read the sign "Sugar & Spice Club". A swift internet search on my mobile revealed it was a brothel in New South Wales.

My skin became clammy. Ju-Long and Qiao had been associates for years. How many illegal brothels had they operated together? How did they know each other? Had they crossed state borders to establish more brothels?

The fact that Qiao was integral to the whole scheme made me cringe. She'd seemed to care. This whole network wasn't a figment of my imagination. The syndicate was real and I'd broken into the head honcho's house. Shit, I was still there.

Resisting the urge to flee Ju-Long's house instantly, I saved albums onto the USB. I glanced towards the staircase, hoping like hell Ju-Long's massive frame would be absent. Before leaving, there was one more search I was desperate to complete.

As I closed down the jpegs, there was a vibration in my pocket. My hand shook as I extracted my mobile and leaped to my feet. I was praying Stewart had rung in plenty of time.

Maria's image lit up on my mobile. Why would she be ringing after midnight? Maybe she'd found out my location, or else she was in strife.

'Hello,' I whispered.

'Did I wake you?' Her voice boomed in the quiet house.

I reduced the volume. 'All good. What's up?'

As I turned back to the screen, a couple of thousand documents appeared. Leaning over the desk chair, I spun through the titles, my fingers trembling.

'Kristin and I can't sleep. We've been planning and wanted your opinion.'

One PDF with a series of numbers appeared on the screen – exactly the evidence needed.

'Yep,' I filled in quietly.

'We think violet and lilac. Lilac for you.'

'Lilac,' I repeated blankly.

'Are you okay?'

'Fine.' I wondered what the hell I could say to her. 'A bit preoccupied.'

'Are you with someone?'

I almost said yes, except she would have bombarded me with questions.

My mind suddenly twigged. 'Lilac's great. I'm exhausted. Can we talk later?' I feigned a yawn.

'Sure, lilac it is.'

Thank God, Maria was so focused on her wedding, otherwise I could have wound up in confession.

Quickly sorting the PDFs by name, I saved the numbered ones as sweat gathered on my upper lip.

A chugging noise made me jolt. The fridge downstairs perhaps? My nerves jangled. Time to skedaddle.

I ejected the disk and drew out the silver USB. As I shut down the computer, the USB slipped out of my fingers. I dropped to the floor and crawled around the thick carpet, shining the torch frantically.

Finally, it appeared under the computer table and I shoved it into my jacket pocket. Inside my gloves, my palms sweated. With my backpack on my back, I sprinted down the stairs and dived towards the front door.

I was about to turn the lock, when voices slithered through the door. Male voices. Chinese tones. My throat tightened. I quickly tiptoed in the opposite direction. Although my head was screaming at me to fly outside, I edged the back door ajar. Stepping onto the patio, I scanned for options.

What looked like a trellis at the back of Ju-Long's property offered the best hope. I tried to calm the pumping in my ears and strained to listen to what was happening out the front. A banging noise got me moving.

After pulling the back door shut, I sprinted over the patio and through the small back garden. My pocket vibrated. *Too bloody late, Stewart.* With a leap, I hoisted myself onto the thick vines creeping up the fence. My foot sunk as a branch snapped under my weight. I reached through the vines and grabbed hold of the top of the fence and shoved my right foot onto the horizontal beam. With that foothold I managed to pull myself up and hold onto the top of the trellis. It was lucky that Ju-Long's neighbours seemed to be asleep, but a bummer no lights guided my way.

The glow of a waning moon marked a rectangular shape below. It wasn't clear if it was a barbeque or a table. I shuffled to the right where the ground looked clear. Swinging my leg over the trellis, I balanced awkwardly on the top, before the woodwork began tilting towards the neighbour's house. Time to leap. I dropped onto what I hoped was grass.

Concrete jarred my knee joints as I fell onto my hands with a thump. Even aikido black belts don't train to fall from that height onto concrete. Pain shot from my left foot up to my groin. Surely, I'd torn or broken something. I managed to push myself upright and straighten my leg. Despite a niggle in my knee, it seemed alright.

Before working out my escape route, I paused to listen. Leaves swirled, the north wind had picked up again, but no voices emerged. Inside my gear, it had become a sauna.

I extracted my torch and checked either side of Ju-Long's neighbour's garden.

A side gate gave me an instant of relief, until torchlight lit up a padlock and wrought-iron spikes. Would I have to unpick another lock to escape? Before taking out my tools, I jiggled the bolt. It slipped under the inadequate padlock.

I jogged around the block, and spotted Stewart's car. Opposite him, Ju-Long's house stood in darkness.

After sprinting across the road, I jerked Stewart's car door open and stuck my head in. 'What the hell.'

Stewart did a double take as I pounced into the passenger seat and yanked the seatbelt across my chest.

'Did you read my text?' he jabbed at me.

'I was a tad preoccupied trying to avoid a head injury as I dropped from great heights.'

He bit his lip.

'*What did it say?*' I emphasised each word.

'I don't think it was Ju-Long,' Stewart edged away from me.

'What?'

'These two guys rocked up in a car. They looked older than the guy you showed me. They went to Ju-Long's door; that's when I texted. But then they drove off.'

Resisting an urge to strangle Stewart, I squeezed my mobile between my shaking hands while reading his text. It would have been a good idea to stop and read it earlier, but by the time it was safe, I was already stranded in the middle of suburban backyards.

'You okay?' asked Stewart.

'Just drive, will you?'

Stewart glared at me.

I jabbed at the road with my forefinger. 'Come on. Get fucking going, you moron!'

Stewart revved the accelerator. 'You can forget having a sidekick next time.'

He pulled out and sped down the street. We turned into the main road and I breathed again.

'Not even a "thank you".'

We cruised over the West Gate Bridge, the lights of the wharves innocently shining. Even though logically it was obvious I was safe now, deep breaths did nothing to calm my jittery heart. I needed to apologise to Stew, but the words eluded me.

We travelled the rest of the way over the bridge in silence. Stewart's hands kept moving, as he fiddled with the window, tapped the steering wheel and scratched his head. The noise and the movement drove me crazy.

As soon as we were off the freeway, an uncontrollable urge to get out of the car consumed me. When we stopped at a red light, I grabbed my backpack and jumped out.

'Thanks, I'll get home from here. See you later.'

Stewart leaned across the passenger seat as I slammed the car door. 'What the hell.'

The lights changed and he took off. I stomped up the road. It was dark, ugly and stank of diesel. Still, the physical movement was an antidote to the pent-up energy. After walking a few blocks, I noticed a white Holden ahead. Zipping down a side street to avoid him was an option, but when I arrived at the car, the adrenaline had dissipated and been replaced with guilt.

Stewart opened his eyes wide as I poked my head in through his window.

'Get your arse in this car!' He had his arms crossed. 'What the hell were you doing?'

'Sorry Stew. It's a long story.'

His mouth was unforgiving.

'What about a beer?' I suggested.

'At this hour?' His voice smarted.

'There's a bottle-o in West Footscray.'

We took a detour and I paid for a six-pack. When Stewart offered me half, I refused.

In the safety of my home, after changing into shorts and a T-shirt, I sank onto the couch. Stewart already had his beer open. I snapped the lid off mine, downed half the tin and began to calm down.

I told Stewart about the photos and connections, then how I'd freaked, thinking it was Ju-Long outside.

My buddy's face morphed from sullen to sympathetic. 'God, Sandi, hand it over to the cops.'

'Totally, as soon as I sort the evidence.'

'You really are completely insane and a stupid fucking reckless bitch.'

I laughed. 'Not sure about the "reckless", but I'll cop the rest.'

He tried to hide it, but a smirk lifted his lip.

'We good?' I eased my arm across his shoulder.

'Don't do it again,' Stew insisted.

I nodded. 'Hey, let's see what he's up to.'

When I rang in to the listening devices, there was silence from the lounge room and snoring from the bedroom. Ju-Long obviously slept without a guilty conscience.

Stewart's mouth dropped open as we listened in. When I hung up, he burst out laughing.

'Can I borrow that accessory next time Ben visits a nightclub? That is the solution.'

I clicked my tongue. 'You might be better off not knowing.'

'Oh my God, look at your hands Sandi.'

My palms and fingers were covered in bloody scratches, so I grabbed some antiseptic and Band-Aids. Once my hands were covered in pink strips, I started up my laptop and inserted the USB.

As Stewart petted Flicker, I opened up the PDF bank account statements. Huge amounts of money were being deposited and withdrawn with Crown Casino being the main recipient of his fortune. Small cash deposits were also being made. Had Maria been right about money laundering? It wouldn't have been surprising given Ju-Long's business. From the evidence in front of me, he was spending more than he earned. Regular overdrawn fees were charged to his account. It seemed to me that he had an out of control gambling habit.

'Hey Stew, were these the men at Ju-Long's door?'

I showed him the photos of Ju-Long's casino associates.

'Maybe. It was a bit dark.' Stew yawned.

'Won't be much longer.'

I searched the ABN website and checked out the proprietor of Club 96. Ju-Long and Qiao weren't listed, but it was mighty close. Qiao's husband, Alistair Payne.

Further research on that website showed Alistair was also the manager of Amsterdam Angels and the Port Melbourne brothel. All of these players were steeped in this illegal industry.

Next, I tried looking up the owner of the brothel in New South Wales but my eyes glazed over.

Stewart was now prone, his head resting on cushions, his eyes closed.

'You can stay here the night,' I said, 'It's too late to go home.'

I was hoping he'd agree; the expedition to Ju-Long's had left me jumpy.

Stewart nodded. 'Yeah, may as well crash here.'

He dragged himself into my bed, while I fed Flicker and turned the lights off.

I should have counted my lucky stars for Stewart's friendship. He'd been there for me even when I'd treated him like a bag of manure. Crawling in next to him, I crashed into sleep before even counting.

29

THE INTEL-GATHERING ESCAPADE AT JU-LONG'S HAD TAKEN ITS TOLL ON MY body and mind. After a leisurely breakfast with Stewart, I allowed myself a day free of PI work, with swimming classes, shopping and aikido my only outings. I felt like a normal person, except for nagging questions about the manager of a string of brothels, the elusive Alistair Payne.

Early the following day, I filled my car with petrol and crossed town to Ivanhoe. Wattlebirds and lorikeets racketed in the bush-lined street as I parked diagonally opposite Qiao Zeng and Alistair's modern mansion.

A couple of hours later, after other households had sped off to school and work, Alistair emerged. Dressed in a black satin dressing gown, he jaunted down the external stairs. Despite a receding hairline, he was good-looking in blokeish way, his clean-shaven face and high cheekbones creating a movie-star quality. Qiao followed behind, dressed in a knee-length red dress with a thigh split that accentuated her slim figure. With letters in one hand, Alistair drew Qiao close to him, running his hand down her spine and backside. He grinned and his whole face beamed. I imagined he had a lot to be happy about, with a business as profitable as his.

They chatted, but despite craning my neck, I missed what they said. Something funny, as Alistair's raucous laughter outdid the lorikeets.

I slid down my seat as Qiao backed the SUV out of the garage, the automatic door descending behind her.

My spirits flagged as Alistair bounded up the steps and disappeared inside. I considered breaking into their garage to install a GPS tracker. Recklessness threatened to take over my logic. Giving myself a lecture about safety and covert choices, I managed to heed my own advice for once and stay put. I hoped Alistair would do more than spend all day catching up on paperwork or whatever he might fancy doing behind bluestone feature walls.

My bum was numb and my back aching from poor car posture when Alistair jogged down the stairs. The garage door crept upwards and a red Jaguar, with Alistair inside, surfed around the windy road.

We drove in the direction of Amsterdam Angels. I wondered why I'd never glimpsed Alistair at any of the brothels he owned. I'd spent more time there than he had. Instead of going to the Richmond brothel as I'd anticipated, he turned into the nearby factory outlet mecca of Bridge Road where cafés and restaurants hummed and the town hall clock tower glowed.

Alistair parked in the only vacant spot on the street and dropped some coins in the meter. As I double parked behind him, he ambled up the road and into a café. I nabbed a free two-hour spot around the corner, before racing back to the main road.

When I arrived outside the café, I glanced through tinted windows and spotted Alistair with his back to me. His companion was a bald guy with a greying moustache and beard, who shovelled down chips in between gulping white wine. My mind raced with possible associations of these men. I grabbed the one spare table out the front, under an umbrella.

When a waiter appeared beside me, I ordered a takeaway latte.

The bald guy adjusted his glasses and wagged his finger at Alistair. There was something routine about their conversation – familiar but not comfortable.

Alistair stuck his hand down behind him, as if his bum was itchy or he was reaching into a back pocket. He extracted a fat wallet. Once he had it in front of him, his body blocked my vision. When he'd finished, the wallet slipped back into his pocket.

The waiter brought my coffee and I handed over the exact cash.

Alistair pushed his chair back; I thought he was about to get up, but then the other guy held up a finger, signalling he had more to say.

A minute later, the bald guy stood up unsteadily. Latte in hand, I tootled off in the opposite direction from Alistair's car, past beauty salons and overflowing restaurants. If I'd had time and money, I could have zipped up the other end of Bridge Road and picked up a pair of desperately needed new jeans, but the question on my mind was who next to follow.

Alistair emerged with a broad smile. He made way for a woman with a pram with a flourish of his arm, before he sailed towards his car. It was too late to follow him. The bald guy stumbled onto the pavement and pressed the button at the pedestrian crossing. He jolted onto the road when the lights turned green. As he headed for the tram stop, I wondered if he was drunk.

I dashed across the road as a tram ground to a halt. The old guy hoisted himself up the front steps and I jumped inside through the middle door. When he chose a seat, I positioned myself behind him. He studied the contents of his wallet as we trundled towards the CBD and passed incongruous palms in the otherwise European tree laden Fitzroy Gardens.

When we arrived at Exhibition Street, my target disembarked. I hopped off the tram on his heels, a wallop of a boiling northerly wind slamming into my face. The temperature must have hit the thirties and the concrete and bitumen radiated heat. As the sun struck my black jeans, they grew heavy and bulky. The bald guy stumbled along the footpath; I stuck to shadows of towering office blocks as we meandered north, through crowds of workers on lunch breaks.

We reached a glass panelled high-rise that glinted with sunlight. My target trudged through rotating doors into the imposing foyer of the Department of Justice and Community Safety.

'Excuse me, sir, I think this is yours.' I tapped him on the shoulder.

He twisted his torso and cocked a lip. 'Hey?'

His red nose was covered in large pimple-like protrusions. I held out a fifty-dollar note with the dour image of our first female politician.

In between his eyebrows, two vertical lines deepened. 'Sorry, love?'

'As you went through the doors, I saw you drop it.'

'You did?' he asked.

I flapped the golden $50 in front of him. 'Definitely. Must have popped out of your pocket.'

He stuck his hands in his trouser pockets, considering the possibility. I scratched my head. 'If you don't think it's yours, finders keepers hey.'

Pulling off my backpack, I scrounged around the contents as though trying to find my purse, but only came across scrunched up paper that had gathered in the base.

The guy brushed the front of his dark-brown jacket, and a

combination of crumbs and dandruff floated to the floor. 'I'm sure you're right. I did have money tucked away.' He gave a phlegmy laugh which ended in a coughing fit.

As he reached out his bloated hand, mine poised midway. I forced myself to give him the note. That give-away was going to leave me begging for donations myself, unless I landed another case soon.

I surmised he didn't want me to see the wad of money he had, because after fingering a square bulge in his jacket, he folded the $50 in half and stuffed it into his trousers pocket.

'Must have good views from your office,' I said.

'From the top floors. Not my office. I'm only on the fifth.'

His breath stunk of alcohol. The Department of Justice and Community Safety obviously expected high standards of their employees: long lunch breaks, drinking on the job, mixing with criminals.

'Secure job at least,' I said.

He nodded, his mouth downturned. 'Yeah, yeah, not too bad, love.'

He took a step backwards.

'Anne Henderson.' I clamped his hand and shook it vigorously.

He hesitated. 'Russell. Thanks. Not many'd do that.'

He tried to withdraw his crusty hand, but I held on. 'Russell Craig,' he finally admitted.

I released his hand. 'Well, hope you spend it wisely.'

He chuckled and stumbled off through the swipe card entrance to the lifts.

As I smugly retraced my steps towards the tram stop, it hit me that I'd parked in a two-hour car spot. A parking ticket was all I needed. Leaping down the street, I pushed myself through thick hot air before waiting anxiously for the next tram back to Richmond.

When I arrived at my VW and saw there was no pink slip sticky taped to my windscreen, I chuckled with relief.

Sliding into the car, I quickly turned on the ignition and air conditioner. The cool air evaporated my sweat, though my cream shirt turned tan under the armpits. Before heading back to the furnace of my flat, I searched for Department of Justice and Community Safety services then phoned their numbers systematically.

'Hi, it's Michelle Tolbert here, returning Russell Craig's call.'

When I rang Small Business Regulation, I found my man.

'I'll just see if he's available,' said the operator.
'Thanks. What's his role again?' I asked.
'He's the Coordinator of Sex Work Establishments.'
I didn't wait to find out if Russell was free.

30

RICARDO SKULKED INTO THE INTERVIEW ROOM LIKE A DEFEATED MAN. Maybe the fact that his left eye had copped a whopping shiner was the reason I'd had to wait 45 unexplained, frustrating minutes in a suffocating interview room. My doodles had become increasingly bleak, with sketches of hanged men etched into a page of my notebook.

It should have been easier to return to remand after my previous visits; instead, I sensed the seething violence beyond the Visitor's Centre walls, corrupting or smashing men, some of whom could have been salvaged. Ricardo might well have been one of them, given the chance.

Ricardo lowered himself onto the chair like an old man, suggesting his injuries were more extensive than the visible one.

'*Buenos días.*' I automatically switched to speaking Spanish. '*Trabajaste hoy?*' 'Did you work today?'

'*Es lo único que me mantiene ocupado,*' he growled. 'It's the only thing keeping me busy.'

'*Qué tipo de cosas haces allí?*' 'What sort of things do you make there?'

'*Tejados, barras. Muchas cosas.*' 'Roofs, rails. Many things.'

My Spanish was flowing. Perhaps I should have returned to Spanish school and nailed the subjunctive.

'How did you get the black eye?' I asked.

Ricardo stuck out his chest like a toreador. 'I can handle myself.'

My compassionate moment vanished. 'What happens here is your business. I want to talk to you about Petal. You and she have something in common, don't you?'

'What do you mean?' he said with hostile curiosity.

'She was a prisoner too.'

Ricardo sagged forward in his chair. The man had control over his words but not his gestures. This time the meaning was as clear as the ocean off the Whitsundays. Ricardo knew that Lee was caught up in the illegal sex industry, that she had been held against her will.

'What do you know about Ju-Long and Qiao?' I asked.

Ricardo squeezed his hands together in an effort to withhold the truth. I had a sense if I prodded, he'd succumb. He needed to confess.

'You knew Petal was unhappy.' I kept my voice mellow.

Ricardo bit his fingernail. 'I knew Tuffy was a bad boss.'

'Petal told you, that one time you went to the brothel?'

He fingered the small gold cross on his neck. 'Luz, my grandmother. They don't know. The first time I went because I was so lonely. I'd never been to a prostitute before.'

It was unbelievable that with everything Ricardo was mixed up in and accused of, he had to maintain a saint-like image with the women in his family.

'The first time I saw Petal, she was beautiful and sweet and she took away some of my pain. I couldn't bear it without Valentina.'

'Why did you give her the mobile? To keep in touch?' I asked.

'One time, I noticed bruises on her stomach. She wouldn't tell me how she got them at first. Eventually, she told me Tuffy had hit her. He made her work long hours and she only slept a few hours a night. One-time he pointed a gun at her head when she was so tired she couldn't stay awake. They made her take drugs so she could keep working. Terrible things. She was scared for her life.'

'Did she tell you she was a student?'

He stood up and circled his side of the room like a caged animal. 'She said she was tricked into coming to Australia. Her family in China were poor, so she went to work in the city. Someone there told her she could earn more money in Australia.'

I indicated the seat opposite. The last thing we needed was a guard to lob in and disrupt his confession.

He grabbed the back of the chair, then sank down. 'Petal begged me to take her away. Sometimes she slept while I was with her. I bought her a phone so she could call me if she needed help.'

Ricardo was finally on a roll. Perhaps the beating he'd been subjected to made him realise he had to cooperate.

'One morning when I was at work, I got a missed call from her. I called her back but she didn't pick up. I tried many times, but she didn't answer. I thought they might have killed her. I couldn't bear to think that she might go like Valentina. So, after work, I went to Club 96.

'I had to wait a long time before they let me into her room. Her throat was red and swollen, like someone had tried to strangle her. Petal cried without stopping. She couldn't talk for a long time, then she told me in a hoarse voice that Snow had found her mobile. Snow was a traitor, she'd told Qiao about the mobile. Snow wanted to one day take over the receptionist job, so she needed to stay on the right side of Qiao. Another time, Petal told me Qiao used to be a prostitute herself, but then she became a receptionist and married an Australian man.'

I thought about how Snow had ingratiated herself with Qiao and Ju-Long on the day I had snuck into the brothel.

'I had to help Petal. She was so sad, so scared. And Tuffy treated her like a dog. Worse than a dog.'

I was torn. I was willing to believe Ricardo had cared about Lee, but it was a stretch to believe this sullen, angry man tried to rescue her.

'Where would you have taken her?' I asked.

'I don't know. I couldn't have taken her home. A hotel maybe. All I knew was I couldn't let Tuffy murder her. That had happened to—'

'That had happened to?' I repeated.

He clamped his lips together.

I thought of Yun-seo and how she'd been savagely beaten for attempting to escape. Had Tuffy had actually murdered someone?

'Valentina,' I stated, without planning.

Ricardo's eyes bulged with horror. 'It's too dangerous for my family.'

'Did your cousins murder Valentina?'

Tears welled up in the bottom of Ricardo's eyes. He held back any noise.

'What happened?'

'I don't know. I shouldn't be telling you this. I don't know what they'll do. You have to make sure Luz and her children are safe.' He took a deep breath. 'More than a year ago, Valentina and I went out for a coffee with two of my cousins, Carlos and Diego. We were driving home, having fun. Valentina and I were in the back seat of Diego's Holden Malibu. At the traffic lights, Carlos – he is a daredevil *and* violent – saw a dealer who hadn't paid up. Carlos jumped out of the car and chased the man down a lane.

'When Carlos came back, he had blood all over his hands and T-shirt. The next day the dead man's photo was in the paper. Carlos must have stabbed him. I knew. And Valentina knew too.'

Ricardo cradled his forehead in his hands. 'Diego was furious. He always covered for his younger brother, cleaned up his mistakes. It was only because he was the youngest that Carlos got away with that sort of shit. When he dropped us home, Diego whispered to me that Carlos was an idiot. Diego said we couldn't let anyone find out. I had to tell Valentina to shut up.

'A few days later my eldest cousin Santo, who's the boss, forced me into his car, and held a knife to my throat. "Feel this. If you tell anyone. If your bitch tells anyone. You, your bitch, your sister, your grandmother."

'He drew the knife from this ear to that ear.' Ricardo indicated with his forefinger.

'Valentina begged me to tell the police, but I don't trust them and I was worried what might happen to her, Luz, my nephew and niece if I did. I told Valentina we had to keep quiet. It was too dangerous to say a word. Every day, I wish I would have gone to the police then, but there's no reason now.'

Ricardo flicked tears away.

'When Valentina disappeared, I tried to find out what happened. I went and confronted Santo. All he said was if I breathed a word about the drug dealer, my family would be dead.'

I took a minute to process everything Ricardo had told me. It became clear. Ricardo had been trying to protect those he cared for. All along.

'I have to tell Maria,' I said.

Ricardo wiped his nose on his sleeve. He straightened up as if gathering himself, ready to go back into the dungeon. 'Just make sure Luz is safe,' he ordered as he aimed a finger at me.

31

IN THE COCOON OF MY FLAT, I PLUNGED INTO BED. OUTSIDE, THE SCORCHING wind had switched to an Antarctic blast. Rain lashed my bedroom window, a gale howled through crevices.

Courtesy of excessive late nights out on the town, my throat burned and swallowing felt like eating shards of glass. I wanted to share Ricardo's revelations with Maria but lacked the energy even to ring her. Instead, the doona enticed me under its cover and I propped my head back on the pillows. Flicker showed she agreed with my decision by snuggling on my lap.

To stop thinking about a looming cold or, worse, the flu, I picked up the opening novel in the sci-fi series Mum had loaned me from the bedside table. Turning the glossy fire-brick red cover, I read the first page and reread it, the blurred words being overtaken with thoughts about Ricardo's connections with his cousins; the murder of Valentina Rojas, and the information about Ju-Long Wang and Qiao Zeng all made shocking sense.

The book lay abandoned on the doona as I grabbed my phone. I hadn't checked out Ju-Long's activities today and that task could be done without effort.

Within seconds of ringing the GPS tracker, a text with a link pinged. His car was at home, even if he wasn't. When I called through to the listening devices in his apartment, silence emanated from both rooms.

As I slid Flicker off my lap, she opened one green eye and reconfigured herself. Powering up my laptop, I wrote up notes about my visit to remand, then checked if there were any updates from Maria. An email from Kat, littered with enticing details and dizzying photos from the Empire State Building, caught my attention. I wrote a brief reply. What was there to tell about my life?

After tapping send, I transported myself back to Ju-Long's house, catching intermittent words from a news bulletin on his TV.

'Collingwood – secured – talented – draft.'

At least now he was at home and awake. I stayed tuned.

'Cold front sweeping – Victoria – damaging winds.' More news.

Good thing Flicker and I were safely nestled in bed.

A bell-like noise sounded through the phone. Had that come from Ju-Long's TV? His scaly voice filled my ear then his words faded. I jabbed "end" and rang in to the device under Ju-Long's bed.

He was talking fast. It sounded like he said "Yun-seo" and seconds later repeated her name. Ju-Long stopped talking and a noise that could have been something or someone being dragged replaced it. My nerves zinged as I thought of Yun-seo. She'd been all right last time I'd seen her, but had she become a liability? The sound of heavy steps made me speed dial back into the bug in the living room and I discerned a jangle of keys.

If Ju-Long was about to dispose of her body, it was time to take action. I yanked on jeans and snapped up my keys, ready to race out the door despite my sore throat and weather warnings.

Still glued to my mobile, a faint rhythmic tapping that could have been rain and a soft scaping hissed through the speaker. As I tried to determine what the sound was, Ju-Long gutturally cleared his throat.

'Yun-seo,' he said, 'tomorrow. Qantas. Three-forty to Sydney.'

He yelled some unintelligible words, but two stood out. 'Cassy? Where?'

My skin turned clammy.

Ju-Long grunted intermittently. 'You useless piece of shit. I'll do it myself.'

A door slammed.

I hung up and dialled Cassy. It went to voicemail. I rushed off a text to her but in my hurry, I typed, *Call me mow*. She'd know what I meant.

The GPS tracker in Ju-Long's Mercedes indicated it was still at his house in South Melbourne, but it would take him 10 minutes to get to Cassy's place, much less than for me. I texted a code to the GPS tracker to alert me of his car's location every two minutes.

After struggling into a thick, tight English coat Mum had bought me online, I flew down the outside stairs. My phone rang. In my hyped-up state, I fumbled getting it out of my coat pocket and it almost slipped onto the concrete steps.

'What's the drama?' Cassy bawled. I could hear women chortling in the background.

'Ju-Long's coming for you.' A sliver of doubt occupied my mind, but only certainty would work with Cassy. I caught a replay of my voice with a one-second gap.

'What? How do you know?' she asked.

'Where are you?'

I heard a muffled conversation. It was unclear if she was speaking to me or someone else.

'Cassy?'

'It's fine,' she said. 'At a friend's. Are you sure?'

'One hundred percent.'

'Okay, well, thanks.'

I shook my head in disbelief at Cassy's blasé response.

'Call you tomorrow,' said Cassy. 'By the way, Jae's still desperate for you to help Yun-seo escape.'

'That's the other thing. Yun-seo, it seems she's being moved to Sydney.'

Background music blared and Cassy's voice broke up.

Under the stairwell, the freezing wind torpedoed through my open coat into my chest and neck. 'Cassy?' I called.

The phone beeped. She was gone.

'Stuff you,' I yelled.

Geez if Cassy doesn't give a shit about the danger, forget it, I ordered myself.

With a foot on the bottom step to my apartment, I had a sick thought. What if Cassy had misheard me or she was so out of it, she didn't realise the risk?

A text on my mobile supplied GPS latitude and longitude coordinates – Ju-Long's car remained in South Melbourne. But what if he'd gone in an Uber to do his dirty work? Even if Cassy wasn't there, what if he was lying in wait for her? A crazy urge to check on Cassy's safety propelled me into the VW.

Pelting rain and buffeting wind slowed me down as I drove over the West Gate Bridge and along the freeway, with only the windscreen wipers doing the fast-paced work. It had been on my to-do list to replace the driver's side wiper; part of the rubber hung off, leaving a stripe of squiggly water right in my line of sight. Blurry lights outlined city buildings, but my attention remained fixated on the road, my hands gripping the steering wheel to keep the car steady.

Along the Esplanade, palm trees quaked. I drove slowly past Cassy's apartment, shrouded in darkness. Ju-Long's Mercedes was still at home according to the GPS tracker. Outside Cassy's there was no sign of the van and nobody on the street.

The rain had eased to showers. I opened the car door but a wave of freezing wind made me yank it shut again. An internal argument raged. Surely Ju-Long would have arrived by now if that was his plan, but it was pointless for me to have come all this way without bothering to check if Cassy's front door was still intact.

Forcing myself out of the car, I tugged at the gate leading to the apartment block. Finding that locked, I hauled my body over the metal fence, nipped around the back of the courtyard and stole up the steps to Cassy's apartment. An automatic light caught me in its glare. If Ju-Long was there, he'd get plenty of advance warning. At the front door, I pressed my ear against the wood, turned the handle, and shone my mobile torch inside a window. All was quiet and undisturbed.

Back in my car, I drooped against the steering wheel for another 15 minutes, waiting just in case Ju-Long was on his way, before driving home.

Tucked up in bed, warm and cosy with Flicker, I sipped a honey and lemon drink and checked out the Qantas website. There was a flight to Sydney at 3.40pm the next day, exactly as Ju-Long had said through the bugging device. The GPS tracker indicated Ju-Long's car was still outside his townhouse.

I couldn't do anything more to help Cassy; she wasn't listening to me anyway. The only thing left was to talk to her boss, Bani, and get her to help Cassy and Yun-seo. That, I thought, as I peered at the time, would have to wait until morning.

32

MY SORE THROAT FADED AS I DEMOLISHED A MASSIVE BREKKIE OF SCRAMBLED eggs and bacon, along with vitamin C and strong coffee. I texted Cassy and stared at the screen, willing those answering dots to appear. With no reply popping up, I checked the GPS tracker. Ju-Long's car had been at his house all night, though that didn't prove he'd stayed in.

As soon as nine o'clock ticked over, I dialled the Coalition's number.

After six rings, a long-winded recorded message cut in. I lay on the bed, with one hand under my head, half-listening. As I was giving up hope of even being able to leave a message, the monotonal voice said, 'If the matter is urgent, call our Director Bani Anand,' and provided a mobile number. I threw myself off the bed and scrounged for pen and paper. The first six numbers flowed from my pen onto the back of an envelope, but I had to hit redial for the rest.

Prepared to leave a message, I was thrown when Bani's sing-song voice answered.

'Hi, it's Sandi Kent here. We met when I was in your office with Cassy.'

'Ah, oh yes. What can I do for you?'

'I'm concerned about Cassy. One of the traffickers knows where she lives and I haven't been able to reach her.'

There was silence, so I continued, 'She's in danger. Also, I've learnt that Yun-seo Kim's being flown to Sydney today, so I'm calling to give you the details so you can intervene.'

There was no reply. 'Hi, you still there?'

'I apologise, Sandi, but I'm not aware of this situation.'

'Do you know about Jae?' I asked.

'It's best if you tell me the details.'

I hesitated. What was going on here? It seemed this information might unwittingly undermine Cassy. I'd hoped my phone call would be a swift, 'Over to you, Bani'. There was no choice now but to keep going, since Cassy's safety was the priority.

'Cassy's been working with a woman called Jae Shin. We rescued her from Amsterdam Angels and now she's in a refuge. Is this ringing any bells?'

The Coalition had struck me as a small enough service for the boss to be across major incidents. Perhaps they were so common, she'd forgotten. I waited for her to make the next move.

'As one of our volunteers, Cassandra wouldn't ordinarily have direct contact with women.'

'On her phone shift.' I wondered what the hell was going on.

'Her phone shift, did you say?' Bani's tone became high-pitched.

As I stared out the window at rubbish bins lining the pavement, Bani's comment registered.

'Cassy's a *volunteer* with the Coalition?'

'That's right. She's been doing a marvellous job assisting with our most recent fundraiser. Can you remind me what your connection to Cassandra is?'

I cleared my throat. 'I'm a private investigator. The Fair Sex Coalition contracted me…'

My mind was racing. Money had been transferred into my account. Quite a lot of money.

'I see,' said Bani. 'Can I get back to you?'

'Hey, Bani, Cassy's life's at risk. I talked to her yesterday but her phone cut out. I don't know where she is.'

'I'll get back to you as soon as I can.' The director left no room for argument.

As I dropped onto the couch, I tried to remember if Cassy had actually stated she worked at the Coalition? Perhaps I'd assumed she did.

While I waited to hear back from Bani, I rang Maria.

As soon as she answered, I blurted, 'Where are you?'

'At Studley Park Boathouse with Kristin. Why?'

'Too much to explain on the phone. Meet you there.'

'It's not a good time. We're in the middle of planning the wedding.'

'When you hear what's happening, *amiga*, you'll agree that seating and flower arrangements can take a back seat.'

I didn't wait for her answer. After diving into jeans and a T-shirt, I hurtled across town.

Opposite the buzzing Queen Vic Market, my phone chirped. I scanned for cops before swiping the green icon. A fine would ruin my Christmas.

'Sandi, it was good of you to let me know what's happened. Can we meet at the office?' said Bani.

'Have you found Cassy?'

'Not yet. We're working on it. We just need a few more details. If you could spare a few minutes.'

'I'm due at a meeting,' I said.

'It's vital.' A twinge of desperation coated her voice, along with a lot of authority.

It made me want to buck, but I reminded myself that I was the one who rang her. 'All right, I can swing by briefly.'

At the next set of traffic lights, I texted Maria about my detour.

I crisscrossed the city, attempting to avoid the congestion. With only days before Christmas, the frenzy was peaking. I hadn't even had the headspace to think about buying presents.

Bani must have been standing in the hall of the Coalition office, because I'd only reached for the doorbell, when the door creaked open.

Bani's cream pants swished as she led me swiftly down the corridor.

Her office appeared lighter than the last time, sunlight streaming through the window.

'Would you like a drink?'

'Thanks, but I'm in a hurry,' I said.

Bani sipped from a mug filled with green liquid. In her other hand flapped a piece of white A3 paper that seemed to contain a table of figures.

Once we were seated at the scratched wooden table, she asked, 'Where exactly is the trafficked woman you rescued?'

'You don't store that kind of info?'

'My service manager is across the practical details. She's unavailable at the moment.' Bani licked her teeth. There was a smudge of maroon lipstick that fought off the saliva treatment.

I gave her Jae's address, and then in response to her follow-up questions cautiously explained about the number of brothels in the ring, and the brothel operators, emphasising Ju-Long's violent behaviour. I omitted telling her that Cassy's mum had hosted Jae for a night. I thought that tidbit might cause Bani to spit Cassy out of the fold.

'You also mentioned there was another woman who was in danger?'

As I explained about the planned shipment of Yun-seo Kim to Sydney later that afternoon, Bani noted down the details.

'We'll follow up. Now, in relation to the payment for your work, exactly when were you paid?' She studied the Excel spreadsheet in front of her.

'Isn't that in your report?'

She peered over her half-rimmed glasses at me.

I could feel my face contorting. 'What the hell is going on?'

'That's what I'm trying to ascertain.' Bani's smile was tight lipped. She tried again to clean her teeth, making use of every available opportunity.

I stood up. 'I have to go.'

'Look, I know you think Cassy's in danger, but it's difficult to gauge without all the information.'

'I've told you everything. I don't get why you haven't called Cassy yet.'

'We need to understand what we're dealing with before following up.'

'Hey, appointed leader of Fair Sex Coalition, I would have thought your employees' welfare—'

'Volunteer's.'

'Whatever. That you might be slightly concerned.'

'Of course, I'm concerned. You don't know how concerned.' Bani regarded me as if she were standing up and I was the one sitting down.

'Cassy isn't a telephone worker here,' I stated.

'No.'

'Was she meant to be involved in getting Jae out?'

'No.'

'Aha.'

The extent of Cassy's deception was stunning. Even though part of me wanted Cassy throttled, I wanted to be the one to do it and not be the snitch, any more than I had already.

'We take this matter very seriously,' said Bani.

'The main issue at the moment is Cassy's safety.' I found myself yelling. 'Do you hear me when I'm telling you Ju-Long's a thug with no conscience?' I shook my head. The conversation was pointless.

Maria had texted. *Waiting*.

Coming, I texted back.

I made for the door. Behind me the click of high heels followed as I stomped down the hallway.

'We might need to speak more,' called Bani.

'I've said enough. If anything happens to Cassy, it'll be on your head.'

33

I sped down Johnston Street to Studley Park where mottled gum trees dominated the view in every direction. In the Boathouse car park, I realised too late it was overflowing. I did a three-point turn and accelerated back up to the main road. Even there, vehicles were banked up for a kilometre. Finally, after spotting a vacant park, I sprinted back down the path, bypassing puddles. As I jogged through pre-Christmas functions in the BBQ area, the scent of sizzling chops made me salivate.

The sound of a splash made me turn. A guy had fallen out of his kayak into the muddy Yarra River and was awkwardly manoeuvring the boat towards shore. The main danger with the Melbourne waterway wasn't drowning; the real killer was the invisible bacteria.

Nearby, Maria dressed in curve-revealing Lycra and Kristin in trekking gear were seated at an outdoor table on the bank of the Yarra.

'Waiting for you is like watching a billy boil,' called Maria. 'After rubbing two sticks together.'

'Latte?' asked Kristin.

I nodded gratefully. She headed off to join a snaking queue at the outdoor café.

'I had to make an emergency detour,' I explained to Maria.

She frowned, unconvinced.

'The parking,' I started, then gave up justifying. 'Anyway, listen to what I've found out.'

Although Cassy's wellbeing was still on my mind, I pushed it underground and focused on my visit to remand, trying to order my jumbled thoughts.

'Ricardo. He finally opened up. He told me he went to the brothel regularly. Some of the stuff he said was hard to believe, but he used the name "Tuffy" instead of "Ju-Long", which means Lee must have talked to him. I reckon he was genuinely trying to help her. Sounds weird, hey. I don't exactly get what happened, but the others who were at the brothel that day were equally, if not more, capable of killing Lee Wu. They're key members of a sex-trafficking ring for Christ's sake. Am I making any sense?'

Maria squeezed her face in concentration. She'd stop me if she needed to.

'On top of that, it seems that Ricardo's cousins murdered Valentina.'

Maria's expressions changed from summer to winter as I filled her in on Ricardo's revelations.

'Wow *bella*, great work.' Maria wrapped her hand around my forearm. 'I'll follow up Valentina's murder with Ricardo asap. It's interesting that he's only mentioned this now.'

'He was shitting himself. Actually, he's terrified for his sister and her kids. The cousins threatened to kill them too, if Ricardo dobbed them in. Which he has now. Can police protection be organised for his family?'

'Not sure. Let me handle it and see where it leads.'

I filled Maria in on the rest of Ju-Long's activities and associates, as Kristin reappeared and slid a coffee in front of me. Maria glanced up and squeezed her hand.

'Beautiful day,' Kristin said before she strolled off towards the suspension bridge. It was astute of her to leave us to talk business.

'Are any of the sex workers willing to make a statement?' Maria continued.

I hesitated and stared up at patches of blue sky for a solution. 'Not sure. It's a bit complicated.'

My phone rang. Bani's name didn't appear, Cassy's did.

'Gotta take this,' I mouthed to Maria as I headed towards the boat-renting kiosk, away from the crowds. 'Cassy. You all right?'

'Depends on what you mean.' Cassy's voice was faint.

'Where are you?'

'At home.'

'No. Ju-Long—'

'Bani told me. How could you? How could you tell her about Jae? She's had it in for me since my interview for the role.'

'Hey?'

'Apparently, she thought my interest was too extreme. How ridiculous. Luckily, the Volunteer Coordinator recognised my skills, my capacity, how useful they'd be for the Coalition.'

'Yeah, well, it would be good to talk that through, but right now, you need to get your arse somewhere safe.'

'Point being, it's not *your* place to contact them.' Cassy's voice was tight. 'This was all going through me. You've been getting your money, so what are you complaining about?'

'Did she remind you that Ju-Long's got your address?'

'She said she'd contact the police if there was any danger. That's not my main issue at the moment.'

Cassy's words interspersed between staccato breaths. 'She's – sacked – me.'

I wondered how that worked if you were a volunteer. No recourse for unfair dismissal, supposedly.

'We had something special, you and me.' Her voice was sharp and cold. 'Thought you could be trusted.'

Before I had a chance to reply, her tone morphed into desperation. 'It's all too much. Just don't know how to keep going. Not sure what to do.'

'What do you mean?' Was she playing me? I couldn't risk it. 'Hold on, Cassy. I'm coming.'

I ran back to the table, and flung a 'Sorry, talk soon,' at Maria before flying up to the car.

I sped down Hoddle Street, the main north–south arterial route, hoping to get to Cassy before she did something stupid or Ju-Long got in first. Cars honked as I shoved my way in front of them.

Fitzroy Street was bumper to bumper. At a red light I checked the GPS tracker. *Fuck.* Ju-Long was there in St Kilda.

My hands clenched the steering wheel as I searched for a park so I could sprint the rest of the way. Every spot was filled. At last, I spun into Cassy's street. The silver Mercedes stood sparkling in the sunlight. I screeched into a no-standing zone, next to Ju-Long's car, leaped out and plonked my palm on the expensive car bonnet. The engine was hot. I bolted towards Cassy's apartment block, dodging pedestrians and discarded beer bottles.

The gate was locked again. I jumped up onto the brick fence and scaled the green metal lacework, before dropping onto the concrete path below. After sprinting through the communal courtyard, where myna birds noisily scattered, I dashed up the stairs to Cassy's apartment. Half-way up, I ground to a halt. Her front door was ajar. Splinters of wood jutted out from the doorjamb and the metal plate angled towards the threshold.

I edged up the rest of the stairs, vigilant for any noise or movement from inside. A poke of my head around the front door revealed an empty corridor. I crept over door shards into the house.

Suddenly, a scream shot through the building. My heart jolted.

'Where's Jae?' A fierce voice exploded through the house.

I flattened myself against the wall that separated the hall from the lounge. Fear threatened to immobilise me; my next step was going to succeed or fail, and failure might get us both killed. I centred myself and thought of Sensei. My arms were shimmering steel.

Cassy's voice was muffled.

'Tell me,' the male voice echoed.

Another scream and a sound like a hammer hitting a vase propelled me into the lounge.

With his back to me, Ju-Long had Cassy bailed up in an armchair. She clutched her forehead with one hand. Relief flowed through me; she was alive. Her breathing was heavy, her upper lip dripping with blood. The bastard must have smashed her lips into her teeth.

I resisted the urge to help her. First, Ju-Long had to be crushed.

I planned to wrench Ju-Long's hair back with one hand and headlock him with my other arm, but the bronze statue on the sideboard flashed into my peripheral vision. Armed with the female nude, I tiptoed towards Ju-Long, my heart bursting through my mouth.

Up close and personal he was more massive than I remembered. His aftershave had been replaced with overpowering sweat, mixed with a metallic stench.

As his hulking form loomed over Cassy, her eyes flicked towards me. Ju-Long noticed and spun around, clenching his fist as I struck him in the temple. His head jolted sideways, a gash above his eye leaked bright-red gore that trickled down his cheek. He doubled over and slumped awkwardly on the carpet.

I dropped the bloodied statue. 'Cassy, you all right?'

With half-closed eyes, she gurgled a response.

My hands shook as I ripped out my mobile from my back pocket and jabbed the Emergency button.

'You have dialled emergency Triple Zero. Your call is being connected.'

Cassy groaned, her head sagging onto her chest.

The operator asked what service was needed. 'Police,' I faltered. Cassy needed more than the cops.

Without waiting for the next question, I burst out, 'The Esplanade, St Kilda. A man's assaulted a woman and he's still here.'

'What number, the Esplanade?'

'I think it's 20. Apartment three.'

Ju-Long wriggled, then struggled onto his forearms and knees. He looked up and studied me closely.

'You.' He groaned as he tried unsuccessfully to stand up. 'I know you.'

'An ambulance. We need an ambulance too.'

'You'll pay.' Ju-Long panted as he clawed his way onto the couch.

With strength from God knows where, he lunged at me. I sprang backwards as his fist powered towards me, but not far enough as his knuckles smashed into my cheek. A wave of nausea erupted from my gut up my throat. A shooting pain stabbed under my ear and my jaw burned like a bonfire.

'Where's Jae?' the thug screamed as he grabbed my arm.

I automatically spun out of his grip, seized his wrist and locked his elbow. There was no way anyone could remain standing with that sort of pressure on their joint. I took morbid pleasure in watching Ju-Long sprawl on the floor. Kneeling next to him, I pressed down hard on his elbow until he yelped. The only way for us to be safe was for me to fracture his joint. I used all my weight. He bellowed.

After having had my jaw smashed by Ju-Long moments before, the effort to down him was too much. A sensation ripped through my head and I willed myself not to faint. As my hands flew to the floor to steady myself, Ju-Long wriggled away towards the hallway wall. He was still too close and his sweaty stench made me want to throw up. I sunk onto the carpet but managed to shuffle on my bum, closer to Cassy.

I tried to open my mouth to whisper to Cassy, but pain shot through my skull. Desperate for the blare of sirens, the only noise I could hear was the strained breathing of three injured people. Cassy was upright, so I guessed she was still conscious. She was insane, getting us into this situation. Hopefully we'd both survive this attack so I could harass her about it later.

Ju-Long leaned against the wall and pushed himself up. His black shoes lumbered into the hall. Where were the fucking cops? I couldn't let him escape. On my knees, with my palms pressed against the armchair Cassy sat slumped in, I forced myself upright and edged into the corridor. Heavy steps clomped down the outside stairs.

With the support of the wall, I stepped sideways to the front door. I eased myself down the stairs, holding tightly to the handrails. Each jolt caused a sharp pain that rifled up my skull. Ju-Long rounded the corner towards the gate, as the sound of sirens finally filled my ears.

On the pavement, out the front of the apartment block, Ju-Long staggered towards his car. There was no sign of the cops; the sirens were fading. I steeled myself against the pain and ran to catch the sumo wrestler.

His car beeped and he yanked open the driver's door as I stole behind him. I grasped his wrist and, as he spun around, kneed him in the balls. It wasn't exactly aikido, but neither was smashing his head with a statue.

He doubled over and crumpled to the ground. As Ju-Long writhed, clutching his groin, I leaned on my car bonnet. Sirens spiked the air and I watched in slow motion as a police car pulled up. I beckoned to the officer in a dark blue vest, his face a blur.

Ju-Long was on his knees with his elbow on the driver's seat. He gave an almighty yell and hauled himself into the Mercedes.

Not again. For God's sake, was I going to have to completely cripple the bastard before the cops intervened?

As I launched myself at Ju-Long a deep voice ordered, 'Move away from that man.'

'He's assaulted my friend upstairs. Don't let him get away.' I sounded like I was drunk, my jaw resisting opening. I stepped back from the skinny cop and let him take my place.

Ju-Long took a swing at the cop but it lacked clout.

As the police snapped handcuffs on Ju-Long, the bitumen slammed into my body.

Once I'd spilled my guts, literally, I felt better.

In an interview room at St Kilda Police Station, a policeman offered me a cup of sweet milky tea, bringing me almost back to my old self. My poor jaw clicked each time I opened my mouth, but at least I could talk.

I revealed all the evidence to Sergeant McCulney, except the bit about breaking and entering into Ju-Long's house.

He grilled me about Ju-Long's injuries, but seemed more impressed than ready to charge me.

My explanation was interrupted by a knock on the door.

'Her lawyer Ms Luisetto is here, sir.'

Maria marched into the room, squeezing newly painted lips together, and clutched my shoulder. Her subtle perfume replaced the musty smell of the interview room. Sitting next to me, she tried to shift the metal chair back from the minimalist table, only to discover it was bolted to the floor.

'Exactly what is the intention of this process?' Her strained voice peaked.

Maria hadn't changed out of her Lycra gear since we'd met at the Boathouse. It shaved an edge off her credibility, but her tone made up for any doubts the cop might have had.

The sergeant sported a wry smile. 'Just a chat, really. Can you suggest anything, so I can get her to repeat her story?'

'I beg your pardon,' Maria said.

'Truth is, we're finished anyway,' said the officer. 'Ms Kent has been fully cooperative.'

'Has she been charged?'

'If you insist, we could charge her with assault,' he smiled, 'but I think we'll manage self-defence. But, look, Ms Luisetto, why don't you flick me an email, 'cos I hear you're employing Ms Kent to do some scoping work. I think that should more or less cover it off.'

Maria peered over her green-rimmed glasses. 'If Ms Kent is here under her own volition, she will choose another time to make a statement about what happened today. Obviously, she needs medical attention before we can proceed.'

As he stood, the sergeant placed his large, wrinkled hands on the back of the chair. 'We're here twenty-four seven.'

If another copper had been talking to us like that, I'd have blown a fuse. This guy didn't rile me. Perhaps shock stopped me thinking straight and Maria was right to terminate the interview.

'The Feds might have other ideas, but that's up to them.' The sergeant blinked, continuing his wry smile.

He saw us out, walking at a jaunty pace towards the constable behind the front counter. 'Can you get the car keys for Ms Kent? And your mobile phone's here as well.' His voice was as jolly as Santa Claus.

The constable reached under the counter and pulled out my belongings.

As we headed out through the automatic glass doors, Maria said, 'Straight to emergency.'

'I just need a stiff drink.'

She wouldn't be shifted. 'I'd stay with you, except I've arranged for Ricardo to make a statement to the police about his cousins. I want to be there.'

'That's way more important,' I said. 'I'll be in good hands.'

Before she dropped me at emergency at the Alfred Hospital, I made her promise to organise to pick up my car and find out if Cassy was all right. The second request met with a stony stare, but she nodded.

34

THE DING-DONG NOISE OF THE DOORBELL DRILLED INTO MY FOREHEAD. Flicker catapulted from the doona into the loungeroom, adopting a defence position under the couch.

As I rolled out of bed, my lower back spasmed and my hips ached. The last time my body had been crippled like this was in autumn, when a friend coaxed me into competing in a triathlon. It took me a week to recover; I hoped this time would be quicker.

The hospital had given me the all clear: nothing broken, just a hell of a lot of bruising and a jaw that clicked whenever I tried to talk, and they sent me home with instructions to take painkillers and anti-inflammatories. It would have been more restorative to self-diagnose and skip the six-hour wait.

I shuffled to the front door. Through the peephole, dark-brown hair, a red scarf and an hourglass figure confirmed it wasn't Ju-Long's associates come to knock me off.

'Wanted to check you were still alive.'

'You could have texted. What if I'd been in bed with a luscious woman?'

After giving me a tentative hug, Maria waltzed through the living room and peeked at my unmade bed. She deposited a cloth bag in the kitchen and handed me my car keys.

Flicker surfaced and pranced up to Maria, who enveloped her in a chatty cuddle. My joints were so stiff, I knew a wander around my flat wasn't going to be the cure. Returning to my bed, I heaved the doona over my battered body.

Maria hovered in the doorway to my bedroom. 'You could have told me what was going on with Cassy.'

'I was about to explain.'

'That you were recklessly crossing town to tackle a known criminal,' said Maria.

'Known?'

'Apparently, he's previously been charged with assault. You could have been killed.' Maria wrung the end of her scarf.

'In case you missed the news, he collapsed after I donged him on the head with a statue.'

Admittedly, Ju-Long had escaped after that, but I was going to relay a condensed version of events at every social opportunity, although maybe not at the next aikido class.

Maria approached the bed and balanced herself on the edge. 'You can't wander around in the fog as if you know where you're going.'

'What the heck is that meant to mean?'

'Please tell me you're not back together with Cassy.'

'Oh, for Christ's sake, Maria.'

'I didn't come here to argue with you.'

'Geez, you're failing spectacularly on that front,' I snapped. 'I don't expect sympathy, but it's a bit much to cop a grilling the day after I've been attacked.'

'Exactly my point,' she said.

My limit had been reached. What with the physical discomfort and Maria harassing me, I needed painkillers: something strong and instant.

After tossing off the doona, I veered towards the bathroom then diverted into the kitchen. From the top shelf of the cupboard, I plucked a bottle of caramel-coloured Johnnie Walker, a birthday present from Stewart. It was only for special occasions. After filling a tumbler with the pungent liquid, I gulped a mouthful.

Maria squeezed past me and studied the blue label. 'That's too good to be using as an analgesic.'

I sank the rest of the medicine, the heat rushing down my throat.

Maria tightened the lid on the whisky bottle. 'You scared the living nightlights out of me. Promise me you'll be more careful in the future.'

'Scrapes have a way of chasing me.'

Maria raised a chiselled eyebrow. We both knew the truth.

'Anyway, I'm going to change career,' I said. 'An air hostess, I reckon. My height would be a plus. Get to travel. Regular income.'

'But *bella*, you get results. Speaking of which, Ricardo Lopez made a statement to the police, regarding his version of events about witnessing his cousin Carlos Perez chasing a suspected drug dealer and returning to the car with bloodied hands and clothes. Plus, Ricardo discussed his suspicion that his cousins murdered his fiancée to silence her. On that basis the police have re-opened both cases.'

Maria drummed the bench with her fingers. 'In terms of the sex-trafficking case, the Federal Police have taken over the investigation. Quite a posse of people you've implicated: Ju-Long Wang, Qiao Zeng, Alistair Payne, Russell Craig, and potentially other associates of Ju-Long's.'

'Thank God the cops have taken it seriously, especially with Jae Shin refusing to make a statement,' I said. 'Do you know how Cassy is?'

'She's stable,' Maria's voice flattened.

'You've seen her?'

'I called the hospital. The nurse wouldn't give me any information but transferred me to her mother, who was by her bedside. She told me Cassy has concussion and a broken jaw, but the prognosis is good. She's having surgery this morning.'

Maria checked her watch. 'Actually, she should have had it already.'

My head started spinning. I held onto the sink, waiting for the dizzy spell to pass.

'Why don't you go back to bed?' suggested Maria.

The couch was closer. I lowered myself gently onto the three-seater and lay down with a cushion under my head.

Sounds of cupboard doors and china dishes emanated from the kitchen.

'Been a bit busy to shop,' I called out, hearing the slur of my words.

My body relaxed and my eyelids drooped as the whisky kicked in. *Thanks, Stew.*

Next thing I knew, Maria was hovering over me. 'Move over.'

Maria hoisted the blinds and sunlight doused the lounge as I yawned myself awake.

On the coffee table, two plates were piled with a gourmet breakfast. I drew in the welcome scent of coffee and reached for the already poured mug. I eased my legs off the couch, pleased I could move without agony.

'Has Ju-Long been charged with assault?' I asked.

Maria joined me on the couch. 'Sex trafficking is a more serious charge, so they're going with that. Other news is, Luz Aitken made her brother tell the whole story. Sad really. It was an accident; well, Ricardo did take a weapon with him into the brothel, so according to the police he should have seen it coming.'

'What?'

'Ricardo unintentionally killed Lee when he was helping her escape.'

'No way.'

'He'd intended to attack Ju-Long and Lee got in the way. Ricardo will definitely serve time; even though it was an accident, the charges aren't much lighter, unfortunately. He's now been charged with the manslaughter of Lee, attempted murder of Ju-Long, and recklessly causing injury. However, since he's confessed and agreed to testify against Carlos, I'm hoping the sentence will be reduced.'

I couldn't help feeling sorry for Ricardo and Luz. 'What about police protection for Luz?'

'The police are keeping a close eye on the cousins. They'd be stupid to try and attack Ricardo's family.'

I worried for Luz and the kids, but it was time to let the case go. After witnessing people's pain so intimately, it was always tough to step away.

I finished off the remaining crumbs on my plate, my body oiled by the nutrients and the medicinal drop of whisky. Picking up the plates, I stood up, a slight wave of dizziness making me clutch the back of the couch.

'I'll do them.' Maria insisted.

'Thanks heaps. I'm going to have a shower and then I have to head out.'

'You can barely stand. Are you planning on driving?'

'I'll be fine. I only had one glass and the chef's contribution has worked wonders in my recovery. By the way, thanks for dropping the car home. Do you need a lift?'

Maria studied me dubiously, as she retied her silk scarf around her neck. 'Kristin's on her way to pick me up.'

'You can pay for a cab if you're so worried,' I said.

Maria pulled out a fifty.

'Nah, only joking.'

'The last thing we need is you losing your licence,' said Maria. 'Imagine you without wheels. That would be a sight for sad eyes.'

I grabbed Maria around her shoulders and squeezed her. 'You're a right pain. Breakfast was perfect. I'll hang here for another hour or so, then I'll be good to go, I swear.'

I saw Maria out. 'Merry Christmas.'

In the shower, steaming water massaged my limbs and back. My body was so covered with impressive bruises that I couldn't see myself hitting the aikido mats anytime soon.

Before leaving home, I checked my bank account, expecting a disaster but instead, $500 had appeared from Maria with the word "bonus". I was chuffed and a bit choked up; it must have been the whisky making me sentimental. Well, I'd earned it, the case demanding "above and beyond" time and dedication. Ideas floated past about how to spend that amount of money. I ditched all the other options; decent Christmas presents for my family was my top priority.

Before shopping, I had two final visits to make.

35

I EDGED THROUGH GLARY WHITE CORRIDORS, GLANCING INTO CROWDED four-bed wards at the Epworth hospital in Richmond. A woman attached to a drip trickled past in a flimsy nightie. The stench of illness behind a veil of antiseptic made me queasy.

My shoulders shivered as a childhood memory surfaced. Propped on a hospital bed, gasping for air, as a man in a white coat shoved an oxygen mask over my nose and mouth.

I clutched a bunch of yellow jonquils in one hand and delved into the side pocket of my backpack with the other. Asthma puffer in hand, I squeezed twice and inhaled the soothing spray.

Further along the corridor Cassy's room appeared: a spacious single-bed ward. Had her father somehow wangled it? I squirmed at the sight of a clear tube that moustached across Cassy's face and entered her nostrils. A thick white bandage looped under her chin and around her head. Her face was a palette of black, blue and yellow; my bruised and swollen cheek nothing compared to hers.

Quietness cloaked the room. Cassy's eyes were closed.

In a grey chair next to the narrow bed, Cassy's mother slumped, her head supported by her hand.

The urge to retreat overtaking me, I took a step back into the corridor.

Beatrice glanced up, grey bags puffing under her faded green eyes. 'Sandi. You came,' she said, as if I was a long-lost daughter estranged from the family.

'Have this chair.' She took up a position in between Cassy's toes and the steel rail at the end of the bed.

Cassy blinked at me.

'How thoughtful.' Beatrice nodded towards the bouquet I'd brought. 'They say the surgery was successful, thank goodness. Her jaw is wired up but it is such a relief. Her father was going to fly back immediately, but now I think he can go ahead and give his paper.'

Cassy would be relieved. The last thing she'd want was her father lobbing next to her sickbed.

I lowered myself gingerly into the still warm hospital chair. Cassy beckoned me with her forefinger, and at my lack of response her fingers grew insistent. I leaned over crisp white linen.

With her lips opening a sliver, she murmured, 'Thanks.'

'I'll let you two have some time together while I find a vase,' said Beatrice.

'I can go,' I offered.

'While you're here, I might go and get a cup of tea as well,' Beatrice said to me.

No doubt, she'd been there all night, watching over her daughter.

'Here's your phone, dear, if you need me.'

Cassy released my hand as she claimed her mobile.

As Beatrice shuffled out the open door with the bunch of jonquils, I pitied her. Not only that Cassy had ended up in hospital, but Beatrice's stooped back betrayed a deeper sense of tragedy.

On the bedside table, a vase of violet carnations generated a faint spicy scent. I flipped the attached card and grimaced at Bani Anand's signature. The gesture was disingenuous. Cassy's injuries could have been avoided if her boss had intervened. Cassy thought Bani's only "crime" was ending her volunteer role. Maybe I'd fill Cassy in when she'd recovered.

I raised an eyebrow. Cassy shrugged sluggishly then began tapping on her mobile, not bothered by the drip attached to the back of one hand.

She handed me the phone, with the notes app open. *Jae texted. She's agreed to testify since Ju-Long attacked me.*

'Wow, wouldn't have predicted that.'

Cassy retrieved her phone. *Yun-seo's been picked up by Coalition.*

'Great.' At least Bani had been of some use.

Maybe see a movie sometime, the next note said.

'A fluffy comedy,' I chuckled. 'You need anything?'

Cassy carefully shook her head. *New career*, she wrote.

I smiled. 'Yeah, me too.'

A nurse appeared at the base of the bed and pulled out Cassy's file.

'Better go. Take care.' I waved my way out of the ward and made a hasty retreat down sterile corridors and emerged into brilliant sunshine.

36

ALTHOUGH I'D ADVANCED TO HIS PERSONAL VISITOR'S LIST, RICARDO'S cheery expression deteriorated as he entered the packed contact area at remand and spotted me with Luz and her kids.

Luz had chosen a table close to a fenced play area. Ricardo weaved past other prisoners and their family members to get to us. Luz's kids seemed unperturbed by the burly blokes in the room.

'*Tío, tío,*' called Nicolás. 'Uncle, uncle.'

One at a time, Ricardo hugged his sister, niece and nephew tightly. I stayed put, carefully positioned on a hard stool.

Re-joining me, Luz drew Blanca onto her lap, as Ricardo took up the empty spot at the table.

'*Cómo va el entrenamiento de fútbol, Nicolás?*' Ricardo asked his nephew. 'How is football training?'

'*Tío*, it's summer, we're not playing,' Nicolás answered in English.

'You still need to practise,' was the Spanish response.

His nephew spun on the stool.

'You need to sit quietly,' Luz told Nicolás as she eyed the prison guards.

'Nicolás is small and strong, like I was.' Ricardo nodded at me. 'His technique is much better than mine was at his age.'

He ruffled his nephew's black hair. 'One day you will play in the World Cup. But you have to practise.'

'Who can I train with?' said Nicolás.

Luz and Ricardo shared a frown. I read it as a silent dig at Luz's husband. Couldn't he pull his finger out and kick a ball with his own son?

'When are you coming home, *tío*?'

The question hovered, all of us adults resisting false reassurance.

'I can play with you,' said Luz.

Ricardo added in Spanish, 'When school goes back, there will be lots of kids to practise with. Remember the exercises we talked about?'

His nephew offered up a sulky look. Ricardo nudged him with his elbow.

'*Sí tío,* I do the stair stepping every day.'

'What's that?' I asked.

'You have to jump on the ball without it moving,' said Nicolás.

'Good boy, and remember the figure eight dribbling too,' reminded Ricardo.

He turned his attention to his niece. 'Blanca, how's school? Are you studying hard?'

Blanca smiled, a broad grin like her mother's. 'I got 10 out of 10 for my last maths test.'

'You're very clever. She can be anything she wants.' Ricardo told me.

'*Mamá,* I want to go on the slide.' Blanca wriggled on Luz's lap.

'Come, *niños,* we'll buy some sweets and then you can go to the play area.'

'But *Mamá,*' protested her son.

'Come on,' Luz said. '*Quieres algo?*' she asked Ricardo. 'Do you want something?'

'*Sí, chocolate,*' he answered.

They headed over to the vending machine. I imagined that one of the bonuses of having visitors was the chance to binge on junk food.

'I told Luz everything,' Ricardo whispered.

I nodded and slipped into Spanish like him. 'The thing I don't understand, Ricardo, is why you didn't tell me it was an accident.'

He stared at me with intense dark eyes that I'd have called fierce on our first meeting.

'You don't understand. I was trying to help her, and then I– I killed her.'

Before we could continue, Luz returned with a Mars bar for Ricardo. He peeled off the wrapping and absently took a bite. When the children entered the play area at the end of the hall, with Luz hovering outside it, Ricardo turned back to me.

'I couldn't forgive myself. I knew the police believed I'd killed Valentina. Of course, they were going to think I meant to hurt Petal too. It was useless to try and explain.'

Ricardo's hand formed a fist. 'On the day we decided she had to leave, Petal packed the few clothes she owned. We made it past the counter, past Qiao. I thought it was going to be okay. We were at the front door, when Tuffy burst out and grabbed Petal. He punched her in the stomach and she doubled over. I hit Tuffy but he's built like a brick wall, it was nothing to him. I couldn't stop him with my fists. That's when I took out the knife.'

Ricardo sniffed and flicked his head. It was still unbelievable to him.

'What happened?' I asked.

Ricardo rubbed his hands along the white table; a gesture that signalled he was readying himself to admit the brutal truth. 'Tuffy dragged Petal back inside the brothel. She was screaming. I attacked him with the knife, but he was too quick. He pulled Petal in front of him. He used her as a shield. Bastard. The knife went straight into her throat.'

Ricardo's voice became choppy. 'My Petal died and I died with her. After everything, first Valentina disappearing and then it was *me* that killed Petal.'

He crossed his arms across his chest and fought back tears; it was unsafe to cry in this joint.

I thought of various inane things to say, but for once decided silence was the best option.

He fiddled with the gold cross around his neck. 'Maybe we'll find out where she is and she can finally be buried properly.'

He placed his elbows on the table and gazed at his niece and nephew as they played chasey around a purple plastic slide. 'I pray Luz and my nephew and niece stay safe. Luz is a saint. I thank God every day for that. I'm so blessed to have such a loving sister.'

The play area gate squealed open. Nicolás had let himself out and sped back to the table. '*Tío*, it's boring in there. I wish I could play *fútbol* with you.'

'One day soon, I hope.' Ricardo clasped the boy's cheeks between his hands. 'Here, you have the rest of my chocolate.'

'Really?' Nicolás hoed into the half-eaten bar.

'I don't want to disappoint my family,' whispered Ricardo to me.

Glancing at glum prisoners, I wished I could promise Ricardo that Maria would get him off.

37

As Stewart wrapped his arms around me in a soft embrace, my resilience evaporated. I realised I'd been holding myself tightly for weeks, since both cases had ricocheted into my lap.

Stewart drew back, his face overflowing with concern as he spotted the blue bruise on my cheek. I'd thought foundation had camouflaged any traces.

'If you think this is bad, you should see Cassy,' I said. 'All I need is a drink.'

My buddy poured us shots of whisky in glasses that had originally been jam jars. I threw back the fiery liquid then collapsed into the springless couch. Beer bottles clinked as I pushed them aside to place my empty glass on the coffee table. The familiar smell of stale beer oozed from the carpet.

'Are you sure you're up to partying?' asked Stewart.

I felt anything but. 'A coffee will pick me up.'

I'd driven over to Stew's house on automatic, the idea of missing our friend's thirtieth not occurring to me. But Stewart was right, I should have been ensconced in bed.

'We'll grab one on the way,' said Stew.

As I tried to find a comfortable position on the couch, Stewart vanished and disco music emanated from his bedroom. I closed my eyes and instantly nodded off.

Stew emerged, magnificently decked out in a sleek purple dress and blue wig, and slowly blinked massive false eyelashes. I couldn't disappoint him after he'd spent – I knew from prior experience – hours plotting his outfit.

First though, I held out an arm so Stewart could crane me out of the sunken couch.

He strutted outside with me lagging behind.

As I tugged the front door closed behind us, his mobile chimed.

'Bloody hell, did I really need to see that?' He wobbled on glittery silver stilettos.

'Maybe flats would have been better.' I grabbed his arm.

He shoved his phone in my face. 'I asked Ben to keep me in the loop. Terrible idea.'

I expanded the image and recognised Stewart's boyfriend. He was standing snug up against a hulk whose neck was enveloped by shoulder muscles. Ben was always smiley, but this time his expression was tense.

'Just my type.' I laughed, trying to take the edge off Stewart's reaction.

We crossed the major intersection of Alexandra Parade and entered bustling Brunswick Street. We dodged two guys walking their bikes on the footpath and two women holding hands. I had a moment of nostalgia for what could have been with Cassy, but sagely let the moment sashay away.

Dinner stragglers exited our favourite Fitzroy haunt, Marios Café, as we arrived. After taking a seat at the bar table facing the street, we ordered coffees from a waiter decked out in a white shirt and black vest, who didn't give Stew a second glance.

Stew jiggled knobbly knees that poked through pantyhose as he studied the photo on his mobile. It was clear he wanted to dissect this new drama with Ben, but I lacked the energy for the intricacies.

'Maybe it's time to ditch him,' I said.

'My thought too.'

'Enough of this being treated like shit. You're too magnificent for that.'

When the coffees arrived, Stewart added three spoons of sugar and stirred his cappuccino swiftly, froth spilling over the side of his cup.

'Maybe we should just get married, have kids and stuff all the losers who can't see the gorgeous queens in front of their eyes.' Stewart adjusted a curl on his blue wig.

'That calls for a photo. You sure are something to behold.' With my mobile, I snapped as Stewart posed left, right and centre.

We hit our friend's thirtieth party venue, and with caffeine in our veins we let loose for the night.

Apart from my family Christmas, I was done with dramas for the year.

ACKNOWLEDGEMENTS

I've had the good fortune to be surrounded by friends and associates willing to encourage me, critique my work and provide practical assistance in the development of this novel.

Firstly, many thanks to Clan Destine Press's Lindy Cameron for the publishing opportunity, as well as the editing team for their advice.

I particularly appreciate Catherine Heath's independent editorial contribution on early drafts and as a significant mentor.

Friends and colleagues have guided me with details about subject matters, including police procedure: Sally McCurrough; Spanish grammar: Maria Majors; swimming techniques: Lindy Marlow; medical matters: Maureen Convey; and IT intricacies: Danos Shukuroglou. Other contacts have been generous with their time and information, including Shirley Wood from Project Respect and Detective Senior Sergeant Jeffrey Maher.

Thanks also to my daughter, Danni Ray, for her early research assistance.

Sue Cole's insider knowledge of the bookselling industry has been invaluable and members of my writer's group have provided insightful feedback and constant encouragement.

My fabulous friends have helped me focus on the goal.

Above all, my life partner Viv Ray has provided valuable feedback and been a steadfast support throughout my journey.

ABOUT THE AUTHOR

Robin Gregory has worked as a social worker in community health and the family violence sector. She lives with her long-term partner and an unpredictable black cat in inner-city Melbourne.

In her spare time, Robin has ridden bareback, picked coffee beans for the Nicaraguan revolution and trekked the Inca trail. She loves visiting Spanish speaking countries and when at home enjoys vicarious travels through her weekly Spanish classes.

www.ingramcontent.com/pod-product-compliance
Lightning Source LLC
Chambersburg PA
CBHW030516020726
47494CB00004B/1116